To LaVerne with love,
Betty Johansen

Out of Darkness

By

B.J. Aaron

1663 Liberty Drive, Suite 200
Bloomington, Indiana 47403
(800) 839-8640
www.AuthorHouse.com

This book is a work of fiction. People, places, events, and situations are the product of the author's imagination. Any resemblence to actual persons, living or dead, or historical events, is purely coincidental.

© 2005 B.J. Aaron. All Rights Reserved.

No part of this book may be reproduced, stored in a retrieval system, or transmitted by any means without the written permission of the author.

First published by AuthorHouse 09/13/05

ISBN: 1-4208-2019-2 (sc)

Library of Congress Control Number: 2004195243

Printed in the United States of America
Bloomington, Indiana

This book is printed on acid-free paper.

*Dedicated with adoration and praise
to Jesus Christ, the Lord of Glory,
who loved me and gave Himself for me.*

To the Reader:

1. Although this novel is a work of fiction, the phenomenon known as the "Toronto Blessing" is real. For more information about it - both pro and con - put "Toronto Blessing" in a search engine on the worldwide web.
2. *Out of Darkness* is the second book in a series. The first, *Darkness Under His Feet*, can be read in its entirety, free, on the internet at www.bondwebs.com/bjaaron .
3. All the characters and events in this book are fictitious. Any resemblance to actual persons, living or dead, or to actual events, is coincidental. Also the town of Deepwater is fictional.

Chapter I

It was not a sinister night. South breezes dipped and soared through streets that echoed with laughter and music. Children played. Teenagers cruised. Lovers rendezvoused.

Even the silver stars that thronged the velvet black sky seemed frolicsome. And the craggy old face of the man in the moon had settled into a benevolent smile on this mild June evening. When tempers flared in a shabby little house at 1809 Tomlin Street, the lunar face never flinched. And hours later, when a knife blade flashed and a young life ended, the moon smiled on.

The first hint of something amiss was the opening and closing of the heavy glass door at the Deepwater Police station. Flossie Bobbsey, who served as non-emergency dispatcher and receptionist on the evening shift, was seated at a desk behind a tall gray counter surrounded by a sea of paperwork. She looked up from her work with a smile and a cheerful greeting on her lips. The smile turned to a frown. No one had entered.

She had learned long ago that anything could happen at a police station. She would have to hurry outside and see if she could catch the joker who thought it was fun to play pranks on the local police.

But the ringing of the telephone diverted her attention. She settled back into her chair and picked up the receiver. "Deepwater P.D.," she said briskly.

"This is Mrs. Randolph White," a familiar voice crackled. "My cat is up in a tree and I can't get her down. I called 911, but they said they don't handle cat emergencies. And don't tell me to call the fire department. They were very rude to me last time I called."

Mrs. White paused a fraction of a second to breathe and Flossie asked, "How long has Tiki been up in the tree, Mrs. White?"

"Oh for a good 30 minutes now. She wanted out. Just for a bit to get a breath of fresh air, you know. And the Huxley's mean Doberman next door chased her up a tree. That dog ought to be put to sleep!" The petulant voice became a shrill whine. "Why do the Huxleys have to keep such a vicious animal?"

She breathed again and Flossie said quickly, "It's late, Mrs. White. Nearly 11:00 o'clock. I don't know if we'll be able to help you or not, but I'll see what I can do."

"Oh, Miss, I hope you can. I don't know what I will do if my Tiki is trapped up in that tree all night. Why, I'll lie awake worrying about her until morning as sure as the world. Won't get a wink of sleep. And then I'll be so tired I'll sleep all day tomorrow and won't be able to sleep tomorrow night." A sob was coming into her voice. "Then it'll be the same thing the next day and the next. Oh, dearie me, what shall I do?" The words trailed off into a soft whimper and then the phone went dead.

Flossie sighed and dialed Ben Walling's phone number. Ben was chief homicide detective for the department, but he was a soft touch for elderly widows in distress. Even annoying ones like Mrs. White.

Ben's wife DeeDee answered the phone. "DeeDee, it's Flossie. I'm sorry to bother you so late, but Tiki's stuck up a tree again and Mrs. White is in tears. I didn't know what else to do but call Ben."

DeeDee's voice was sympathetic. "The poor dear. Don't worry; I'll send Ben and Davy right over. Tiki loves Davy and he'll have her out of that tree and home safe in just a few minutes."

Flossie set the receiver down with a sigh of relief and a smile at the thought of little Davy Walling. Davy must be about eight now, the same age as her youngest grandson Bryce. And probably an animal lover, just like Bryce. She hadn't seen Bryce in nearly a year now, since his family had moved to San Diego, and she missed him desperately. She missed them all.

"Get back to your paperwork, Flossie," she told herself sternly, "before you start blubbering all over it."

She bent determinedly over her desk, the mysterious opening and closing of the front door forgotten, until she caught movement out of the corner of her eye. She had believed she was alone in the big room and she reacted before she could stop herself.

Screaming, she leaped from her chair. It rolled backward a few inches, then toppled over and crashed to the floor.

With her heart racing she faced the intruder. It was a child - a toddler - wearing nothing except a bulky diaper. At her unexpected reaction, he let out a howl of terror and plopped onto his diapered bottom.

"Oh, baby," Flossie gasped. "You darling thing. I'm so sorry I scared you."

She scooped him up, cooing and cuddling him as only a grandmother can, and would have quickly quieted him if blue-uniformed officers hadn't piled into the room, some of them with guns drawn. He began crying again and clung to Flossie's neck.

"What is it?" "What's wrong?" "Where'd the kid come from?" the officers asked, striding about, looking down hallways and opening doors.

"Are you all right?" Nancy Montgomery asked Flossie. She was in charge during the graveyard shift that was coming on duty.

"Of course. The child startled me. I thought I was alone in the room and then - bam! there he was like a tiny spook."

"Here's his diaper bag," said a young officer, bringing a blue and white plastic bag behind the counter. "Where are the parents?"

"Search me," said Flossie. Then she remembered the door. "Wait. About ten minutes ago the door opened and closed, but no one came in. I was about to go see who was outside, but the phone rang and I forgot about it. Maybe someone put the little boy and his diaper bag inside the door and left."

"Who?" Nancy asked.

Flossie shook her head. "I never saw him before. Do any of you know him?"

The assembled group gazed at the child who had quit crying and begun sucking his thumb. With his other hand, he was clinging to Flossie's gray curls. One by one they shook their heads.

"What in creation are we going to do with him?" Flossie asked, trying to sound detached. But she was a mother bear guarding her cub.

"Call Children's Services," Nancy said with a shrug. "Nothing else we can do."

"No!" Flossie surprised even herself with the fierce tone of her voice. "I'm taking him home, at least for tonight. I'll not have him kept up for hours, passing from one pair of strange hands to another."

Nancy looked doubtful. "He has to go to the hospital to be examined first. After that..." Her voice trailed off.

"Okay." Flossie took charge. Looking around she chose a handsome young officer who, she knew, had a two-year-old of his own at home. "Miguel, you can drive us to the hospital, and..." She rummaged around in her roomy handbag and extricated her car keys. "I'll phone when I'm home and you can have someone drive my car over." She handed Nancy the key ring.

Nancy accepted the keys reluctantly. "And tomorrow?" she asked.

"Tomorrow I'll take him to Children's Services myself," Flossie promised.

Nancy nodded. "Okay, we'll go through the diaper bag and check for finger prints," she said. "We'll send the child's things to you with your car, but I think we'd better hang on to the bag itself for awhile."

"Good idea," agreed Flossie. She hooked the strap of her handbag over her shoulder and asked, "You ready, Miguel?"

"Yes, ma'am," he replied and followed her into the night.

Rescuing Tiki from a tree and a vicious Doberman during the wee hours of the night was an enormous adventure for Davy Walling. He had been easily roused by his mother and pulled on blue jeans and sneakers in a matter of moments. Now he was abuzz with excitement as he and his Dad made the drive to Mrs. White's home in Ben's tawny brown compact pickup.

"Do you think Tiki's hurt?" Davy asked anxiously.

"Are you kidding?" said Ben heartily. "Tiki's the fastest cat in the west. I bet she was up that tree in such a blur the dog thought he needed glasses."

Davy laughed at the idea of a Doberman in glasses. He chattered happily and Ben, tired after a long, frustrating day, felt his spirits rising to match Davy's mood. The father and son, both blonde-haired and brown-eyed, doted on each other. They laughed at each other's jokes and cheered for the same sports teams so, after a companionable drive through the balmy night, they arrived at Mrs. Randolph White's house in high spirits and eager for any challenge Tiki might present.

But Mrs. White didn't answer Ben's knock. She had no doorbell, so he banged louder. He was hesitant to yell for fear of disturbing her neighbors.

"Maybe she's in the back yard trying to get Tiki to come down," Davy suggested.

"Of course," Ben agreed. "Do you remember where the gate is?"

"Sure. It's over here." Davy beckoned and led the way, but he had to wait for his Dad to reach over the gate and unlatch it.

"Mrs. White," Ben called as they stepped into the yard. "Are you here?"

"Who is it?" Mrs. White's crackly voice preceded her ashen face, as she peered into the darkness. "Who's there? I'm calling the police." Her voice trembled with terror.

"It's Ben Walling, Mrs. White. Davy and I came over to get Tiki out of the tree."

"Oh, thank God." The shriveled little woman sank into a canvas lawn chair and clasped her hands over her heart. "I'm so glad you're here!"

Ben knelt in front of her and she held out her hands to him. He took them both in his and tried to warm them. It was like trying to melt ice cubes. "I'm sorry we didn't call first, but I thought you knew we were coming."

"No. The lady said she would try to get somebody, but she sounded kind of...well, I didn't think anyone would come."

"Next time, don't bother calling the station. Just call me. Then if you can't get me, call the station. Okay?"

She nodded, looking so grateful Ben wanted to cry. "Promise me," he said sternly.

"I promise," she said and a smile brightened her face.

Ben kissed her hands and gave them back to her. "Okay. Davy's dressed for tree climbing. Let's see what we can do about Tiki."

Mrs. White turned her attention to Davy, who was watching her solemnly. She held out her hand to him. "Aren't you a dear little boy?" she asked.

"Yes, ma'am," he said shyly, letting her hold one of his hands in both of hers while she beamed at him with unabashed admiration. "Well, no ma'am," he added. "Not really. I like Tiki. I'm glad my Dad let me come help her."

"I'm glad, too," Mrs. White said softly and released his hand. "Here you go. Put a handful of these in your pocket. They're Tiki's favorite treat." She held out a smelly cat delicacy and Davy wrinkled his nose as she dropped them into his shirt pocket.

Then Ben gave him a boost into the ancient mulberry tree that shaded Mrs. White's small back yard. Davy scooted up the thick, friendly branches he had climbed three times before. Tiki, a black and white feline of uncertain parentage and an air of royalty, mewed a welcome as he approached.

Watching from the ground, ready to spring into action if Davy missed a step, Ben shook his head. It seemed as if that stupid cat came out here, climbed this tree and staged a sit-in every time she was lonesome for Davy.

Davy gave Tiki one of the kitty treats from his pocket, picked her up and climbed down almost as nimbly as if he had both arms free. At the top of the trunk, Ben swung him to the ground and Davy proudly delivered Tiki to Mrs. White.

"Nope. We're going home to bed before I collapse," Ben said. But he did turn around and retrace their trail, staring long and carefully up every street they passed.

What he failed to do was drive up a murky alley half a block off Mabry Lane where a big, black car had merged into the shadows and parked.

Ben, driving past the end of the alley was saying to Davy, "I was proud of you tonight, son. You did something nice for somebody and didn't expect to be paid for it."

"I got paid for it," Davy said, still scouring the dark streets with his eyes while his Dad stared at him.

"What do you mean?"

Davy looked at him then. "Helping Mrs. White made me feel good," he explained. "Isn't that why people take drugs and drink beer? To feel good?"

"That's what they say."

Davy smiled wisely at his Dad. "Maybe they ought to do something nice for somebody instead."

Ben's grin covered half his face. "Somebody's doing a good job of raising you, kid. You must have some kind of mother!"

Davy tried to suppress a little half grin. "My Dad's not too bad, either."

Ben turned onto Mabry Lane and the black limo glided silently out of the alley onto Tomlin Street. The head lights came on and the big car drove rapidly away two minutes before the first patrol car arrived and began methodically prowling up and down every street and alley in the area.

Chapter II

At Carlyle Memorial Hospital, Joel Trent, the hospital's departing CEO, put down a handful of papers he had been studying for the next day's board meeting. He wanted his last board meeting at Carlyle to go smoothly. And he wanted every file and report to be in order for his successor. Well, things were as perfect now as he could get them, so he might as well close up shop and go home.

He sank back in his chair to enjoy a sense of accomplishment and his eyes fell on the framed photograph of Tobi Kirkland that was so new to his desk it sometimes startled him to see her emerald green eyes smiling at him. He touched the glass that covered the photo and imagined he was touching the soft masses of her red-gold hair. But when he caught a glimpse of his balding pate in the glass's reflection, he winced. "What does she see in me?" he asked himself for the thousandth time.

It frightened him when he realized how much Tobi meant to him. Ever since his divorce, over a decade earlier, he had avoided romantic entanglements, remembering how marriage had transformed a beautiful, soft-spoken woman into a nagging shrew. And, although a sense of failure dogged his steps over the broken marriage, he had breathed a sigh of relief when Rachel married Paul Hudson and the full weight of her tedious, whining childishness had been transferred to Paul's shoulders.

Even after Rachel married, he had shied away from women until the day he idly picked up an edition of the *City Crier*, the local newspaper, and found a column on the editorial page about gentleness. Gentleness! He gazed at the photo of the writer at the top of the column. Her name was Tobi Kirkland and she was city editor of the *Crier*.

Joel folded up the newspaper and took it home where he read and reread the column. Was it possible that the city editor of a newspaper could be gentle? And was it possible that a woman - even a woman possessed of monumental gentleness - could marry and retain her gentleness? Perhaps, but he had been burned once. Wouldn't he be a fool to make himself vulnerable again?

The answer was yes, of course, but it was too late. Joel's preoccupation with Tobi had drained him of good sense and, when he learned she was single, he became consumed with a desire to meet her. To date her. To know her.

Joel smiled, remembering their turbulent early encounters. If he'd had any sense left, their first meeting would have been their last. But his passion for her, perhaps intensified by many years without close female companionship, had taken control and he had pursued her as ardently and foolishly as Don Quixote had tilted with windmills.

Joel resisted a desire to kiss the photograph and picked up the receiver of his telephone instead. He shouldn't call her so late. But he did. And he didn't admit, even to himself, that he wanted to know how she would react to the late night phone call. That he wanted to observe her in every disagreeable situation possible until he learned whether gentleness were only a facade with her or if it went as deep as her heart.

"Hi, Joel," she answered the phone. "Why are you still at the hospital?"

"Being compulsive, I guess," he said, realizing suddenly how tired he was. "I decided I needed to recheck all my figures and the wording in the reports. I want everything to be perfect for my last board meeting."

"You must be exhausted."

"I am and I know you are too. I'm sorry for calling so late. Were you asleep?"

"Not yet."

He hesitated before he said, "Look, I know it's ridiculous at this hour of the night, but would it be all right if I come over for a few minutes?"

"Of course. Joel, you can come over any time. I thought you knew that." The excitement in her voice at the prospect of seeing him assured him that she was sincere.

"Thanks. I'm heading out right now."

As his custom was, Joel walked through the Emergency Room on his way to the employees' parking lot. In the ER lobby, a middle-aged man guiltily crushed out a cigarette in his empty coffee cup, then snapped at the little girl with him to sit down and shut up. Joel's lips fairly twitched with angry words, but he restrained himself. It was too late and he was too tired to speak calmly to an insufferable idiot smoking in a hospital! Better to find the receptionist and sic her on the selfish lout.

The emergency room was a labyrinth of curtained cubicles. Behind one curtain, a machine beeped angrily, and anguished voices spoke in urgent whispers. One other cubicle was closed and silent. The rest stood open, waiting for the next patient.

Joel strode to the nurses' desk. "Martha, there's a man smoking in the lobby," he said. "Why don't we have a receptionist out there?"

Giving him a frazzled grimace, she said, "I'll take care of it."

As Martha disappeared into the lobby, the curtain of the silent cubicle was flung aside. A woman with iron-gray curls and an exasperated expression looked him up and down. "Are you the doctor?" she asked irritably.

"No, ma'am, but I do work here. Joel Trent," he said, holding out a hand, which she shook briefly. "Have you been waiting long?"

"Probably not as long as it seems," she admitted, "but I do need to get this baby home to bed." She nodded toward the toddler who was sleeping peacefully.

"Is he sick?" Joel asked curiously, observing the child's healthy appearance.

"No. He was left at the police station around 10:45," Flossie said. "Nobody knows who he is. You wouldn't happen to know him, would you?"

Joel studied the rosy face, framed by thick, damp, black hair. For a moment he hesitated. There *was* something familiar about the child.

Finally he shook his head. "He's a beautiful baby, but I've never seen him before. You say he was left at the police station?"

"That's right. I'm Flossie Bobbsey, by the way. I'm the dispatcher on the evening shift for the P.D. Somebody opened the front door, put the child and his diaper bag inside, then disappeared.

"What are you going to do with him?" Joel asked.

"Take him home for the night," said Flossie firmly, "then take him to Children's Services in the morning."

Joel nodded. "Poor little, fella'. I wonder what happened to his folks."

"I wonder what happened to that doctor," Flossie said, glancing at her watch.

"I'll see if I can round him up for you," Joel said. "Please let us know if there's anything we can do to help find this youngster's parents."

"Thank you, Mr. Trent," Flossie said, "but I guess that problem will pass to Children's Services tomorrow."

He nodded. "I guess so. Well, I'll see what I can do about getting a doctor here."

"That would be a great help," she said approvingly.

After consulting Martha, Joel made a phone call to radiology where the ER doctor had gone with a patient. Then, anxious to get away before another problem arose, he stepped out of the hospital into the warm night. Feeling suffocated, he yanked off his tie and wrenched open the top button of his shirt. Breathing easier, he got into the navy blue SUV he had driven off the new car lot ten years earlier, turned the air conditioner on high, and headed for Tobi's house.

Tobi opened the door before Joel could knock. Her house, as cool as an ice cave, and fragrant with the scent of a vanilla candle, beckoned to him. She took his hand and led him inside. Shutting the door behind them, she threw her arms around him and scattered feathery kisses over his neck.

Laughing and shivering with goose bumps, Joel captured her face in his hands for a long, satisfying kiss. Tobi tightened her embrace as he kissed her and her body softened and melted into his. His arms enclosed her and drew her closer. The heat and frustration outside this sweet, silent sanctuary were beginning to drain away.

Kissing Tobi was the most intoxicating experience Joel had ever known. And he hated himself for it, but he often struggled to remember if he had ever had such intense feelings for Rachel. It wasn't right to compare Tobi to a woman he now classified with hags, crones and shrews, but he seemed unable to stop himself. And he lived in a terror that Tobi would realize how much power she held over him. What would she do then?

She spoke in a muffled voice he couldn't understand and he realized that, after the kiss, he had enclosed her in a suffocating embrace. "What did you say?" he asked, loosening his hold so she could come up for air.

"Are you hungry? Thirsty? May I get you something?"

"No thanks. I want to talk a few minutes and then I'll get out of your hair."

She smiled impishly. "I like having you in my hair."

"Don't tell me that," he whispered huskily, kissing her briefly again. "You may never get rid of me."

She followed him toward her green-and-gold sofa and blinked in surprise when he sank into the recliner, instead, and pulled her into his lap. She nestled into his arms, and waited for him to begin. They usually sat on the sofa but, when something was bothering Joel, he wanted her in his lap. She wasn't sure why. Maybe her nearness was reassuring to him. Or perhaps her facial expressions distracted him from his train of thought.

Whatever was troubling him tonight, he was in no hurry to discuss it. "What's wrong?" she finally asked.

His arms tightened around her. "I'm going away for a week or two."

"Going away where?"

Her voice held only surprise and curiosity. No shock. No anger. No rebuke. Joel breathed easier. "To Dallas."

"Why?"

"I have an uncle there who knows a retired seminary professor who's willing to give me some time this summer, showing me where Charismatic doctrine is wrong in its interpretations of New Testament passages. I think I need to go. I want to understand exactly what I believe and why."

His voice sounded breathy and Tobi knew he had reached the part he was nervous about. "I joined a Charismatic church because of Rachel. Then I began to see some problems in Charismatic doctrine because of your influence, but I need to find my own way. It's not that I don't respect you and your beliefs, but..."

Tobi sat up and turned toward him so she could study his face. His heart sank when he saw the deep wrinkles in her forehead.

"Joel Trent, you don't have a clue how much I believe in you, do you?" she asked with mock severity.

"What do you mean?" He was afraid to imagine that she might not be furious with him. For going away. For declining to accept her beliefs just because they were her beliefs. For any of the hundreds of things men do that infuriate women and the men never understand why.

"You get this nervous, somber tone in your voice like you're about to tell me you have only two months to live. Then all you say is that you're going to Dallas. I'll miss you like crazy but, if that's what you've decided to do, then do it. I trust your decisions."

She could see that he needed a few moments to digest this little speech, so she snuggled back into his arms and waited. "I thought you'd be furious," he said at last.

"Why?"

"We were going to move to Westley in two weeks and take over Dad's newspaper. He's ready to retire. You're half packed. You don't have a job. What are you going to do while I'm lolling around Dallas in some esoteric analysis of the New Testament?"

Tobi shrugged. "I don't know. I'll pray about it."

"That's it? You'll pray about it? You're not going to yell at me and tell me I'm an insensitive, selfish lout?"

Tobi laughed out loud. "If you ever turn into an insensitive, selfish lout, I'll be the first one to yell at you. Until then, I better not catch anybody telling such monstrous lies about you."

"You don't want to hang around Rachel, then," Joel muttered.

"I'm not Rachel," Tobi said, suddenly understanding why he was tense.

"Thank God," Joel said fervently, holding her closer. "Thank God!"

Tobi had a frightening notion that she could be happy vegetating in Joel's embrace for the rest of her life. Surely she would grow bored of it eventually and be ready to do something else. Surely! But at this moment in their young relationship, she could imagine no greater joy than being in his arms.

Even so, she soon realized there was something else on his mind. "What else?" she asked.

"Hmm?" He murmured absently.

"Is there something else you're worried about?"

"Are you sure you want to know?" he asked. "It's not anything you should have to be concerned with."

Tobi's fingers went to the tense muscles in the back of Joel's neck and she began massaging them as deeply as she could in the limited space available there. "Tell me," she urged.

He took a deep breath. "I'm probably borrowing trouble, but I'm afraid Rachel is going to give Paul the boot. Then she'll be calling on me every time she needs something. And Rachel *always* needs something."

"What makes you think she and Paul are going to break up?"

"Do you remember the morning after Gracie's appendectomy when Paul stood up to her?"

Tobi smiled at the memory. That morning was the first time Joel ever held her in his arms, exactly as he was doing now. "I remember," she said. "What about it?"

"Rachel doesn't tolerate that kind of treatment very well. She expects everyone around her to salute and obey her slightest whim. Gloria and Gracie think Paul's getting a gut full. If he quits fawning over her, she'll send him packing."

"Is that what happened to you?" Tobi asked.

"Indirectly. When I'd had all I could take, I joined the Navy. Went off to sail the ocean blue, leaving her alone with two babies. She moved to Deepwater because her parents lived here then and, when I got out of the Navy, Paul was waiting in the wings."

"I'm so sorry," said Tobi, working diligently on muscles in his neck and shoulders that seemed to tense up again as quickly as she rubbed the knots out of them.

"Don't be sorry. The day she married Paul Hudson was the happiest day of my life," he said in a voice that sounded anything but happy.

"Except for Gloria and Gracie," Tobi said softly.

"Except for Gloria and Gracie," he echoed brokenly. "I should have found a way to stick it out for their sakes - at least until they were grown."

"I know that's true," Tobi said, "but I'm glad you didn't."

"I am too." He grinned suddenly and kissed her, but with a fervency that was less intense than usual and she pulled away suddenly to glare at him accusingly. "There's something else bothering you, isn't there?"

His face fell. "How can you already know me so well?"

Tobi had no intention of explaining that she loved him with all her heart. Not yet. So she ignored the question. "What's wrong? No wonder you're so tense. You're carrying the weight of the world on your shoulders!"

"Not quite the whole world," he said.

"Tell me about it." She went back to kneading the muscles in his neck.

"There's going to be an evangelist holding meetings over at the Living Vine the rest of this week," he said, referring to the Church of the Living Vine, which had been his church home until he met Tobi. "The girls are beside themselves with excitement. They believe he's going to get the whole town saved and turned on to Jesus."

"And..." Tobi prompted.

Joel gazed into her emerald eyes with a heartsick expression on his face. "He's been to Toronto. His goal is to spread that darkness to every corner of this nation."

"The 'Toronto Blessing'?" Tobi asked.

He nodded.

A tidal wave of weakness swept through Tobi. Her hands went limp. "Dear God, have mercy," she whispered.

"I have to go at least once," Joel said, "If I don't, how can I talk to the girls about it?"

A surge of revulsion that felt much like nausea hit Tobi next. Was there no end to the sacrifices a parent was required to make for his children?

Joel's next question blind-sided her. "Will you go with me?" he asked.

Tobi hesitated. She had believed there was nothing Joel could ask of her that she wouldn't gladly do for him. This thing she would do, but there

"Oh, you precious child, thank you!" Mrs. White said, kissing Davy's blond hair. "I can't thank you enough." She cradled Tiki in both arms and scratched behind her ears. "What a naughty, naughty girl you are!" she fussed affectionately at the cat. Tiki purred and smiled.

"Good night, Mrs. White," Ben said. "I'd better get this young 'un back to bed."

"Good night, Ben. Good night, Davy. I wish I knew some way to show you how grateful I am for your help." She followed them through the gate into the front yard.

"It's thanks enough to know that Tiki's safe," Ben assured her. "Right Davy?"

"Yes ma'am," said Davy eagerly. "That's all we want - to know Tiki's safe."

She watched them with eyes full of tears, as Ben began backing the pickup out of her driveway. Still rolling backward, he glanced at Mrs. White and waved one more time.

"Stop, Dad!" Davy shrieked.

Ben slammed on the brakes, as a huge, dark car slid past them on the street. It had no lights on.

"Where did *that* come from?" Ben gasped as he watched the shadowy form gather speed and turn the next corner with tires squealing.

"It just turned off that street," Davy said, pointing.

Ben glanced in the direction Davy indicated, then put his own vehicle into motion. "Hang on," he told Davy, as he backed into the street and slammed the gearshift into Drive. The pickup flew to the next corner and turned, but the mysterious car had disappeared. Ben drove several blocks, peering both directions at each intersection, but the ghostly car was gone.

Disgustedly he pulled out his cell phone and called the police station. When the night dispatcher answered, he asked for Nancy Montgomery - pronto!

"This is Ben Walling," he said tersely when she came on. "I nearly plowed into a dark, luxury car just now. It came off Tomlin Street onto Mabry Lane, then turned right onto Hanover. It's running without lights. I tried to catch it, but I was too slow. I couldn't get the make or model, but maybe the guys on the streets can watch out for it."

Nancy acknowledged the information and disconnected. Ben grinned. She was one sharp woman!

"Are we going to keep looking for the car?" Davy asked. He was still squinting diligently at every car that passed.

would be no "gladly" about it. "Couldn't we just hike through Siberia in the dead of winter?" she asked plaintively.

He smiled and shook his head.

"How about if we take on the Sahara Desert during the dry season?"

"You don't have to go," he said resignedly.

"But I will," she said, nuzzling his neck, "because I would rather be at that disgusting meeting with you than anywhere else without you."

"Really?" His face lighted up.

"Oh yes." Her voice was low and provocative. Her eyes smoldered with desire for him. And this time, Joel kissed her with an eagerness that told her his troubles were, at least temporarily, forgotten.

"I'd better go before you kick me out," Joel said finally. "Thanks for letting me come by."

"I'd like to pray for you before you leave," Tobi said. "Do you have time?"

Joel nodded. "Of course."

Tobi smiled into his eyes and kissed his cheek before she began to pray softly, but so close to his ear that Joel easily understood every word. "Father, thank You for bringing this wonderful man into my life. Tonight I'd like to ask You to equip him with Godly wisdom in the board meeting tomorrow, then when he goes to Dallas to study Your Word and in every aspect of his relationship with Rachel, Gloria and Gracie. Help him to know that You're with him - directing his steps, putting words in his mouth and guiding his thoughts - so that he will be filled with Your peace that passes understanding. Let his rest be sweet tonight. And be his joy and strength all day every day. In Jesus' name. Amen."

There was an intimacy and childlike confidence in Tobi's voice when she prayed that made Joel think God would hear and answer her prayers if He heard no other. And when she prayed for him in that tender voice, his heart ached, his throat closed and his eyes burned with unshed tears. He wanted to pray for her, too, but he couldn't get his voice box to cooperate. If it meant half as much to her as her prayers meant to him, he was cheating her out of a remarkable blessing.

He coughed and cleared his throat, but it was no use. If he started to pray for her, he would cry instead. Then she would know he was hopelessly smitten with her. And he would be at her mercy.

"Next time," he finally told her, feeling like a clod, "I'll pray for *you*. When you pray for me first, I get so choked up, my throat won't work. I'm sorry."

"It's not a business transaction," Tobi said gently. "I prayed for you because I wanted to - not so you would pray for me."

"I know. But I want to. And I do pray for you every day." Suddenly he grinned ruefully. "In fact..." He paused. Why was he spilling his guts? What if he offended her? He should shut up before it was too late. But Tobi was waiting patiently for him to finish his sentence, so he did. "Sometimes I start thinking things I shouldn't be thinking about you...yet. And when that happens, I pray for you instead."

A smile lit up Tobi's face. "Then I hope that happens to you as often as it does to me, because it means you're praying for me a lot."

He stared at her for a long moment. Was she saying what he thought she was saying? A coy little smile and the hungry desire in her eyes told him she was. "I think I better get out of here," he said with some urgency.

"I think that's a good idea," Tobi agreed.

She walked him to the door where he paused for one last, lingering kiss. But it didn't linger long. A picture flashed across his mind and he pulled away from Tobi suddenly to say, "Gracie!"

"Where?" Tobi asked, looking around.

"Not here," he said. "It's that baby! He reminded me of Gracie."

"What baby?"

"There was a baby - a toddler, actually - at the hospital who had been left mysteriously at the police station this evening. When I saw him I knew I didn't know him, but he looked familiar. I just realized why - Gracie looked a lot like him at that age."

Frown lines creased his forehead as he tried to understand why the unknown toddler should bear a resemblance to Gracie. Maybe Rachel still had relatives in town. He should probably call her tomorrow and ask. He shuddered at the thought.

Tobi's head was on his chest and her eyes were closed. He kissed her hair. "Good night, Tob. I'll call you in the morning. We'll have to go to Living Vine tomorrow evening because I'm leaving for Dallas Friday."

She nodded sleepily. "Okay. Good night, Joel."

From the door she watched the tall, athletic figure stroll across her yard. "I love you, Joel Trent," she whispered. "I love you."

Chapter III

Joel walked into his office the next morning with a vast sense of foreboding. He had to call Rachel. He *had* to! He thought of her high, whiny voice and her endless prating about imaginary persecutions, and groaned soulfully.

He sat down at his big, mahogany desk for only a moment, then got up and roamed around the red-carpeted office. Pausing in front of his diplomas, he straightened them - one for his Bachelor's degree in journalism, the other a Master's degree in business administration. They had been perfectly aligned before he "straightened" them. Now they were cock-eyed. Not noticing, he moved on to the picture of the soccer team he had coached the preceding fall and picked out Davy Walling, Tobi's nephew. Cute kid!

A glance out the window gave him a view of a parking lot. Nothing on it was stirring. He sighed. If it had to be done, better to do it and be done with it. "Eat a bucket of frogs every morning, and your day can only get better," he muttered, sitting down again.

"You're not getting ready to call Rachel this morning, are you?" Joel's secretary Vi Crofton stood in the doorway of his office studying him.

Joel turned a pitiful face to the sympathetic woman in her mid fifties who typed his letters and reports and, in every way, smoothed the path before him. "How did you know?"

"First you groaned out loud. Then you roamed around your office. Now you're muttering to yourself. I don't know of anything else that can get you so edgy. Do you want me to call her for you?"

"Yes," he said sorrowfully, "but I won't do that to you." Then he grinned, remembering Vi's last conversation with Rachel, after which she reported that Rachel had spent 45 minutes bawling like a mama cow with an udder full of milk and its baby lost on the back 40. "I'm dialing now," he said, jabbing the numbers viciously. "God forbid that she doesn't answer and I have to go through this again."

But Rachel answered and Vi returned to her desk. "Rachel, it's Joel. Do you still have any relatives in town with a baby? A toddler, actually." He went straight to the point.

"Good morning to you too," she said sarcastically.

Of course. She was a stickler for protocol. Now he would get a lecture on courtesy - why didn't he show her the same simple courtesies he would show complete strangers?

He held the receiver away from his ear until it quit whining. When he put it against his ear again, he heard only silence. "So do you?" he asked.

"I'm waiting for my apology," Rachel said stiffly.

"I apologize," he said, knowing he could only prolong the agony if he refused.

"Now," she said, sounding pleased with herself, "why do you want to know about babies or toddlers or whatever it was?"

"A toddler - maybe 18 months old - with thick black hair and a sweet face. When I saw him, I thought he looked familiar. Later I realized he reminded me of Gracie at that age."

"Well, who is he? Why do you want to know if I'm related to him?"

"He was left at the police station last night and no one knows who he is. I thought I should call you and ask if he might be the child of a relative."

To his surprise, Rachel did not answer. She had an entire repertoire of annoying conversational devices. Silence was not one of them.

"Rachel, are you there?"

"Where is the child now?"

"I guess he's been turned over to Children's Services. Or he will be today. Do you think you know who he is?"

"Of course not!" The familiar whine had returned to her tone. "Can't a mother feel sorry for a poor, lost lamb? I don't have to know the child to care about his welfare, do I?"

"No, of course not. Well, thanks anyway."

"Joel, wait!" The whiny tone had been replaced by Rachel's drill-sergeant voice.

"What, Rachel?"

"The girls say you're coming to the revival tonight."

"What about it?"

"I haven't seen you in church lately. Are you backsliding?"

"I'm going to another church."

There was a short, ominous silence before she said, "Another church?"

"That's right."

"There's not another church in this town worth attending. I hope you don't think I'm going to allow you to lead our daughters away from the truth."

"I would never lead anyone away from the truth," he said sincerely, then added firmly, "I have a board meeting this morning. I have to go." He yanked the phone away from his ear and jammed it back into its cradle before he could hear her next complaint. She would rake him over the coals about courtesy again the next time he saw her.

His phone rang. Maybe she was in a raking mood right now. "Vi, would you get that? I can't take any more of her this morning," he called plaintively.

"I've got it, boss," Vi called cheerfully. "Joel Trent's office," he heard her say. A long silence ensued. Rachel was putting her through the wringer. He buried his face in his hands. One "I do" and he was still paying for it almost two decades later. Vi was paying too.

What ever possessed men to get married in the first place?

———

Flossie had risen early in spite of her late hours the preceding night - actually, her early hours that morning. She made short work of her preparations for the day - a shower, a few swipes of makeup, and a handful of dishes hidden in the seldom used dishwasher. She was at the back door with one hand on the knob and two loaded garbage bags in the other hand when she heard a wail from her bedroom where the toddler had slept on a pallet on the floor.

Leaving the garbage bags at the door, she flew through the house to his side with a joyful step. "Good morning, you sweetie pie," she cooed. "How did you sleep? I hope the floor wasn't too awful hard."

The child quit crying and gurgled happily instead. When she bent over to pick him up, he lifted his arms to her, then settled against her breast with an arm around her neck. "What a precious little doll you are," she murmured. "Your poor Mama must be beside herself with grief, not knowing where you are."

Flossie laid him on the bed to change his diaper and considered her last words. What if his Mama did know where he was? What if it was his Mama who had abandoned him at the police station? She studied the cherubic face and shook her head. No way. The mother who was raising this cheerful, trusting child didn't abandon him. She loved him too much for that. Flossie knew it was true because the child knew it was true. It was written all over his chubby little face.

"Well, how about some breakfast?" she asked, completing the diapering and swinging him into her arms again.

He stared straight into her eyes and said, with a question in his voice, "Ma-ma?"

Her heart shuddered. "Your Mama will be back real soon. I just know she will." Flossie said the words and prayed they were true.

The child ate a bowl of apple cinnamon oatmeal hungrily and drank milk out of a small plastic mug that Bryce had used when he was a toddler. Then Flossie dressed him in a yellow sunsuit that had been in his diaper bag. It took some searching to find the car seat all her grandchildren had ridden in, but finally she located the pile it was buried under, washed it off, and secured it in the back seat of her car.

Her energy was already waning and the sun was high in a cloudless sky when she carried the child to the car. "Looks like we're revving up for another scorcher," she told him, as she strapped him in.

At the Court House, Flossie wielded her most authoritative voice. "I need to see Max," she told the receptionist in Children's Services.

"Do you have an appointment?" the girl asked, studying a calendar in front of her.

"No, but please tell him it's Flossie Bobbsey."

The girl shrugged. When she picked up the phone, Flossie let out a silent sigh of relief. If she could get to Max, she would have no trouble convincing him to let her keep the baby for a few weeks. And since he was the director of this department, the child was as good as hers. At least, he was hers until a parent or other relative could be located.

It took an hour to photograph, fingerprint and fill out papers. Flossie stepped back into the sunlight feeling more lighthearted than she had in years. She shopped for diapers and another set of play clothes. She would stock up on baby food on the way home, but first the police station.

The receptionist during the day shift was named Tanya something. She greeted Flossie warmly, but with some surprise. "You're a few hours early, aren't you?"

"Just a few. I'm looking for child care, and I don't know where to begin. So I thought I'd come by here and see if I could round up an idea or two."

"Is that the baby from last night?" Tanya asked. She held out her hand to the child and he latched on to a finger. "Aren't you adorable?" she said, smoothing his dark hair with her other hand. "Oh, Flossie, what a sweetheart! What are you going to do with him?"

"Keep him two weeks. Then, if no one has claimed him, he'll go into the system."

"Oh no!" Tanya wailed. "Surely his mother will show up before then."

"I'm betting she will if she can," Flossie agreed, trying not to sound morbid.

Tanya's eyes widened. "You don't think she's...she's...

"I'm trying not to think," said Flossie. "I just know whoever is raising this little tyke is doing too good a job not to be crazy in love with him."

Tanya nodded. "Well, I don't know any baby sitters since I don't have a baby yet, but maybe somebody in the back will have an idea. There are several young dads and Sue's child is just now old enough for pre-school."

Flossie nodded. "Wish me luck.'

"Luck!"

But Flossie hadn't picked up a single lead by the time she reached Ben Walling's desk. She almost didn't stop and disturb him, knowing both of his children were school age, and his wife, a teacher, was home with them in the summer. But Ben looked up and hailed her. "Flossie, where've you been? I miss you since you started working evenings."

"Yeah, I miss all you spit-fire day cops, too," she grinned. "Listen, thanks for getting me off the hook with Mrs. White last night. I don't know what I would have done if DeeDee hadn't agreed to send you over there."

Ben's expression sobered instantly. "I'm the one who should be thanking you," he said. "She could have fussed around that back yard, fallen, broken a hip, and never been discovered until it was too late. I'm so glad you let me know she needed help."

"You must be some kind of saint," said Flossie. "She's the whiniest old widow in town. I wouldn't have been surprised if DeeDee had yelled at me and slammed the phone in my ear at the very name of Mrs. Randolph White. What makes you so fond of her?"

Ben smiled sadly. "She reminds me of my grandmother. Grammy died in a nursing home a month after she fell and broke her hip. I didn't get to come to the funeral. Dad was stationed in the Philippines at the time, and he was the only one who flew home for the funeral. I always felt... Well, I didn't have a sense of closure, and it haunts me when I hear about an elderly person with a problem. I always think I'd do anything to make sure she doesn't break a hip." He smiled ruefully. "Pretty juvenile, I guess."

"Pretty sweet, I'd say," Flossie contradicted.

"Ah, sweet...," he mused, "just what I always wanted to be. Sweet!"

"Don't knock it!" Flossie said. "Being sweet is what drives the women wild."

"Thanks for the tip. I'll try it out on DeeDee," Ben said with a wink. "Is that one of the grandchildren?" He nodded at the dark-haired toddler.

"No, this is the baby that was left here last night. I'm looking for child care for him while I work. It's either that or I'll have to take vacation time now and won't be able to visit my own grandkids next month."

"I thought that child was at Children's Services," said Ben.

"I just left there. He's in my care for two weeks and, Lord willing, his Mom or Dad will show up by then. Otherwise, it's foster care."

Ben made a face. "We'll have to help you pray for his family to come back."

"Thanks. Pray hard," said Flossie. "You wouldn't happen to know where I could find some cheap, reliable child care for a couple of weeks, would you?"

"Well..." Ben thought a moment. "You know, I just might." He picked up the telephone receiver and began punching in numbers.

Tobi was walking past the phone when it rang and she picked it up on the first ring, hoping it would be Joel. Instead, it was Ben, calling from the police station. "Listen, Tobi, when is it you're planning to move?"

"I'm not sure. It was going to be two weeks, but Joel may not be ready for a month."

"Hey! That's good news. Maybe your sister, your niece, and your nephew will postpone their crying for awhile when they know you'll be here two extra weeks."

"What about my brother-in-law?" she asked. "Are you crying your eyes out over me?"

"I'm afraid there's no hope for me. I'll be crying over you for the rest of my life."

"In that case, I'd better stay. But you'll have to adopt me since I don't have a job."

"Well, what d'ya know. I have a lady right here who has a job for you. Hang on."

Tobi frowned at the phone at this unexpected development.

"Hello," said a pleasant voice.

"Hello," replied Tobi.

"Ms. Kirkland. My name is Flossie Bobbsey and I'm looking for someone to take care of a toddler for a couple of weeks from 2:30 P.M. to 11:30. Is there any chance that you'd be interested?"

Tobi's mouth had dropped open. Now she pushed her chin up with her hand and tried to think of a response.

"Ms. Kirkland? Are you there?"

"Is this some kind of joke?" Tobi asked. Ben Walling was going to pay if he was pulling some stupid practical joke on her!

"Of course not! Why do you ask?"

"Flossie Bobbsey is a fictional girl in a series of children's books."

"Oh. I forget sometimes," said Flossie. "Not many people seem to remember the Bobbsey twins any more, so I've kinda' gotten out of the habit of explaining. My parents named me Hortense after some ancient ancestor. When I married Fred Bobbsey, I had a head full of blond curls. So his buddies in the department started calling me Flossie. I liked it better than Hortense, so I kept it, even if my hair *is* gray now."

Tobi was still frowning when Flossie finished. "Listen," she said, "if you're helping Ben pull some ridiculous prank on me, you should know that he may not live over it."

"It's no joke," Flossie protested. "I'm an old, gray-haired grandmother with a problem. I need to know if you can help or not because, if you can't, I have to find someone who can."

"Okay," Tobi relented. "Tell me about it."

Flossie told her tale and asked Tobi to come to her house around 2:00 that afternoon to get acquainted. After this first day, she would bring the child to Tobi around 2:30 each afternoon. Tobi would bring him to Flossie's at bedtime and stay with him there until Flossie got home around 11:30. It wasn't a lucrative job, but Flossie assured her it would pay richly in satisfaction. "This is the most adorable child you'll ever see in this county, now that *my* grandkids have moved to San Diego," she promised.

After receiving Flossie's blessing on her plan to leave the little one in the church nursery for an hour or two that evening, Tobi hung up. Her heart felt light. Two weeks with an adorable toddler! She smiled toward Heaven and said, "Thank You, Lord. I never would have looked for this job, but I can't wait to start!"

The phone in her hand rang again, startling her. "Hello," she said into the receiver.

"Hi, Beautiful! Are you waiting for me?" said a familiar voice.

Kent Grantham. His movie-star handsome face flashed across her mental screen. She closed her eyes and tried to erase the picture. It was replaced with the memory of his steely gray eyes - eyes dark with deadly intent.

"Kent," she said, trying to make her voice steady. He had been in jail a couple of weeks now for the murder of his stepfather, Hugh Mansett.

Since he hadn't called her after his arrest, she had assumed she wouldn't be hearing from him again. At least, not until she faced him at his trial. "Where are you?" she asked weakly.

"I'm holed up in your local institution of incarceration, of course, thanks to that brother-in-law of yours."

"Well, it was either you or me," she said, remembering her horror upon hearing that Hugh had been killed with a gun registered to her. And later, her horror upon learning that Kent had been the one who had framed her for the murder. Kent who had pretended to be a dear friend for many years. What a Judas he was!

"I guess you'll never forgive me for doing that to you, will you?"

While Tobi tried to think of an answer, he went on. "Of course not. Why should you? Look, I don't have much time. I called to ask you if you would come by the jail and see me tomorrow."

"No!" slipped past her lips before she could stop it, but she had to add, "What for?"

"It's pretty lonely in here. I know you should hate me, but your religion doesn't allow you to hate anyone, does it? So I was hoping you'd come by and brighten up my life."

She was shaking her head, but he couldn't see that. "I'll have to think about it," she said finally. "I don't really want to see you again, Kent, but I feel sorry for you. Maybe..."

"I don't need your pity," he said and his voice sounded hard and angry. "If you can't come as a friend, don't come at all." Then the dial tone buzzed in her ear.

She pushed "end" on her portable phone and sighed. A friend? What was he trying to pull now? Surely he couldn't imagine that she was stupid enough to think of him as a friend after he had tried to frame her for murder! She couldn't think of even one reason why she should visit him in jail. Except that, as always, she had to consider whether she might be able to sow some seed that might one day bring him to the Lord.

"You're a fool, Tobi Kirkland," she said out loud. "You've been trying to sow God's Word in that man for years, and for what? All he does is use and manipulate you."

She would pray about it. And she would mention it to Joel although she already knew what he would say. She let Joel's image form in her imagination. She could already see the hurt in his hazel eyes and the worried creases in his forehead when he heard she was considering a visit to Kent in jail. He wouldn't like it. In fact, he would hate it.

Tobi sat down in her recliner and tried to imagine the whole scene with Joel. How angry would he get? Would he try to convince her not to see

Kent? Might he even order her not to make the visit? Hmm, it would be interesting to see how he would react.

Suddenly she was determined to visit Kent, not because she wanted to see Kent, but because she wanted to know what Joel would say. What he would do. As a result of his disastrous marriage, he had his issues. But she'd had her own disastrous marriage and she had issues, too. She had no intention of ever marrying again without finding out what she was getting into. She couldn't afford to pass up this chance to test Joel's reaction to an unpleasant situation.

The phone rang again, and she answered it resignedly. But her mood brightened when she heard Joel's voice.

"Is the board meeting over?" she asked.

"Just finished."

"How did it go?"

"It was pretty tough," he said. "They offered me a big raise if I would stay and, for a few minutes there, I couldn't remember why I was leaving."

"What did you tell them?" Tobi asked.

"That leaving Carlyle Memorial is one of the hardest things I've ever done."

"Are you sorry you're leaving?" asked Tobi. "You should stay if you've changed your mind. I could find a job somewhere."

"I know you could. But I want to go. Dad's newspaper has been a life long dream of mine. Carlyle has been a great job, but it's not in my blood the way the newspaper is."

"Well, I'm glad the hospital board recognizes how valuable you are," she said. "That should make you feel good."

"It makes me feel good *and* bad," he said. "I'm glad they want me to stay but, at the same time, it's that much harder to leave." Suddenly he changed the subject. "Look, what about tonight? Do you want to stop at Cleo's Kitchen for a bite on the way to church?"

"I'd love to, but you may not like the idea so well when you hear about my new job."

"Your new job? Already? And what does it have to do with our stopping at Cleo's for dinner?"

Tobi couldn't keep the excitement out of her voice. "Do you remember the toddler you told me about last night? Well, I'm going to be keeping him from 2:30 in the afternoon to 11:30 at night for the next two weeks. So he'll be with us tonight."

"You're kidding!" Joel's voice sounded almost as excited as hers. "I'm sorry I'll be in Dallas. I could help you entertain him if I were going to be here."

"Really?" Tobi was amazed. "You'd like that?"

"Sure, I would. He's a cute kid. And he's welcome to join us tonight for dinner."

Tobi's heart warmed and her eyes misted, as they finalized their plans for the evening. When she had met Joel's secretary Violet Crofton, Vi had said of Joel, "I fall in love with him every day and, if you don't watch out, you will too." Tobi had been infatuated with Kent at the time and furious with Joel. Yet Vi's words had been prophetic, for here she was falling in love with him for the hundredth time.

Chapter IV

Tobi arrived at Flossie's house in the stifling heat of early afternoon. No one responded to her knock, so she went around to the back yard. Flossie was there, rearranging sprinklers.

Tobi gazed longingly at the sparkling droplets of water dancing upward into the simmering air. Oh to be a kid again, playing in the back yard sprinklers! She flirted with the idea of making one wild dash through the closest sprinkler, but contented herself with pausing in the shade near the house. "Hello!" she called.

"Oh!" Flossie looked up with a start. "I didn't hear you. I'm nearly through here."

When two new patches of lawn were being watered, she pushed her hair back and breathed a sigh of relief. "One of these days I'm going to break down and put in a sprinkler system. I'm too old for this scrabblin' around in the heat."

"That does sound like a good idea," Tobi smiled.

"I just put the baby down for a nap, and I'm calling him Johnny. He has to be called something besides 'baby' all the time," Flossie said. "It looks like the person who shoved him into our lobby could have pinned his name on him somewhere. It doesn't seem right to deprive him of his own name."

"Maybe..."

"Maybe what?"

"Maybe the person didn't know his name."

"No! No-no-no!" Flossie put her hands over her ears. "I'm not going to believe his mother has been killed by some maniac."

"Of course not," said Tobi soothingly. "I'm sorry. I shouldn't have said that."

"But how could you keep from thinking it?" asked Flossie forlornly. "It's all I could think about last night. What if some monster has killed the mother of this baby?"

"A monster would have killed the baby, too," said Tobi.

"I know," said Flossie, "but sometimes I'm so terrified for him I can hardly breathe."

Tobi put her hand on Flossie's shoulder. "I'll pray," she said. "I've already started, and I'll keep on. I'll pray really hard for Johnny's mother."

When Flossie looked up, there were tears in her eyes. "Thank you."

Flossie's house was cool and comfortable. It was neat, but not too neat. Tobi liked what it told her about the kind-hearted, grandmotherly woman.

"Right this way," Flossie said, leading Tobi through a short hall. "He sleeps on a pallet in my bedroom."

But when they stepped into the room, the pallet was empty. "What in the world...," Flossie began. "He was sleeping like a log!" She looked in the closet and the bathroom and under the bed. "Johnny!" she called, as she searched. "Where are you, sweetie?"

"Flossie, look," Tobi said. She was standing by the window, holding the curtain aside. "The screen is cut and the glass is broken."

The next half hour passed in a fog. Tobi dialed 911 to summon both the police and an ambulance when Flossie collapsed in a storm of tears, clutching the child's new play suit to her breast. Five minutes later police officers burst through the door and found Tobi on the floor, holding Flossie in her arms and weeping with her.

It wasn't until Flossie had been settled in a bed at the hospital and received a sedative that she was calm enough to tell her story. She had given Johnny some lunch, rocked him a few minutes, and sung him to sleep. After putting him on his pallet, she carried the two garbage bags abandoned that morning at the back door, to her dumpster in the alley. On the way back inside, she had moved her sprinklers, greeted Tobi, and visited with her a few minutes before returning to the house. "It couldn't have been more than ten minutes," Flossie kept saying. "But I shouldn't have left him. Not for a second..."

She was inconsolable, even when Tobi swore up and down it must have been Johnny's mother rescuing him and not a kidnapper stealing him. Finally Flossie's doctor told Tobi and the roomful of police officers to be on their way. They all trooped out of Flossie's room, but Tobi lingered. And when the doctor left, she stole in quietly and sat in the darkened room, holding Flossie's hand and praying for her and little Johnny.

Joel was shuffling through papers on his desk, throwing some away and setting aside the ones that needed to be filed, when Vi appeared in his doorway. She tapped lightly on the door jamb, and he looked up.

"Paul Hudson called," she said.

Joel groaned. "Oh no."

"He wanted to come see you and I gave him an appointment at three," she said, concern darkening her brown eyes. "Shall I call him back and tell him you can't see him?"

Joel sighed. "No, of course not. Paul's always welcome here. He's one of the great liberators of my life."

"Why? Because he married Rachel?"

Joel nodded. "That's right. I probably owe that man my sanity."

"Then, why did you groan when I said he called?"

"I'm afraid he's going to give her back."

Vi laughed. "Well, I told him I thought you'd be free around three."

Joel sighed again. "Okay."

Vi was out on an errand when Paul arrived. Joel heard the door open and close and went to greet Paul, who was standing just inside Vi's office.

"Paul!" Joel said heartily. "Come on in. It's great to see you. Any time!"

Paul looked relieved. "I wasn't sure if it was a good idea or not. I don't suppose current spouses have much to do with ex-spouses."

"Are you kidding - I'd rather see you than Rachel any day!"

Paul smiled ruefully, and Joel's heart sank. It was true - Paul wanted to get rid of Rachel. Or Rachel wanted to get rid of Paul. It was one way or the other.

Joel led Paul into his office. Two armchairs, upholstered in velvety, red fabric, waited invitingly for visitors. Joel sat down in one of these and Paul took the other.

"So what's up?" Joel asked.

"Well, I'm thinking about joining the Navy," Paul said.

Joel laughed. "It worked for me."

"Thanks to me," said Paul. "I'm afraid lightning won't strike twice in the same place."

"It could happen," said Joel. "She's still a beautiful woman. We guys are suckers for that kind of beauty."

Paul nodded. "Nobody knows that better than you and I."

"Is there some way I can help you?" Joel asked.

"Probably not," said Paul. "Maybe I just want to vent to someone who knows what I'm talking about. I'm frustrated, and I don't know how to deal with it."

Joel nodded. "I remember that feeling."

"Do you know," said Paul, "that she wants me to change my middle name?"

"Why?"

"Well, it's Avery, and there are no Averys in the Bible. It's not spiritual enough."

"So what does she want you to change it to?" asked Joel. "Jesus?"

Paul snorted. "Probably."

"I know what you mean," said Joel. "When I found out she was seeing a Paul, I thought, 'Of course! Paul wrote half the New Testament - a Paul would have to be more spiritual than a Joel who wrote only one book of the Old Testament'."

"Right," said Paul. "And I'm sure she named the girls - Glory and Grace."

"That's right," agreed Joel. "She really did want to name Gloria 'Glory.' I put my foot down on that one - told her to give the child a name that sounds like a name. She has to live with it the rest of her life."

"Did you do that often?" Paul asked. "Put your foot down?"

"I tried at first," Joel said, thinking back. "But her punishments were so intense and lasted so long that she trained me pretty quickly to do exactly what she wanted."

"Would you consider changing your name if a woman - any woman - asked you to?"

"I guess it would depend on how I felt about my name," said Joel.

Paul shrugged. "Avery is a family name, my grandmother's maiden name. I don't want to change it. Besides, there's something about the idea of Rachel thinking she should be able to change something as fundamental as my name. Why should I let her get away with it?"

"Can't you just let the whole thing drop?"

"*I* can, but she won't. It's a terrible thing to say, but... You wouldn't repeat any of our conversation to anyone, would you?"

"Of course not," said Joel.

"Sometimes I think she's crazy. Do you know if there was ever anybody in her family that was - you know - a little off...or all the way off?"

Joel leaned back in his chair and thought. "If there was, I don't think I ever heard about it."

"Well, what about this... I've been trying my whole married life to understand why Rachel is the way she is. Do you have any idea what makes her think she should be able to have everything she wants, when she wants it?"

"Oh, that's easy," said Joel. "Her older brother Preston died when he was 10 and she was five. Rachel was all her parents had left and they spoiled her shamelessly. Her mother told me the story herself. She said by the time Rachel was in her teen years, she was set in granite. Nobody could put a ripple in her rock-hard core of selfishness."

Paul was shaking his head and frowning. "Are you sure about that? She told me her parents were very strict and hard on her."

"I only know what her mother said and, according to her, they weren't strict. But they *were* over-protective. Maybe Rachel interpreted protectiveness as strictness."

Paul nodded. "That sounds like the spin Rachel would put on it," he agreed.

Joel had a thoughtful look on his face. "I remember one Christmas Eve... Everyone else had gone to bed and I heard somebody stirring around. I got up and found her Mother in the den. Heidi was pacing around, weeping. I wasn't surprised. There had been a big blow-up about...something...I forget what. Rachel demanded to have her way. Rachel got her way. And the whole household went to bed in a snit."

Joel paused, frowning. "I'll never forget what Heidi told me that night. 'We lost one child to leukemia, and, as a result, we ruined the other one. It's like we've lost both children.' She was only in her forties, but she looked old and tired. She and Gordon both died in their early fifties. He had a heart attack, then she just seemed to fade away - of course, you already know that. I used to wonder if they both died of broken hearts."

Paul nodded soberly. "Maybe having kids isn't all it's cracked up to be. Maybe I should be grateful Rachel refused to have more children. I resented her for a long time because she refused to have a child with me. I nearly left her over that a few years ago."

"Why didn't you?"

"Probably because she would get half of everything we own. I'm the only one who works - she even has a part time housekeeper and cook - but she would get half. I could never bring myself to do it. So I've learned to avoid her as much as possible."

"Doesn't that tick her off?"

"Sure. Or it did. But I quit listening to her ranting. When she started, I left." He grinned. "And that made her go ballistic, but I wouldn't hang around to listen to her explosions. When she started, I walked out. So she finally quit. Now we live in detente."

"Which is probably the best you could hope for with Rachel," Joel mused.

Paul shrugged. "So far, it's the best I can do. Look, I've taken enough of your time, and I have a patient coming at 3:45 to have her braces adjusted. I'm supposed to tell you the girls can stay with you for a few days if you like. Rachel and my niece took off on a whim. Went shopping in Dallas."

Joel's face brightened. "I'd love that! But I'm leaving for Dallas myself tomorrow. It would be great to have them with me. We could go to Six Flags, maybe a water park... But I may be gone a couple of weeks."

Paul looked worried. "Rachel gave me strict instructions to pick them up for church. She says you're attending some dead church and she's afraid you'll take them with you."

Joel didn't answer for long moments. Finally he said, "Ya' know, Paul, maybe it's time we quit enabling Rachel."

"Enabling?"

"Yes, you know, like the family of an alcoholic cleaning up his messes so he can continue to drink without dealing with the consequences."

"What are you suggesting?" Paul asked doubtfully.

"Let's quit letting her always have her way. You're smart to walk out on her when she rants and raves. I can do the same thing - hang up on her. At least we wouldn't have to listen to her."

"So you're saying you want to take Gloria and Gracie to Dallas with you for several weeks without clearing it with her?"

"Right. And if she doesn't like it, she can pick them up and take them home herself."

"That's easy for you to say. You don't have to live with her."

Joel nodded. "You're right, so I'll let you make the decision."

Paul's eyes widened. "Really? Well, that's good of you. Look, I have to tell you one more thing. Rachel says if you're sleeping with your secretary, the girls are never staying with you again."

A thundercloud crossed Joel's face, but he kept his temper. Paul wasn't the enemy. "Tobi's not my secretary - she was filling in for Vi for a couple of weeks. And I'm not sleeping with her."

Paul took a deep breath. "Okay. Let's do it. Let's see if we can *force* her to grow up. You take Gloria and Gracie to Dallas with you. And when she starts telling me what a clod you are, I'll walk out on her."

The two men shook on it.

"Joel?"

It was Tobi's voice in the outer office, and she sounded upset.

"Tobi!" Joel was at his office door in one long stride. He saw immediately that she had been crying and with three more strides, he had her in his arms. "What's wrong?"

"The baby...the toddler. He's gone! Somebody kidnaped him! Poor Flossie is heartbroken. Nobody even knows who he is, and now he's gone!"

Tobi had been trying very hard to be strong for Flossie, but now she allowed herself the luxury of crying on Joel's shoulder. As he sheltered her in his arms, Joel explained briefly to Paul about the child who had been left at the police station the previous night.

Realizing Joel hadn't been alone in his office, Tobi quickly pulled herself together and apologized. "You were in a meeting! I'm so sorry. You should have said something..." She wiped her eyes with the back of her hand.

"It's okay, Honey," Joel said, handing her a Kleenex. "I was talking to Paul Hudson, and we were finished. You remember him, don't you? He came to the hospital the morning after Gracie's appendectomy. With Rachel. Paul, this is Tobi Kirkland."

"Oh, Rachel's husband," Tobi said, then looked alarmed. "Is something wrong? Gloria? Gracie?"

"Nothing's wrong," Joel reassured her. "We were having a powwow about Rachel. Now tell us about the little boy."

Tobi recounted the afternoon's experiences for them. When she finished, Joel asked, "So Mrs. Bobbsey is here in the hospital now?"

"That's right. She's in room 210."

"I'll have to stop by and see her," said Joel. "Look, Paul, you'd better run. Didn't you say you have a patient at 3:45?"

"That's right." Paul consulted his watch. "It was a pleasure meeting you, Ms. Kirkland." He offered his hand, and she shook it with a warm smile.

"Please call me Tobi," she said.

"Thank you, and I'm Paul."

He hurried from the room, then. When the door shut behind him, Tobi asked, "Is he a doctor?"

"An orthodontist," said Joel.

"What was he doing here?"

Joel smiled wearily. "It's a long story, but the bottom line is that he's fed up with Rachel."

"Really?" Tobi studied his face curiously. "You got it backwards then. Last night you were worried Rachel was going to dump him. Is he thinking about leaving her?"

Joel grinned. "He said he's thinking about joining the Navy, but he's afraid no one would come along and rescue him the way he rescued me."

Tobi's eyebrows arched. "Poor Rachel."

"Poor *Rachel*!" he nearly yelled. "Rachel's not poor. She's the one who's ruining everybody else's lives."

Tobi shrugged. "I know. But it must be terrible to feel so rejected."

Joel snorted derisively. "She doesn't feel rejected. All she feels is entitled."

Vi returned then, and Tobi greeted her enthusiastically. Soon she was telling Vi the story of the kidnaping, and Joel stole away to check on Flossie.

Chapter V

At Cleo's Kitchen that evening, sitting in a booth across from Joel, feather-soft butterflies fluttered about Tobi's stomach as she held up the menu, pretending to read it. What was she afraid of anyway, to generate such a flock of winged harbingers in her mid-section? She wasn't worried that Joel would yell or throw things. She mused over the problem for a few minutes, and finally decided she was afraid his reaction would, in some way, cause her to love him less. Or respect him less. Or...

Joel, enjoying the delectable fragrance of cinnamon rolls wafting through the restaurant, glanced up from his menu and saw her face. "What's wrong?" he asked in amazement. Only a few moments ago she had been the picture of tranquility.

"Wrong?" Tobi asked. "What do you mean?"

"Your face is all bent out of shape! What are you thinking about?"

Tobi gulped and took a deep breath. Here was the opening she needed. "I was thinking about Kent Grantham. He called today and asked me to visit him at the jail."

"Kent Grantham, the movie star?" Joel asked with contempt.

"Kent Grantham, the professional assassin," she corrected him.

He studied her, trying to read her. She was unreadable. "Are you going?"

"Yes. I think I will."

Color flooded his face. "Why?" he asked, with ice in his voice. "Tobi Kirkland, are you mad? You're still in love with him, aren't you?"

Tobi had imagined many possible responses from Joel, but not this one. Her mouth fell open and her eyes popped out. Then she began to laugh.

Her response befuddled him. "What are you laughing at?" he asked, trying not to betray his rising anger in his voice.

She shook her head and forced down the laughter bubbling up in her. "Just exactly how stupid do you think I am?" she gasped.

"I don't think you're stupid. What are you talking about?" He slid out of his side of the booth and scooted in beside her. "Tobi, are we in the same conversation?"

"I'm sorry, Joel. I didn't think you would like it if I went to see Kent, but it never occurred to me that you could imagine I was in love with the jerk who tried to frame me for the murder of his stepfather."

"Oh." Joel let his head rest against the wall behind their booth while he took some deep breaths and let his emotions calm. "You're right, of course. It was a stupid thing to say. I'm projecting my faults onto you. I once married a woman because she was beautiful, so now I assume you're hung up on Kent because he's the hunk of the century."

Tobi's arm slid under Joel's arm and her soft hand clasped his big one. "He's not the hunk of the century, Joel. Not in my eyes, anyway. You are."

"Oh, Tobi..." Words failed him. He knew he wasn't half as handsome as Kent Grantham. How could Tobi pretend anything different? Was she mocking him? She wasn't blind. So how could she say...

"What's wrong?" Her arm was still threaded through his and her mouth was very close to his ear. If it had been any other woman, he would have felt trapped. Suffocated. But because it was Tobi, he felt warm and wanted.

"I know that's not true," he said, facing her head on and gazing into her eyes, trying to find the truth there. "I'm practically bald. And my face is... Well, it's just a face, nothing special. Plus I'm big. And awkward sometimes." His voice had begun low and grown softer and softer.

"Are you saying that I'm lying to you?" she asked, puzzled.

"Not exactly. But I *know* that next to Grantham I look like Frankenstein."

Tobi forced back a smile at the imagery because she could see how serious Joel was. She had no idea how to answer him, so she sent up a silent SOS to Heaven: "Lord, I don't know what to say. Am I supposed to tell him the truth or let him think I'm passing out cheap flattery?"

It took a fraction of a moment for her to decide to opt for truth. "Joel, I'm going to say something, because I have to. Remember that - I would never have said it now if you hadn't forced me."

"Say what?" He frowned.

"In my opinion you're the handsomest man alive. And that's my opinion because I'm in love with you. I'm not lying when I say that you're a trillion times more attractive to me than Kent Grantham could ever be."

He gazed at her in wonder. "You're in love with me?"

She blushed and said, "Desperately. But, Joel, please don't think that means I'm prowling around you, trying to figure out how to get you to the altar. Love is one thing; marriage is quite another. We haven't known each other long enough to know what we should...do...well, you know... in the future..." She turned huge, green eyes on him, beseeching him to understand.

Joel's throat closed, making speech impossible. He simply sat in the booth, gazing dumbly at Tobi, trying to make sense of her words.

After a long, long moment, Tobi's head dropped. "I'm sorry, Joel. I shouldn't have said that. But I didn't want to lie, so what else could I do?"

"Oh, Tobi!" Joel's powers of speech returned in a rush. "Oh my beautiful, precious Tobi. Don't be sorry. I've never heard more wonderful words in my life!" Unhooking his arm from hers, he pulled her into a tight embrace. "I love you, too. I love you so much! And it scares me out of my mind..."

Someone cleared her throat at his shoulder. "Look, I waited as long as I could, but I really have to take your order now." The waitress looked apologetic, but determined.

The Church of the Living Vine was a young church, constructed in a modern style of gray brick. It consisted of several buildings, all made of the same materials and in the same modern style. Between two of the buildings, but toward the rear of both, was a carport where the church staff parked. All these things Tobi saw at a glance, but her gaze paused on a cross atop the steeple. It was a beautiful, gold cross, but the evening sun flooded it with a blaze of glory that hurt her eyes, and she looked away wincing.

As Joel and Tobi walked hand-in-hand toward the sanctuary, the butterflies returned to Tobi's stomach. She hadn't been to a church of the Charismatic persuasion in over a year and her revulsion at the prospect nauseated her. She didn't want to go. She didn't want to hear the lies, the great, swelling words, the pompous boasting. She didn't want to remember how completely she had once bought into this belief system herself. How it had decimated her life. And how much she had loved believing the lies.

Joel opened a heavy, glass door. "Ready?" he asked.

Tobi smiled bravely and nodded. She was as ready as she could get.

The frosty-cool, front lobby of the church was a beehive of activity. Several children were racing about with adults in pursuit. Near a long table, four or five people were examining materials the evangelist had brought to sell. And two people were using cell phones.

Joel and Tobi skirted the bustle but, as they approached the back door of the sanctuary, they were intercepted by the pastor and the evangelist. "There you are, Joel!" exclaimed Rev. Emory Morel, his deep voice belying his diminutive appearance. "About time you got back here, you old backslider! Come meet our speaker for the evening."

As introductions were made, Tobi studied the two men. Rev. Morel she had already met. He was little, round, and bald. Instead of a person, he should have been a joke. But he took himself very seriously. And his companion, Rev. Joshua Moses, was tall - as tall as Joel - with bushy, brown hair that was beginning to recede noticeably. His eyes were dark and intense, yet he did not seem half as serious as his companion.

Rev. Moses shook hands with Joel, then turned to Tobi and took both her hands in his. "Miss Kirkland! It's always a pleasure to meet a beautiful woman, and you are without a doubt the most beautiful woman I've met in this little burg."

Tobi was watching Rev. Moses with amusement, but Joel saw Rev. Morel's eyes roll ceilingward. Undoubtedly, he had already heard that line this evening. Joel looked at Tobi, then, to see how she was receiving Moses's flattery and was gratified to realize how thoroughly unimpressed she was with the big, self-confident preacher. She removed her hands from his grasp, smiled slightly, said, "Thank you," and turned toward the sanctuary.

Apparently Rev. Moses received her rebuff as a challenge, for he retrieved one of her hands and turned her back toward himself. "Please wait, Tobi... May I call you Tobi?"

Her slight smile turned into a slight frown. "I don't care what you call me," she said contemptuously and removed her hand from his grasp again.

"Please, tell me about yourself," he said in his most beguiling voice. "How long have you been saved? May I pray for you about anything? Talk to me. Please."

Tobi's frown deepened. What was this man's problem?

Reading her expression, he sighed. "I'm sorry. Of course, it's none of my business. It's just that I'm always on the road, and I don't have any family except the good people I meet as I travel. And so, I like to find out a little bit about them. I like to pretend they care about me as much as I care about them."

Seeing that Tobi wasn't taken in by his blarney and that Joel wasn't going to speak for her, Rev. Morel spoke up. "Tobi is Joel's secretary," he said. Then he stopped in confusion. "Well, she was. Joel has just resigned as CEO at the hospital, so I guess she doesn't work for him any more."

"Actually," Joel said, "she only filled in for my secretary for a few weeks when Vi was ill. Tobi's not a secretary; she's a journalist."

"No!" exclaimed Rev. Moses in mock amazement. "Well, you are far and away the loveliest reporter I've ever set eyes on, Tobi. I suppose you work for the local newspaper?"

"Not right now," Tobi said. "I'm between jobs."

Moses's eyes lighted up. "Is that a fact? Listen, I'm glad to hear that because I could use some help. Would you be interested in working a few hours a day for me while I'm here? Of course, it wouldn't be journalism. It would be more like a secretarial position."

"Joshua, don't be ridiculous," Rev. Morel said. "We'll get you any help you need. My secretary is at your disposal. You mustn't hire someone from outside the church. It would cause hurt feelings."

"Oh, you're not a member of the Vine?" Rev. Moses asked.

"No," she replied shortly.

"Well, you know," Rev. Moses said to Rev. Morel, "perhaps I could persuade the young lady to look on your church with favor if I were allowed to hire her for a few days." He returned his attention to Tobi. "I'd certainly like to try."

"*That* won't happen," she said flatly, "but I do need a short-term job."

Joel's eyes widened in surprise, then he frowned. "Tobi," he said, putting an arm around her possessively, "you don't need to do this. If you need money..."

But she interrupted him, "I know I don't need to," she said. "But I think I'd like to try it. It's only a few days." She turned her attention to Rev. Morel. "Of course, I won't do it if the pastor asks me not to."

Rev. Morel shrugged and shook his head. "No, no! You go on and take the job - it's between you and Joshua." His eyes flickered to a group entering the lobby and he excused himself to go greet them.

"Well, then, are you a morning person or a night person?" asked Rev. Moses.

Tobi eyed him coolly. "As it happens, I have already made plans for tomorrow morning, Rev. Moses, so it won't be convenient for me to start before tomorrow afternoon."

"Splendid! Splendid!" he boomed enthusiastically. "I happen to be a night person myself, so I'll meet you here at the church at - shall we say 2:00 P.M. tomorrow?"

"I'll be here," she said, turning with Joel to move into the sanctuary.

But Rev. Moses stopped them with his words. "And would you consider $20 an hour adequate pay?" he asked.

Tobi's eyes widened. "Who wouldn't?"

"What is it exactly you're expecting her to do for you?" Joel asked suspiciously.

"Typing, transcribing - the same things she did when she worked for you, I'm sure," said Rev. Moses. He favored them with a toothy smile and went to join Rev. Morel.

"I don't trust him," Joel whispered, as he led her to a back pew. "I wish you wouldn't work for him. I don't want you anywhere near him."

"It's only a few days," she said. "If it were longer, I wouldn't do it."

"He's a wolf in sheep's clothing," Joel said darkly. "I can smell him. Why do you want to work for him anyway? Do you need the money that bad?"

Tobi shrugged. "Of course I can use the money, but it's more than that. I think I want to see if I can find out what makes him tick."

Joel frowned. "Why?"

Tobi shook her head. "I don't know why." She turned puzzled eyes on Joel. "I'll have to think about it."

A young couple stopped then to speak to Joel and meet Tobi. The conversation continued until the service started. When the pastors entered, the lights in the room brightened and Tobi steeled herself. She knew what was about to happen. A music leader would draw the congregation into an almost trance like state with a mind-numbing repetition of spiritual songs and choruses. Hearts and minds would soar heavenward on a warm swell of beautiful music. It would feel wonderful. And everyone would be receptive to any drivel the evangelist might choose to spout.

"Almost everyone," Tobi amended silently, wishing she had brought ear plugs.

In spite of her best efforts to resist, Tobi quickly began to feel buoyed by the music. Fast, happy choruses came first, followed by soaring worship songs that focused the congregation's hearts and minds on God. It was this opportunity in every worship service to offer the Lord a musical, "I love you," that had first attracted Tobi to the Charismatic sect. And it was this quiet interlude of communing with God that she missed the most after she returned to the church of her childhood.

As the words of the last song faded, the pianist continued to play quietly and the congregation waited expectantly. They didn't have long to wait. Almost immediately a man at the front of the crowded sanctuary began to speak. "It is good, my children, that you have come this night to hear my servant speak. Hear him well. He speaks for me."

Tobi closed her eyes tightly and tried not to listen. It was this part of the service that distressed her most, the part where a mere man pretended to speak for God, where the congregation listened without rebuking him. And yet they walked away as if nothing supernatural had happened. So which was it? Was God speaking or not? If He was, why didn't everyone fall on their faces? Why didn't they write down His precious words and memorize them? But if the words were merely from a man pretending to speak for God, why didn't the pastor hush him and rebuke him?

She didn't realize her cheeks were awash with tears until she felt Joel's arm around her. He pulled her close and whispered, "What's wrong?"

She didn't answer, but pressed her ear against his chest and tried to position his arm so it covered her other ear. "Dear God," she prayed urgently, "please help me not to hear. I don't want to hear."

Not receiving an answer, Joel wrapped his other arm around her and let her snuggle into his chest. Thus cocooned, Tobi was able to tune in to the steady rhythm of his heart and tune out the ponderous, pompous voices around her. She prayed silently and waited as men and women around the congregation presumed to speak for God. Most of them spoke in plain English, but one used the meaningless gibberish these people called "tongues" and Tobi called "jabber." If she had been forced to listen to this blasphemy, Tobi's distress would have grown with every word. Instead, she emerged from Joel's arms as everyone sat down, feeling safe and warm.

Suddenly, she felt Joel's hand on her chin, lifting her face so he could study her eyes. "We don't have to stay," he whispered. "Do you want to leave?"

Tobi's heart and soul screamed, "Yes! Yes! Let's leave," but she shook her head. "I'll be all right," she assured him.

He studied her face, as if he didn't believe her, so she added, "Really. I'm fine!"

He looked troubled, but he settled back in his seat to listen.

Rev. Moses read Ephesians 5:18, "Don't drink too much wine, for many evils lie along that path; be filled instead with the Holy Spirit, and controlled by him." [Living Bible] Rev. Moses then began preaching his autobiography. He spoke of his disappointment when injuries prevented a promising career in professional football. How he had become an alcoholic and how alcohol had consumed his life.

"But now I've found a better high!" he exulted. "When I found Jesus, I found out that alcohol could carry me only halfway to the sky. And then it would always kick me off my cloud. But since Jesus came to live in my heart, I live on a Holy Ghost high. Now, I can sail all the way to the sky and never crash."

Then he began to tell of things he experienced in a church in Toronto, Canada, and other churches around the United States. "You may find yourself in a gale-force wind, right here in this room," he warned. "Or you may step into a river of power, a river of the Holy Spirit, flowing through the room." He talked of uncontrollable laughter. Of people roaring like lions or barking like dogs. People suddenly too weak to stand. People laughing hysterically for hours at a time. People trembling all over as if possessed with some kind of nerve disease.

After nearly an hour of such reminiscing, Moses' loud, raucous voice grew low. "What you have to understand," he said, speaking with the authority of a prophet standing on Sinai, "is that these wonderful things cannot happen to you unless you are willing to be filled with the Holy Spirit. Unless you are willing to let God's Spirit control you as a puppeteer controls a puppet.

"I know how you may be feeling because I wasn't willing at first. I hesitated. I wasn't sure it was really of God. But finally, I released myself. I told the Lord, 'Take me. Take all of me. I surrender myself to you.' At the very moment I said those words, a power hit me - a power like liquid velvet, pouring through me and out of me and all around me. I threw back my head and began to howl like a wolf. And then I laughed. I laughed for two hours and, when I stopped, I was free. And clean. And fresh.

"I promised God I would spread this wonderful anointing to everyone I meet. And I've kept that promise. It's why I'm here tonight. Who wants to experience what I experienced? Who wants a chance to be healed and cleansed and renewed?"

Apparently he saw a raised hand in the audience because he said, "Don't raise your hand. Get out of your chair and come up here. If you want the highest high you've ever experienced, get up here tonight. Get up here right now..."

The pianist began to play softly, as Moses put his hands on the first person in a line that was forming at the front of the sanctuary. In a matter of minutes, the room was in chaos. The pianist was playing louder and louder. Moses was putting his hands on people and shouting his prayers. Recipients of these prayers were behaving like lunatics. Some fell on the floor, shrieking with laughter. Some roamed about roaring or howling or barking. Some danced. Some sang. One actually developed a tremor from head to toe.

When she had seen all she could bear, Tobi looked at Joel. His face was sober and his eyes dark. He returned her gaze. "Let's get out of here!" he said.

No one seemed to notice as they stepped into the aisle and walked through a back door into the lobby. Before either of them could speak, their attention was drawn to three people already in the lobby - Paul, Gloria, and Grace.

"Mom's going to be furious if you make us leave now," Grace was saying. "I didn't even get a chance to go forward. I want Pastor Moses to pray for me."

"Pray!" gasped Paul. "He wasn't praying. He was forming a circus!"

"I don't care what you say," Gloria said. "I'm going back. You can't make us leave."

"Sure he can," Joel said, leading Tobi toward the threesome. "If we have to, we'll find some fish nets and toss them over your heads and drag you out of here."

"Dad!" Grace exclaimed. "You're here! Please let us stay. You'll stay with us, won't you, and take us home afterward? Please, please, please."

"Not on your life," Joel said sternly. "That..." he nodded over his shoulder toward the sanctuary, "...is the most unholy display I've ever had the misfortune to witness. We're getting out of here *now*!" He put an arm around each girl and walked them out the door into the balmy night, with Paul and Tobi following.

When they were outside, Joel asked, "Are you two packed and ready to go? I want to leave early in the morning."

The sulky expressions left Gloria's and Grace's faces. "I'm ready," said Gloria.

"I will be," said Grace. "Can we go shopping while we're in Dallas, Dad? Tina McGregor says Dallas has the best shopping in the whole world. Can I buy a new wardrobe for next fall? I want to be the hottest girl in school next year."

"May," Joel corrected. "*May* we go shopping? *May* we buy..."

"Right, right," Grace said impatiently. "*May* we?"

"Well you're welcome to spend whatever money you have," Joel said cheerfully.

Both girls' heads swivelled as one to look at Paul. Tobi, watching the scene with interest, smiled to herself in the darkness. A broken home was a terrible thing to live with, but there was something to be said for having two, hard-working, doting Dads.

Ignoring the girls, Paul shook hands with Joel. "I'm glad you came along when you did. Since I've never had kids myself, I'm always afraid I'll do the wrong thing."

"Don't be afraid," Joel said. "You stick by your guns, and I'll back you up."

"Dad," Gloria's horrified voice broke in, "whose side are you on?"

Joel glared at her. "Paul and I are both on *your* side, and don't you forget it," he said. "And let's get something else straight while we're at it - that sideshow in there was no more Christianity than I'm Kevin Costner. And if you ever meet that freak Moses on the street, you turn around and go the other direction. Now, let's get out of here!"

He resisted the temptation to watch his daughters clamber into Paul Hudson's shiny silver sedan. Instead, taking Tobi's hand, he started toward his SUV, but the wistful expression lingered on his face. "They're both crazy about you, Joel," Tobi said quietly when they were settled inside and buckled up.

"Who?" he asked.

"Gloria and Gracie," she said. "I'm sure they care about Paul, but he'll never take your place in their hearts."

"I know," he said, but his voice was sad.

"You love *your* Dad, don't you?" she persisted.

He shrugged. "Of course I do."

"Could anybody ever take his place in your heart? Could anybody even come close to taking his place?"

He turned the key in the ignition, then looked at her for a long moment. "No," he said, smiling slightly at some secret knowledge. "No, not even close."

She nodded knowingly. "Me too. My Dad was my hero of heroes. I'll adore him as long as I live. And Gloria and Gracie will always love you the same way. I can see it in their faces every time they look at you. In fact, they may love you more because they've had to be separated from you so much."

"You don't really believe that do you?" Joel asked, searching her face.

"I really do," she answered. "I know what it means to a girl to have a great Dad."

He pulled onto the quiet street that led away from the Church of the Living Vine and drove in silence for several long minutes before he said longingly, "But I'm not a great Dad. I've let them down in every way that matters."

Before she could reply, he said urgently, "Tobi, if it hadn't been for you, I might have gone to the Vine with them tonight and swallowed all that bull - hook, line and sinker." He took his eyes off the road long enough to give her a long, agonized look. "It scares me spit-less to think I might have actually believed all that hocus-pocus was the Holy Spirit."

When she answered, Tobi's voice was thoughtful. "Joel, do you pray for Gloria and Gracie? Do you pray for yourself to know and do God's will? I don't mean praying those things as a habit, but actually being willing to make any change in your life or doctrine that God wants you to make?"

He thought about it for several moments before he said, "Yes, I believe I do."

"Then give God some credit. It's no accident that you quit going to that church when you did. And it's no accident that you're not in there right now with a big wad of Joshua Moses's bait down your throat. You pray. God answers your prayers. That's why your girls are safely on the way home. That's why you're not in the sanctuary right now, grubbing around in the carpet for a touch from some false god. And that's why you're a world-class Dad."

Joel reached over and took her hand. "I hope you're right," he said fervently.

When they reached Tobi's place, Joel walked her to the door, but he wouldn't come inside. Instead, he put his arms around her and said, "Tonight, I'm going to pray for *you*, then I'm going to go home and finish packing."

Tobi smiled up at him with trusting eyes, as he continued, "But first, I have to tell you..." He hesitated. "Well, I can't tell you. I don't know what words to use." There was another pause, in which Tobi waited until he said falteringly, "Thank you for telling me that you love me. It means everything to me to know that. And I'm so grateful that now I can tell you I love you, too."

Unexpectedly, a wide grin lighted up Tobi's face. "I'm grateful too," she said. "I would have hated it if I'd said, 'I love you,' and you'd said, 'Oh gross!' "

His answering grin met hers in a long, tender kiss. Then Joel prayed softly, "Father, I never wanted to love another beautiful woman as long as I lived. And then you brought the most beautiful woman in the world into my life. I can't help loving her, and I can't stop thanking You for sending her to me.

"Be with Tobi while I'm in Dallas. Guide her and guard her. Be her strength. Be her song. And bless her with every spiritual blessing in heavenly places in Christ Jesus.

"Thank You, Father, for my beautiful, precious Tobi. Thank You for letting her love me. In Jesus' Name. Amen."

Joel's heartfelt words flowed over Tobi like a caressing balm. Tears filled her eyes, and it was all she could do to whisper, "Thank you, Joel. That was the most beautiful prayer I ever heard."

They clung to each other for several minutes. Finally, Joel stirred and said quietly, "Tobi, would you do me a big, big favor?"

"What?"

He seemed to be fumbling with his belt and Tobi watched, frowning, until she realized he had taken his cell phone out of its carrying case, which was hooked to his belt. "Would you please take this and keep it with you whenever you're with Rev. Moses?" Joel asked pleadingly. "I don't want to sound like a scaremonger, but that man makes my skin crawl. I can't bear to think of you alone with him."

Tobi accepted the little phone and gazed up at Joel with a radiant face. "Joel Trent, if I loved you any more, I'd explode. Thank you. I'll try not to run your bill up too high."

He laughed, giddy with relief that he hadn't offended her. "That's the least of my worries. You'll need to get a charger for it." He took the phone back and held it under the porch light. "If you want to call a number - 911 for example - punch in the numbers, then push this large button in the center. Okay?"

She nodded. "Okay."

"I'll get you the instruction manual, so you can put it through all its paces. And Tobi?"

She looked up expectantly.

"I'll pray for you every day. I promise. And I love you like crazy!"

"I love you too," she said.

His lips, warm and gentle, touched hers one more time before he strode away. Tobi hugged his cell phone, then realizing what she was doing, laughed at herself and went inside.

Chapter VI

The next morning Gloria and Grace had pulled a mountain of mobile luggage onto the front porch when Paul came to check on them. "Are you sure you don't want breakfast before you go?" he asked.

"No. Dad said we'd eat on our way out of town," Gloria told him. "Do you think Mom is going to be mad at us for going?" Her face was troubled, for she was a peacemaker and would have liked to get her mother's stamp of approval on this trip before they left.

"Who cares?" Grace said flippantly. "She's the one who didn't call, so she can just live with it." She, taking after her mother, was more willful and self-absorbed than Gloria.

"I'll try to smooth it over with Rachel," Paul said to Gloria. Then he continued, "Look, I hope you girls know by now I would never try to buy your love." At the word "buy," he had their full attention. "But I do love you because you're great kids, so I'd like to give you some spending money." He handed each of them a hundred dollar bill.

"Oh Paul! It's not even our birthdays!" shrieked Grace. She threw her arms around him and gave him a resounding smack on the cheek. "Thank you!"

Gloria thanked him next with a hug and a kiss and a "You're the greatest!"

Joel drove up in the midst of this love-fest and the girls descended on him next. "Look what Paul gave us!" Grace called, waving her hundred dollar bill. And "Can I drive?" asked Gloria, holding out a hand for the keys. They both hugged Joel and began transferring their luggage to his vehicle.

Joel joined Paul on the porch. "You're much too generous," he said. "You'll make me look like a miser."

Paul looked chastened. "Look, I didn't mean to..."

But Joel interrupted. "No, no! It's okay. Thanks to you, maybe they won't be begging so hard for *my* hard-earned cash. Look, what about Rachel? Did she blow a fuse when you told her I was taking the girls out of town for a couple of weeks?"

Paul shrugged. "We never heard from her, and I won't know where she's staying until she calls."

"Well!" Joel's voice revealed his amazement. "Maybe she's beginning to trust you after all these years."

"I'd like to think so," said Paul with a grimace, "but it's more likely they've had some kind of trouble. I've been worried about them."

"Who did you say she's traveling with?" Joel asked.

"My niece Patrice. She's the dental hygienist in my office, and she never showed up yesterday morning. Then suddenly Rachel called and said she and Patrice were going to Dallas shopping." Paul's expression was worried. "That's not like Patrice. She's very reliable. I almost had the feeling Rachel was kidnaping her."

Paul's concern was so obvious Joel was hesitant to leave. "Is there anything we can do?" he asked. "We don't have to leave today if you want us to help you find her."

"Oh no!" Paul forced the worry lines out of his forehead. "She'll call when she's ready. She's probably punishing me for...I don't know... something I did wrong yesterday or last week or ten years ago. Who knows?"

Joel knew Paul could be right. Rachel did like to carry a grudge. So he gave Paul a card with the address and phone number where they would be staying in Dallas and turned to go. Seeing Gloria in the driver's seat, he called over his shoulder, "Pray for us."

Paul grinned. "You've got it." He watched them pull away, then went inside for a cup of coffee and a glance at yesterday's newspaper. On his way to the kitchen, he retrieved the paper from the easy chair where he had tossed it, unopened, the previous day. A picture of the lost toddler dominated the front page. "Do you know this child?" the headline asked.

"Trevor!" Paul gasped. He scanned the story before hurrying to the telephone. But he didn't pick it up. Who would he call? Not every hotel in Dallas. He realized immediately that Rachel wouldn't have gone to Dallas, anyway. It took only a few moments of thought for him to decide she could have only gone one place - to his parents in Green Bay, Wisconsin, to Patrice's grandparents.

His hand lingered on the phone for only a moment. Then he looked at his watch. The office would open in 30 minutes. And since it was Friday, his staff would have scheduled a light day. His receptionist's sister-in-law's best friend was an ace travel agent. She would have him on his way to Green Bay five minutes after his last patient walked out the door. He hurried into his bedroom and packed an overnight bag.

Tobi's phone rang at 9:00 o'clock. "Good morning, love" Joel said when she answered.

Tobi frowned. "Where are you? I thought you would be long gone by now."

"We are," he said. "I'm using Gloria's phone. I wanted to tell you that I stopped and picked up another cell phone for myself. So consider the other one yours - do anything you want with it."

"Oh Joel, you're too good to me," Tobi protested. "How can I ever thank you? I *am* going to pay for it."

"We can talk about that later. Right now, I'm just grateful you were willing to take the phone. I would have been too worried to leave town if you hadn't."

Tobi smiled to herself. He *had* been jittery about offering to leave his phone with her. "I thought you seemed nervous about that," she said. "You've been listening to too much feminist propaganda."

"Well, I didn't want to insult you," he said, "and ever since women's lib, I don't know what's insulting and what's not."

"I love it that you want to take care of me," she assured him. "Everybody needs to be taken care of sometimes, and normal people know that. It's just the Amazon nation that doesn't know any better."

The doorbell rang then, and Tobi said, "Hang on. There's someone at the door."

"That's the other thing I wanted to tell you," Joel said. "I arranged to have a cell phone charger and instruction manual delivered to you."

Tobi thanked him again and jotted down his new cell phone number. Then she hung up and went to answer the door. A few minutes later she had unwrapped the charger and attached Joel's phone to it. Grinning broadly, she dialed DeeDee's number. She and DeeDee talked at least a few minutes every day. Some days they talked a lot of minutes. Whatever it took to keep them involved in each other's lives.

"Morning, Sis," Tobi greeted her.

"Tobi! Where are you?" DeeDee asked, eying the number on her caller I.D.

"I'm at home," Tobi said. "I'm using Joel's cell phone. He made me take it because I'm going to be working for a jerk this afternoon. Joel thinks he's the boogey man."

"Oh no." Tobi could hear the dismay in her sister's voice. "What have you gotten yourself into now?"

Tobi gave DeeDee a blow-by-blow account of the events at the Church of the Living Vine the preceding evening, including the short-term job she had accepted with Rev. Joshua Moses. Although a night had passed, her disgust over the nature of the service was undimmed. "Do you think people who are *really* saved could believe the Holy Spirit is inspiring that kind of foolishness?" she asked DeeDee.

"I'd like to think not," DeeDee said, "but we're not their judges."

Tobi felt heartsick every time she remembered the ugly behavior she had witnessed in the sanctuary of the church the previous evening. She wanted desperately for someone to convince her that true believers would never get caught up in such an irreverent hoax. But DeeDee had not witnessed the service herself and was more concerned about Tobi's new employment. "Joel's right - this guy sounds like a sleaze," she said pleadingly. "Why would you even consider working for him?"

"It's hard to explain," Tobi said. "And you probably won't understand, because you were never involved in the Charismatic movement. But ever since I got out of it, I keep trying to figure out why people join it, because I want to know why I joined it. I don't think I'm stupid. So what was wrong with me that made me fall for such preposterous lies?"

"Oh, Tobi, everybody makes mistakes. Why do you have to analyze it to death? Just thank God you're free and go on about your business."

Tobi sighed. "How can I turn my back on such darkness without trying to show somebody else the way out?"

"Do you think this Moses person is looking for a way out?" DeeDee asked.

"Oh no!" Tobi wasn't deluding herself on that point. "But if I can get a glimpse of what makes him tick, it might help me understand somebody else someday. And I might be able to help that person."

"So now you're a Caped Crusader, sent to save the world from charismania? Is that it?" DeeDee asked.

Tobi sighed. "Of course not. Not the world. But maybe somebody. Someday."

DeeDee sighed too. They had reached an impasse, and she would be wasting her breath if she tried to persuade Tobi not to take the job. At least she would have Joel's cell phone. "Thank You, Lord, for Joel," she thought.

Tobi asked DeeDee to pass the number of the cell phone on to Ben and hung up. DeeDee didn't say it, but Ben would have the number and have it memorized before Tobi went to work at 2:00 that afternoon or her name wasn't December Margo Kirkland Walling.

Later that morning, Tobi pulled into the parking lot of the big, grim building that housed the county jail. She sat in her car staring at the building. She didn't want to go in. She didn't want to see Kent. She hadn't actually told him she was coming. So why not turn around and leave? She gritted her teeth and opened her car door.

Kent Grantham looked gaunt and unhappy in his prison garb. His dark hair was shorter than usual and the light had gone out of his eyes. "I didn't think you were coming," were his first words to Tobi.

"I didn't think I was either," she said.

He had started to sit down, but now he stopped and looked at her. "So why did you? If it's just to look at the poor, pitiful jailbird, forget it." His voice was harsh.

"Oh Kent, you know better than that." Her voice and her face were soft. She sat down and he followed suit.

"If you're here because you think you can talk me into accepting your religion, you're wasting your time." His voice was firm, but the harshness was gone.

"I've pretty much given up on that," Tobi said sadly. "Even if you told me you believed, how could I trust you?"

"Good!" he said, sounding more cheerful. "I'm glad we see eye to eye about that. Finally."

Tobi's heart sank, but she gave no sign. "So, how are they treating you here?"

"Like a prisoner," he said. "I have to admit, since I found out what a hole this place is, I've felt lousy for trying to put you in here. I am sorry for that, Tobi."

His voice sounded uncharacteristically penitent, and it was hard not to believe him. "Then why did you do it?" she asked.

"What? Kill Hugh? Or frame you?"

"Both."

"Well." Kent's answer was slow in coming and, when it did, she realized it was because Kent detested giving Hugh so much as a scintilla of praise. "He knew too much, and he was a powerful writer. We couldn't let him live."

He looked rueful as he answered the second question. "I framed you because it was the most efficient way to get the job done. It never occurred to me that some ragged police force in this backwater hamlet would look beyond the owner of the smoking gun."

"Maybe they wouldn't have if it weren't for Ben," Tobi said.

"Maybe not. Anyway, I'm glad you're not in this place," he said, sounding as if he meant it. "And I want you to know that, if you change your mind, my offer still stands."

"What offer?"

"To join our group. To be part of the army that's going to save this lousy planet from itself."

"You'll never understand," Tobi said, "that Jesus already did that."

She expected him to take offense at her statement. Instead he grinned, finally looking more like the real Kent. "We're both trying to do the same thing, aren't we?" he asked. "We just can't agree on the method."

She thought about it, then looked at him with new understanding. "Yes, I guess we are. Do you think that's why we've always been drawn to each other, because we have the same goal?"

There was a faraway look in his eyes when he answered. "I don't know about you, but it's more basic than that for me. I've always had trouble separating you from my first love. When I met you, I thought April had been reincarnated as Tobi Kirkland and come back to me."

"April?" Tobi asked, stunned. She had never heard of this first love named April.

"April," he repeated, almost reverently. "She was even named after a month, same as you. April and October. She was 16 when we started dating and she had green eyes, the same color as yours. Her hair was red too, not a dignified red-blond like yours, but flaming red."

"Where is she now?" Tobi asked.

He took a deep, sighing breath. "She committed suicide when she was 17. After the funeral, I found out her step-father had been raping her twice a week for a year. When she got pregnant, she didn't tell anyone. She just killed herself."

"Oh, Kent, how horrible!" For a moment Tobi couldn't get a breath, as she imagined the agonies April must have suffered all alone.

A satisfied expression crossed Kent's face. "Don't worry. The step-father paid."

Tobi's eyes widened. "You don't mean you...?"

"Who else?"

Tobi staggered to her feet. "I have to go. Kent, I can't cope with... you."

"Look, Tobi." She stopped and looked at him. "If you ever need anything from me, I want to know it. I'd like to try to make up for what I did to you. I don't know where they'll send me after the trial, but you can get in touch with me through my Mother. And you know where she is." He paused and shrugged. "I guess that's all I wanted to say."

Tobi nodded and turned to go. She couldn't thank him for his generous offer - she didn't want anything from him. She would never want anything from him. But she turned back before she reached the exit. "So you're going to have a trial?"

He smiled winsomely, looking as handsome as he ever had. "You don't think I'm going to make it easy for them do you?"

———

In the parking lot, as she approached her red sports car, Tobi saw that someone was using it for a desk - someone tall with thick, blond hair. Ben Walling, of course. Her brother-in-law had a notebook open on the roof and a cell phone attached to his ear. He was taking notes as he talked.

Tobi took a position next to him and waited for him to get off the phone. When he did, he flipped the notebook closed, slid it into his pocket and turned his attention to Tobi. "And how is everyone's favorite assassin today?"

"I don't think he likes being in jail," Tobi said.

"I didn't think he would. Did he have anything interesting to say?"

"Anything interesting like what?"

"Oh, like, he's gonna' make his break tonight and he wants you to bring the getaway car." Ben's tone was light, but his eyes were intense.

"Is that why you're here? Because you think Kent told me something you should know? How did you know I was here anyway?"

Ben answered her question with a question of his own. "What do you think the chances are that Kent is going to quietly vegetate in that cage without trying to escape?"

Tobi eyed him doubtfully. "And you think he's going to tell me his plans for the Great Escape?"

"Probably not," Ben acknowledged, "but I get a call whenever he has a visitor. And when I heard Tobi Kirkland had come calling, I thought I'd ask you what he had to say."

Tobi reviewed the conversation and her eyes grew troubled. "He told me about another murder he committed," she said. "That's when I left. I suddenly couldn't stand the sight of him another second." Her voice sounded close to breaking.

Ben was excited. "Really? Tell me! The more convictions we can pile up against him, the better chance we have of keeping him off the streets."

Tobi told him about April, the lost love of Kent's life. "He didn't really tell me much. If I'd known you were interested, I'd have let him keep talking." She shrugged. "Why didn't you say something?"

Ben smiled at her fondly. "Well, I didn't want you to feel pressured to see him again. He's put you through enough grief already, and I didn't think he was likely to tell you much, you being related to a copper, you know."

Tobi nodded. "Thanks. That was pretty sensitive of you, but I won't let your fellow officers know you've got sensitivity. We wouldn't want to ruin your reputation."

"Why, ma'am, that's real sportin' of you," he drawled. "I appreciate your discretion."

She gave him an impish grin. "Well, I do owe you. If it weren't for you, I would probably be in that cage instead of Kent."

"Aw, maybe not." He ruffled her hair to keep from hugging her, right out in the middle of the public parking lot. "So, why exactly did you go see Kent?"

"I guess he's bored," Tobi said. "He called me yesterday and asked me to come."

"Did you get any sense at all that he was saying good bye?"

Tobi frowned. "What do you mean?"

"Maybe he's about to make his break, and he wanted to see you one more time before he goes. Or dies trying."

Tobi's eyes widened. "Is that what you think?"

"I don't think. I have no idea how to analyze a sociopath. But it seems important to consider all the angles where Grantham is concerned."

"He said he didn't know where he would be sent after his trial," Tobi said, trying to remember his words. "And he said I could contact his Mother to find out where he was. So maybe he's going to wait and see how the trial turns out."

"Maybe." Ben sounded skeptical. "What about this April? What do you know about her?"

"Just what I told you."

"I mean, before today what had he told you about her?"

"Nothing."

Ben studied her face. "Do you think there ever was an April?"

Tobi looked surprised. "Why would he make it up?"

"Number one, lying is as normal as breathing for him. And number two, to provide an excuse for his fixation on you."

"Why does he need an excuse?" Tobi asked.

"Hey, remember me? No expert on sociopaths," Ben hedged.

"So who is?" Tobi retorted, then continued to wait for an answer.

Ben sighed. "Okay, but remember, you asked."

Tobi nodded.

"He's a user. Maybe he thinks you make a good patsy. Maybe he wants to keep the door open in case he ever has another chance to use you."

Tobi looked forlorn. "I had to ask."

"Never mind. You're onto him now. If he contacts you again, let me know. We always want to know what's on his mind."

Tobi got into her car and was about to drive away when she remembered. "Ben, wait! What about the little boy? Have you found him or found out who he is?"

Ben shook his head despondently. "Not a peep. The paper splashed him all over the front page yesterday, and we've had some calls, but nothing definite."

"What about Flossie? Is she all right?"

She will be, Ben said brightening. "Her son came for her. He's taking her back to San Diego with him for a vacation. She'll use some sick days and then her vacation days out there. Being around her grandchildren will help her bounce back."

"She may stay there," Tobi said thoughtfully. "The way she reacted to losing a child she barely knew makes me think she'll have a hard time leaving her grandchildren after a few weeks."

Ben sighed. "We'd hate to lose her, but it might be the best thing for her if she did stay. She nearly bottomed out last year when they moved to San Diego."

Tobi waved and drove away, resolving to remember Flossie and the lost toddler in her prayers.

Chapter VII

Tobi's visit with Kent Grantham left her feeling blue. The thought of an afternoon with Joshua Moses multiplied her gloom. But she arrived at the Church of the Living Vine promptly at 1:55. The church lobby, which had been bright and pulsing with energy the previous evening, was silent and shadowy now. Walking across the sinister space softly, almost on tiptoe, Tobi glanced uneasily at the darkened sanctuary where last night's howls and wails might still saturate the carpet, the pews, even the song books.

With a shudder, she turned her attention to the hall beyond the lobby. It looked dark and spooky, too, but she could see light spilling out of an office halfway down the hall. Trying to keep her breathing natural, she hastened toward the light, tapped on the half-open door, and entered the brightly-lighted room.

Joshua Moses was sitting at the computer. "Ah, there you are!" he enthused, looking up. "Glad you could come." He vacated the secretary's chair and held it for her.

"Where is everybody?" Tobi asked, looking around the empty office. She accepted the chair and positioned herself in front of the computer screen.

"Emory is making hospital visits, then he's going home until time for tonight's service. Lou - the secretary - left so we could use her office."

"Oh." Tobi tried to hide her distaste at the prospect of being alone with him.

"Look," said Rev. Moses, "the first thing I'm going to do is go lock the front doors. Otherwise, half the town will parade through here this afternoon. Be right back."

He was gone before Tobi could protest. She looked around nervously. It was all she could do to tolerate being in the same room with Rev. Moses. She certainly didn't want to be *locked* in this place with him.

But he was all business when he returned, flashing his 100-watt smile for her. "I can't tell you how fortunate I feel to be in the Lord's service. You are exactly the person I need to help me out with this project, and He knew I needed you."

"What's the project?" Tobi asked, turning her attention to the computer screen.

"My autobiography," said Moses. "People keep begging me to write it, so they can take it home and read it. But I'm no writer. As you can see, I have gotten it typed, but it's in desperate need of a professional touch to add some sparkle and pizzazz!"

"I'm a newspaper writer," Tobi protested. "We're not big on sparkle and pizzazz."

"That's okay," said Moses quickly. "It also needs a lot of work on the grammar and the...the...well, the whole thing is too...fussy."

"You want the writing to be tighter?" Tobi asked.

"Tighter! Yes, exactly!" Moses exclaimed. "So what do you think? Would you be willing to work on it?"

Tobi nodded. "Why not?" She turned her attention to the screen.

"Look, while you're doing that, I believe I'll get some shopping done. Do you need anything before I leave? Would you like me to show you around the church in case you need the bathroom or the kitchen or whatever?"

"Yes, thank you," Tobi said.

After giving her a quick tour of the building, Moses asked, "Anything you need before I go?"

"Yes, I was thinking...," Tobi said. "What if I make some changes you don't like and you want to go back to the original? Maybe I should print it out first, and make my changes on the printed pages. Then the original would still be intact until you approve the changes."

"Oh no, that's not necessary," he said with a wave of his hand. "You're working on a disc. I have several copies of the original back home at Houston. But it's downright considerate of you to think of it. Anything else?"

She shook her head and smiled. "No, I'll get right on it."

Suddenly his hand came up and landed softly on her cheek. He gave her a gentle caress, grinned, and disappeared out the back door, locking it behind himself.

Tobi's smile turned to a frown. He didn't have any business touching her like that. He didn't have any business touching her, at all. She shivered, repulsed at the memory of his touch, and all her misgivings returned in a rush.

She walked to the secretary's office and surveyed the scene. She didn't want to do it. She didn't want to sit down in that chair. She didn't want to use that computer. Most of all, she didn't want to pore over the life story of Joshua Moses.

She took a deep breath, closed her eyes, and stepped over the threshold. She had said she would do it, so she would. But when the Rev. Mr. Moses returned, she would make sure he understood he was to keep his hands to himself!

"Oh, Tobi, don't be an idiot," she chided herself, as she seated herself at the computer. "He probably doesn't know how to keep his hands to himself. And if you say anything about it, he may think you're flirting with him."

She grimaced at the thought and shivered as she turned her attention to the computer screen. Moses's autobiography was tragic. His father had been an alcoholic, his mother a sickly woman, who wore herself out trying to support the family *and* her husband's alcohol habit. Young Joshua had expected football to be the ticket out for himself and his mother. But an injury in a car wreck his senior year had kept him from receiving a football scholarship. After that, he had struggled to complete a business course at a community college. Then his mother died, and he had lost the will to live.

By the time Tobi had worked her way through Moses' grim youth, her heart was heavy and her eyes were wet. She had made many changes in the manuscript. Moses definitely wasn't a writer. His grammar was atrocious and his choice of words tended to be repetitive. But he had managed to tell a compelling story and Tobi tried not to lose his flavor and style completely as she corrected his grammar and reworked his sentences.

"How's it going?"

The hearty voice directly behind her startled Tobi so much she leapt to her feet and whirled to find the big evangelist standing inches from her. "Oh! You scared me half to death!" she gasped. "How did you get in here without making a sound."

He laughed jubilantly. "I didn't know I did. Sorry about giving you a fright."

Tobi didn't think he looked sorry, at all.

"So, are you making any headway?" he inquired again.

Tobi nodded. "I'm up to your mother's death. You had a really sad childhood. I'm sorry you suffered so much."

He shrugged. "Water under the bridge." He nodded at the computer screen. "I'll look this over tonight. Can you come in again tomorrow, or do you keep Saturdays sacred for shopping?"

"What time is it?" Tobi asked, feeling disoriented. "Is it already time to go?"

"Four forty-five," said Moses. "I'd say you've done a good day's work."

"Okay. Well, let me save this then," she said, sitting down and tapping a few keys, before she swivelled around in the chair to answer his question. "Sure, I can come in tomorrow. What time?"

"How's two?"

"Fine." She picked up her purse and stood. "I'll see you then."

"You're not going to be here for the service tonight?" he asked, sounding hurt.

"No, I've had quite enough of...*that*," she said firmly.

His eyebrows arched. "You didn't enjoy it, then?"

"Enjoy it!" she exclaimed. "I was horrified!"

Moses sat down and made himself comfortable. "Why were you horrified?" he asked, sounding genuinely interested.

Tobi shook her head. "I don't want to talk about it," she said. "We aren't going to agree, so what's the point?"

"The point is that I'm interested in *your* viewpoint," he said with a smile. "Would I be right to assume that you were embarrassed to see the power of God demonstrated in His people last night?"

"I didn't see the power of God last night," said Tobi. "Whatever was going on here last night had nothing to do with the power of God."

"Really?" His calm voice was silken. "How can you say that?"

"I've spent a lot of time in churches like this one," Tobi said, "so I've thought a lot about God's power and how it's revealed in His people."

"And what did you decide?" Rev. Moses' voice sounded amused.

"I believe the main reason God imparts power to His people is to help us live a holy life," Tobi said.

The evangelist's eyebrows went up again. "A *holy* life? Well, you are quite the hoity toity, aren't you? Don't you believe God invests His power in healing His people? And providing for our needs? And protecting us?"

"Yes, of course," said Tobi. "But I don't believe He does it dramatically and instantaneously the way He did when Jesus and the apostles were alive. That was a special time - a unique dispensation of His power - but it ended when the last apostle died."

Moses shook his head. "I'm sorry that one so lovely can be so wrong. But, of course, you have the right to be wrong. And I suppose you're going to say it wasn't the Holy Spirit, but demon spirits at work here last night?"

"I had no intention of saying one way or the other," Tobi said, "but, since you brought it up, I will say there's no way the Holy Spirit was involved in that...that freak show I witnessed here last night."

Did some of the warmth leave his eyes as she spoke? Tobi wasn't sure. His face remained calm and, when he replied, his voice was still serene. "Well, as you said, we're not going to agree about these things. Thank you for coming." He put his hand into his pocket and pulled out some bills. "Here's your pay for today's work."

Tobi hesitated, then put out her hand to receive three 20-dollar bills. "Thank you, Rev. Moses," she said. "I'll see you tomorrow."

"Please call me Joshua," he said.

She nodded. "Okay."

He had to unlock the front door with a key to let her out. She waited impatiently as he twisted the key in the lock. Finally, the door swung outward, and Tobi stepped past him into friendly sunshine. Walking away from the grim, dark world inside the Church of the Living Vine, she had never been so grateful for hot, blinding sunlight in her whole life!

———

It was around 10:00 o'clock that night when a small, dark figure on a black, nearly invisible bicycle rode slowly up and down Tomlin Street, paying special attention to the sad looking house at 1809. Only one room in the front of the house had a light on - no TV - and the small home was as still as death.

After counting, for the third time, how many houses 1809 was from the corner, the dark figure turned into the alley behind the Tomlin Street houses. He leaned his bicycle against the fence behind the first trash dumpster he came to, then ran noiselessly along the alley to the fifth house. The fence guarding the house at 1809 was new and sturdy.

He would not try to enter the yard. He would not even touch the fence for fear of triggering an alarm. Instead, with one last look around, he pulled out a big, plastic gun that had been secured at his waist, took careful aim, and shot a multitude of fluorescent pellets onto the roof of the house. Then, as swiftly and silently as he had come, he retrieved the bicycle and disappeared into the darkness.

Across town, Tobi's phone was ringing. Joel and his daughters had arrived safely in Dallas and gotten settled in his Uncle William's home. Now, his Aunt Jen had Gloria and Grace in the kitchen, baking cookies, and Joel had wandered out into the back yard. Finding a chaise lounge on the porch, he had made himself comfortable and dialed Tobi's number.

"Hi, Joel," she said, trying not to sound breathless with excitement, at the sound of his voice. She settled herself in her recliner, smiling expectantly.

"Hi, Tobi. I was afraid you would be out on a date with the fancy evangelist."

"No you weren't," she said. Her smile turned into an exasperated frown. "You know I can barely stand the sight of him."

"Well, I figured he spent the afternoon sweet-talking you, and he might have changed your opinion of him," Joel said.

"As a matter of fact," Tobi said, "I do feel a little kinder toward him than I did before. I was working on his autobiography, and it's really sad. I feel sorry for him."

"Sorry for him," thought Joel. "Good. Keep feeling sorry for him, and I've got nothing to worry about." Aloud he said, "And what did the movie star want?"

Tobi had to stop and think. Her visit with Kent Grantham seemed like a distant memory. "I'm not sure I ever figured out what he wanted," she told Joel. "I guess he's lonely. Ben thought..." She hesitated.

"Ben thought what?" he prodded.

"Well, I'm not sure about that either. Ben was waiting for me by my car when I left the jail because he wanted to know what Kent had said. It almost seemed like he thought Kent was telling me goodbye."

Joel frowned. "What does that mean - that he's going to commit suicide?"

"No, Ben's worried that he might attempt an escape."

"And what do you think?" Joel asked.

"I don't know what to think about Kent," she said. "One thing's for sure - he wasn't going to listen to any more talk about Jesus. He made that clear at the very beginning."

"I'm sorry, Tobi," Joel said. He suddenly felt ashamed for the jealousy he had wasted on Kent, who didn't even know the wonder and joy of knowing Jesus. "Do you think there's any hope for him now?"

"I guess there's always hope," Tobi said. "I'll just have to keep praying for him."

"I'll pray for him, too," Joel promised. "It sounds like he needs it."

Tobi agreed, then turned the conversation to a lighter vein. "How was the trip?"

"It was great. It's been a long time since I've been on the road with Gloria and Gracie. I'd forgotten how much I like them."

"You're blessed to have them," Tobi said, and the sadness in her voice hurt Joel's heart.

"Listen," he said, changing the subject again, "I want to tell you what I was thinking about on the road today."

"What?"

"Well, that sideshow last night - a lot of people believe the Holy Spirit is responsible for all that hocus-pocus. And that's the sort of thing that can happen when we start claiming we're receiving new revelation from God. I'm finally beginning to understand why you're so opposed to the Charismatic movement."

Tobi's eyes widened. "You're right! I hadn't thought about it exactly that way, but what better reason could there be for rejecting the whole idea of 'tongues'?"

Joel sighed. "Some people will say not to throw out the baby with the bath water. Just because a few people are misrepresenting God, doesn't mean all of them are."

"Of course you're right," Tobi said, "but it's harder all the time for me to understand how so many people - so many *good* people - can fall for such darkness. Such horrible deception!"

"Both of *us* did," Joel observed.

"Don't remind me," Tobi said and her voice was thick with sorrow. "It's one of the greatest regrets of my life."

"Well, I don't regret it," Joel said firmly. "If you hadn't been involved and gotten delivered, you might not have been able to convince me to step back and take another look at my beliefs. I'll always be grateful to you for that, Tobi."

"Since you put it that way," Tobi said with a smile he could hear in her voice, "I guess I'm grateful too."

As Joel and Tobi finished up their phone call by whispering a few sweet nothings to each other, Paul Hudson was turning a familiar door knob in Green Bay, Wisconsin. The front door of his parents' home was locked, so he fished a key out of his pocket and turned it in the lock. Moments later, Rachel looked up with a shriek as he seemed to materialize in the den where his family was gathered.

"Paul! What are you doing here? Where did you come from?" she gasped.

"The better question is, 'What are *you* doing here?' " he observed, gazing from his wife to Patrice to his Mom and then his Dad.

"Paul!" Ellie Hudson dropped the needlework she had been doing and rushed to embrace her son. "We didn't know you were coming."

"Neither did I," Paul admitted.

Next, Alex Hudson engulfed him. Paul's father had been a linebacker for the Green Bay Packers in his younger days and he greeted his son with a bear hug that knocked the wind out of Paul every time.

Rachel came and planted a dutiful kiss on his cheek, then drew him down onto the dark green, leather couch between herself and Patrice. Paul turned his eyes onto his truant employee but, before he could speak, a toddler with curly, black hair, wearing blue summer pajamas, leaped into his arms with a glad cry.

"Trevor, my boy!" Paul cried, cuddling and cradling the child. "Well, you have created quite a stir back home." He looked at Patrice, then, and was silenced by the agony on her young face. All the stern lectures he had rehearsed on the airplane vanished before her grief. He handed Trevor to Rachel and took Patrice into his arms, where hot, silent tears rolled down her cheeks and soaked his shirt.

Chapter VIII

Between 3:00 and 4:00 A.M. Saturday, the phone next to Ben Walling's bed jangled him awake. He grabbed for it and knocked over the night table beside his bed. The phone, a lamp, an alarm clock, his wallet, and a handful of change crashed to the floor.

"Who is it?" DeeDee asked sleepily.

"I don't know," Ben growled, groping along the floor in a futile effort to find the telephone. "Would you turn on a light?"

When DeeDee's lamp clicked on, he spied the telephone handset where it had skidded to the wall and halted. He scooped it up and said, "Yeah?"

DeeDee watched his face darken and his eyes narrow. "How?" "When?" "Where?" "How long ago?" and "What time?" were his contributions to the conversation, as his voice grew softer and angrier with each utterance.

When the conversation ended, he tossed the handset onto the bed and began pulling on the clothes he had worn the previous day. "Call Tobi," he said. "Tell her not to answer the phone or the door until I get there. Grantham has escaped."

Buttoning his shirt, he could see the "How?" forming on DeeDee's lips. "I don't know all the details," he replied before she asked, "but he got deathly ill this evening. When none of the local doctors could diagnose him, a Med Evac helicopter was called to take him to Dallas. Thirty minutes out, the chopper was intercepted by a military helicopter and forced to land. Now they're thinking Grantham's symptoms might have been caused by some drug his lawyer slipped him this afternoon."

Ben was pulling on his shoes now. "Two men in military garb loaded Grantham into their helicopter and shot up the blades of the Med Evac. Then the military chopper headed for Deepwater. Nobody knows why they're coming back here, but I'm going to get Tobi, just in case."

"When did all this happen?" DeeDee asked, getting out of bed and pulling on a robe.

"About 15 minutes ago."

"How do they know?"

"The radio in the Med Evac was working. The pilot reported as soon as Grantham's chopper lifted off."

"If Tobi's not home, Kent will know where she is," DeeDee cried, trying to quell her rising panic. "None of us will be safe with him on the loose."

Ben was one step from the bedroom door, but he came back and enfolded DeeDee in his arms. "Stay calm, Sweetheart," he whispered soothingly. "I'll get Tobi and be right back. After you call Tobi, watch the yards, but *don't turn on any lights.* Got it?"

DeeDee nodded, taking slow, deep breaths.

"Good girl," Ben said. He kissed her lingeringly. "Remember, I love you."

"I love you too."

Ben made the drive to Tobi's house in record time. When he arrived, he circled the block slowly, then drove up the alley. Every shadow looked like a lurking human form. Every movement was Kent Grantham lifting a deadly rifle into shooting position. By the time he parked in front of Tobi's house, his heart was racing.

Leaping from his pickup, he sprinted toward the front door. When he was halfway up the sidewalk, Tobi emerged and hurried toward him. "Have you seen anything strange this evening?" he asked as she approached. "Anything, at all?"

"No, it's been a..."

She paused in mid-sentence and listened. There was a gentle thrumming sound coming from somewhere. Somewhere in the air. She and Ben searched the skies. As the sound grew louder, both of them faced east straining to see through the darkness.

Suddenly Tobi pointed. "There! What is...," she began, but an explosion cut her off.

Instinctively, both Ben and Tobi dropped to the sidewalk. "What in thunder!" Ben gasped. The explosion had turned into a fireball on the east side of town. As they watched, it faded to an orange glow.

"Come on!" Ben said, leaping up. He hauled Tobi to her feet and pulled her to his pickup at breakneck speed. As they sped through silent streets toward that eerie orange glow, Ben said, "Listen, you'd better call

DeeDee." He fumbled in his pockets a moment before he realized he'd left without his cell phone. "I don't have my phone," he said. "Do you have yours?"

In answer, Tobi opened her purse and pulled out the cell phone Joel had left with her. She punched in the Wallings' number and told DeeDee about the explosion.

After a short conversation, she held out the phone. "She wants to talk to you."

DeeDee's voice sounded small and remote. "Do you think the explosion has anything to do with Kent?" she asked.

At the wheel of his pickup, Ben was nodding. "Don't ask me how," he said, "but it was a military helicopter that picked him up. And we could hear a helicopter right before the explosion. There has to be a connection."

"Ben," DeeDee's voice was stronger and more insistent now, "I don't want to be here. I'm scared. I'm going to take the kids and..."

"And go where?" Ben asked when she hesitated.

"I don't know." Her voice quavered.

"Wait." Ben stomped the brake and slammed the gearshift into Park. He opened the door and stepped out into the night to listen. In a moment, he slid back under the wheel and resumed driving. "DeeDee, Tobi and I could hear the helicopter before. I can't hear it now. I think it's gone. But if you want me to, I'll come get you and the kids and take you... somewhere... Wherever you'll feel safe."

There was a long silence. Then DeeDee said, "Never mind. We'll stay here unless I hear a helicopter headed this way."

"Are you sure?" Ben kept his voice sympathetic. He was itching to get to the action, but his family's safety and peace of mind were more important to him than any disaster.

"Ben, you don't think it's a terrorist attack, do you?" DeeDee asked.

"In Deepwater, Texas?" he laughed humorlessly. "I don't think any self-respecting terrorist ever heard of Deepwater."

"Okay. Call me soon, so I'll know you're all right."

"As soon as I can," he promised before he cut the connection.

Ben handed Tobi the phone as he turned onto Mabry Lane. "Now, I've got to figure out what to do with you," he said frowning.

"Don't you think I can help?" she asked.

"It doesn't matter, I can't take you there until I know what's going on. Besides, we don't know where Grantham is."

Tobi nodded. "I can stay in the truck," she offered.

Ben didn't like the idea, but he didn't have a better one until he noticed a light in the window at Mrs. Randolph White's house. "Wait here," he said, swerving into her driveway. He opened the door of the pickup and dashed to the porch. Almost as soon as he knocked, he heard Mrs. White's crackly voice. "Who is it?"

"Mrs. White, it's Ben Walling. I need you to do me a favor."

Mrs. White threw open the door. Her rumpled face was puckered into more wrinkles than usual. "Oh, Ben, come in, please. What's happening?"

"I can't come in, but I'd like to leave my sister-in-law here for awhile if that's okay. She's knows as much as I do about what's going on and she'll tell you about it."

Hearing the urgency in his voice, Mrs. White's demeanor changed. Some of her wrinkles smoothed out, as she beckoned eagerly to Tobi in the pickup. "Of course, Ben. I'd be honored if there's anything I can do for you."

Impulsively Ben leaned over and kissed her cheek, as Tobi approached. "You ladies pray for us, will you?" he asked.

"You know we will," and "Of course we're going to pray," Tobi and Mrs. White told his back, as he raced toward his pickup.

"Now, dearie, my name is Lorraine White, but you call me Lori. Okay?" Mrs. White said, leading Tobi into her cozy living room.

"Okay," Tobi said. "And I'm October Kirkland, but you call me Tobi."

"All right, Tobi. You sit wherever you want to and tell me what the ruckus is about."

The two women settled in Mrs. White's faded comfortable chairs, and Tiki came out to inspect the visitor.

Ben was able to drive only two blocks on Tomlin Street before he had to abandon his vehicle. Immediately he could see that debris from the blast had damaged cars and houses several blocks away from the explosion. Scraps of wood and metal littered the landscape. One car's windshield was shattered. It looked like a war zone.

As he drew closer yet, the fire seemed to be a living thing. It was an inferno hurling tidal waves of heat into his face. The erratic firelight cast swirling shadows across his path - shadows that writhed at his feet, coiling and clinging. Ashes mingled with oxygen in the air - choking him, blinding him. He wanted to turn and run. Let the fire win. Let it devour the whole block, the whole town. Who could fight it?

"Lord, give me grace," he murmured. "Give me grace to go on."

The fire department was already on the scene, working furiously to contain the blazes devouring three houses in the middle of the 1800 block of Tomlin, as well as one across the alley from 1809. No one was being allowed to work the fire except the firefighters clad in their protective gear, so Ben located Sergeant Owen Ferguson, the senior police officer at the scene, and asked how he could help. Ferguson gazed at him grimly through smoke-reddened eyes, then said, "You're homicide - as far as I'm concerned you can do your thing. Find out how this nightmare started. And when the fires are out, we'll help you count the bodies." He turned away without waiting for a response.

Ben looked across the street. A handful of civilians were watching, but others were arriving every minute. He tried to memorize those who were already present. They were the ones who were most likely to have been eye witnesses.

Walking toward the closest group of spectators, Ben took out his notepad and turned to a clean page. He found everyone eager to tell him what they knew. They wanted to help and, if they weren't allowed to fight the fire, they would talk to the police. Ben was soon scribbling names, addresses, and tidbits of information as fast as he could write.

Several people had heard a helicopter approaching and two had actually seen it. One was an older men with impaired vision, but the other was a high school biology teacher who had been out doing some night observation of the local fauna.

"I had just gotten home," he told Ben, pointing down the street to his house, "and I heard this droning overhead. It was like somebody had a gigantic electric mixer and was trying to beat the air into a lather. I went out into the middle of the street to see if I could tell where the sound was coming from, and suddenly a helicopter appeared. Right over there." He pointed toward the burning homes.

"I think it had been flying very high," he continued, "and it suddenly dropped out of the sky right over that house in the middle." He indicated 1809. "First a light shone down on the house, then the helicopter starting rising again and I saw streaks of fire coming from it. Then the house exploded. The helicopter must have been shooting rockets. Or missiles. Or something..."

He paused a moment, remembering the devastating sight, then continued with a sigh. "I know I should have watched, but all I could think of was getting my wife and kids into the car and away. So I ran and unlocked the front door and then I realized the helicopter was leaving. I could still hear it faintly, but the sound was getting softer and softer. I

Out of Darkness

ran back into the street and tried to find it, but I never saw it again." He shrugged, looking defeated. "I guess I'm not exactly the hero type."

"What are you talking about?" Ben asked heartily. "So far, you're the only person I've found who actually saw what happened. Your information is invaluable to me."

The teacher looked pleased. "Well, I'm glad I could help a little, at least."

"One more question," Ben said. "Do you know which way the helicopter headed?"

The teacher shook his head regretfully. "I couldn't tell."

"I know," said the older man, raising his hand like a child in a classroom. "It went that way." He pointed toward the southeast. "I couldn't see the thing clearly, but I could tell which way it was going when it left."

"Good work," said Ben, patting the old man's shoulder. "Have you told anybody else which way it went?"

The man shrugged. "Nobody asked."

Ben nodded. "Too busy fighting fires. Look, all of you, please sit tight. I'm going to give this information to the officer in charge. Then I'll be back."

Sergeant Ferguson looked perplexed when Ben grabbed his armed and pulled his ear close so he could make himself heard above the din. "It was a helicopter shooting missiles!" he shouted. "It was headed southeast when it left."

"What?" Ferguson yelled.

"All of this..." Ben waved toward the burning homes. "It was caused by a helicopter shooting missiles. When the chopper left, it was headed southeast."

Ferguson's face brightened. "Good work, Walling! I'm on it!"

When Ben returned to his group of informants, a teenage boy had been added to their number. The teen was trying to pull away, but several pairs of hands were restraining him. "What's wrong?" Ben asked. His strong grip closed on the youth's thin arm and the others released their hold.

"This one is always roaming around at night," volunteered one of the neighbors. "We think he knows something."

Ben looked at the boy. He was a nondescript youngster with short, brown hair and a lean build. "What's your name?" Ben asked.

"I ain't sayin' nuthin'," the boy replied sullenly.

"He's Tyson Banning," a man in the crowd said, and the boy glared at the speaker.

"Why don't you want to talk to me, Tyson?" Ben asked.

Tyson stared at the ground.

"What's his problem?" Ben asked the bystanders.

"He's a trouble maker," someone said.

"He was probably out stealing cigarettes or buying marijuana," said another voice.

Ben looked at the boy's angry face, then drew him away from the group. "Look, Tyson," he said confidentially, "I don't have time to take you downtown right now. But if you won't tell me what you know, I'll have to come back later today and take you to the police station and get you to talk to me."

The angry expression on Tyson's face was replaced with an anxious one. "You can't do that! My Mom doesn't know I'm out. I don't want her to know I left the house."

"Okay, then tell me what you know now and I'll send you home to bed," Ben said.

"I don't know if I know anything," said Tyson, finally losing his sullenness. "It sounds stupid, but I think I saw...I think I saw little lighted rocks on one of those houses."

"Which one?" asked Ben.

"1809."

"What about the other houses? Was anything on their roofs?"

"No," the boy said firmly. "I looked."

"Do you think these lighted rocks might have been there last week? Or last month? Or even longer?" Ben asked.

"They weren't there last *night* - well, I guess it's night before last now," Tyson said with certainty. "I notice things. I would have noticed."

"When you say lighted rocks, do you mean electric lights?" Ben asked.

"No, 'course not. But they were shiny."

"Like fluorescent?"

"Yeah. Like that!" The boy seemed pleased to be understood.

"Okay. What else did you see tonight?"

"Nuthin'. Honest, Officer." Tyson's voice held a note of pleading.

Ben studied the boy's face. He wasn't sure Tyson had told him everything he knew, but he didn't have time to pry it out of him, so he held out his hand. "Thank you for your help, Tyson. If you think of anything else that might help us, call the police station and ask for Ben Walling. Okay?"

Tyson shrugged. "Sure." He shook Ben's hand briefly, then turned away and disappeared into the darkness.

Ben returned to the Tomlin Street residents and asked, "Who lived at 1809?"

Several shrugged. Most looked blank. "Well, his name was Ocelot or Lynx or Puma, or something like that," someone finally volunteered.

"It was Lynx," said the old man who had seen the helicopter leaving the area. He lived at 1812 and had a good view of the house at 1809. "Actually, he had a real name, but I forget what it was. He wouldn't answer to anything but Lynx."

"What are you talking about?" someone asked. "When did you ever see enough of him to find out what he would or wouldn't answer to?"

"Well, when he was looking to buy the property, I talked to him," said the man. "He was real interested in the neighbors, whether they were nosy, whether there was a lot of vandalism in the area. Seems like he was pretty partial to his privacy. He wasn't going to take the place if there were a lot of busybodies on the street."

To Ben, it felt like pulling teeth, trying to learn anything about the man named Lynx who had lived at 1809 Tomlin. According to the neighbors, there had been a lot of activity at 1809 when Lynx first bought the house. Trucks and vans were coming and going for several weeks, first remodeling the inside, then delivering furniture. However, nobody had seen inside the house after the work was finished.

"I went over one time to see the place," said the woman who lived at 1815. "I baked him a pie. Thought sure he would invite me in when I brought it to him. Instead, he closed the door behind him and came out on the porch to talk to me. In about two minutes he said he had to go - he was in the middle of a big project. And he went inside with my pie and closed the door in my face. I never tried to darken his door again!"

Nobody seemed to know what kind of work Lynx did, but all agreed it had something to do with computers. They didn't know when he came or went because he kept his car in the garage and had painted the windows in the garage door black.

"But he didn't keep regular hours, I can tell you that," said the woman from 1815. "I'm retired so I'm home all the time, and I pay attention to what's going on around here. Sometimes he would leave at 6:00 A.M. and not come back for a week. Sometimes he would be gone 10 minutes. You never knew when he would be coming or going."

"What kind of car did he drive?" Ben asked.

The woman shrugged. "It was brand new - a sports car - and it was black. That's all I know."

Ben interviewed people individually and in groups for nearly two hours, but he learned little more about the helicopter attack or about the inhabitant of 1809 Tomlin. When he noticed the eastern skyline turning pink, he realized he had forgotten to call DeeDee. He winced, hoping she hadn't been lying awake all this time, waiting for his call.

"Listen, do you know if the phone lines were damaged in the explosion?" he asked the biology teacher who, like many others, was waiting for the fires to be extinguished so they could offer their assistance.

The teacher pulled a cell phone out of a pocket. "This one is working," he smiled. "You're welcome to use it."

"Thanks." Ben smiled gratefully and walked away from the crowd so he could hear.

DeeDee answered on the first ring. "Ben? Is that you?"

"Yes, I'm fine. I'm sorry I didn't call sooner, but I got involved." He gave her a quick rundown on the situation, then said, "I'm going to stop in a little bit for breakfast, but I'm not going to try to sleep any more today."

"Tell me when and I'll have your breakfast ready when you get here," she said.

Ben glanced around. "I guess I'll leave right now. Maybe when I get back, we'll be able to actually get into the rubble and find out...well, whatever there is to find out. Oh, I almost forgot - I left Tobi with Mrs. White. I'll stop by for her."

"No, don't," said DeeDee. She called an hour ago and said they were going to bed. "She's going to call me when she wakes up, and I'll go get her."

"Thanks, my love. Did I ever tell you that you're the perfect cop's wife?"

"Did I ever tell you that you're the perfect cop?"

Ben grinned. "See you in 20."

Chapter IX

When the sun rose that Saturday morning and beamed down on Deepwater, it revealed a pile of dark rubble in the 1800 block of Tomlin Street. Every house adjoining 1809, including the one across the alley, had been decimated. Others had been damaged, but were still standing.

The official count was three dead. The house at 1807 had been empty, recently vacated when its owner moved and listed it with a real estate office. The young family that lived at 1811 had been on vacation for a week and weren't expected back for another week. The retired couple who lived across the alley from 1809 had been killed and so, presumably, had Lynx. Police officials and fire investigators combed through smoking ruins and interviewed neighbors all day in order to reach these conclusions.

Ben Walling was doing his best to gather information about the mysterious inhabitant of 1809 who seemed to be the primary target of the deadly helicopter. But information was hard to come by on a Saturday. Eventually he learned that the owner of the property at 1809 Tomlin was named Lincoln Nix.

"Lincoln Nix. Lynx," he muttered to himself. "Must be the same guy." This information was a disappointment. He had been hoping Nix was a renter and the owner of the house might have some information about the tenant. "Coffee," he muttered to himself. "Gotta' get some coffee and wake up."

Tobi left Mrs. Randolph White - Lori - with kisses and hugs late that morning. They had become fast friends in a few short hours. Praying urgently for a shared need and passing the tense hours of a night that bristled with unnamed terrors had knit their souls together. Tiki rubbed against Tobi's legs affectionately and yowled mournfully when she rode away in DeeDee's minivan.

But DeeDee was not at the wheel. It was her 16-year-old daughter Alison who had arrived to pick up Tobi. "Hi, Aunt Tobi," she said as her aunt climbed into the front passenger seat. "Have you heard any news? Is this the most exciting thing that ever happened in Deepwater or what?"

Tobi smiled fondly at the teenager, whose hair was the same red gold color as her own. "It's pretty exciting, I guess. And completely horrible."

Alison nodded solemnly. "Yeah. I guess some of those people died. Dad didn't seem to know yet how many."

"Have you seen him this morning?" Tobi asked.

"No, but he came home for breakfast before I was up, then went back to work right away. Mom told me what he said before she went back to bed. She didn't get much sleep last night. I think she stayed awake worrying about Dad."

"So what do we need to do? Does your Dad or anybody else need help?" Tobi asked.

Alison shook her head. "Right now they're trying to keep people away until they can finish their investigation. Mom said to bring you home and put you to bed."

"No," Tobi said firmly. "I want to go home - to my place. I couldn't sleep, and there's nothing for me to do at your house."

"But what about that murderer - Kent whosit?" Alison asked. "Mom said he escaped last night, and maybe he'll come after you."

"I know," Tobi said, "but I've been thinking about it and praying about it, and I don't believe he's after me. I think your Dad was right. I went to see Kent yesterday and Ben said maybe he wanted me to visit him in jail, so he could say goodbye."

Alison glanced at her aunt as she drove. She and Davy would have been happy for Tobi come and live with them forever. But she wasn't in the habit of arguing with her elders, so she merely asked, "Are you sure?"

"Yes," said Tobi. "I've got dirty dishes in the sink, and I've got to get them washed before my kitchen fills up with roaches and mice."

Alison made a face. "Ugh."

Tobi cleaned up her kitchen in short order, but was too restless to do anything else except pace and worry. Why had Kent's mysterious apocalyptic organization destroyed a few houses in the middle of a quiet residential neighborhood in the tiny town of Deepwater, Texas?

She struggled with her memory. What had he told her that dark day a month ago when he abducted her? She had been so terrified she had been unable to concentrate on his words. But she remembered that he believed he was helping save the world from itself, and that his organization believed it was all right to commit murder in order to advance their agenda. Who had lived on Tomlin Street and what had they known? Was it someone Kent had met in jail? Someone he had met while he was working briefly on the local newspaper? And why was that someone a threat to Kent and his group? Had Kent revealed something he shouldn't have in an unguarded moment? Knowing Kent, she dismissed the possibility. But then, who? And what? And why? And how?

When it was time to report to the Church of the Living Vine for work, Tobi felt a sense of relief. She didn't want to think about the disaster for awhile. She wanted Ben to figure it out and explain it to her. The whole puzzle was giving her a headache.

The front door of the church was locked. Now what? Tobi knocked and waited. No response. Should she try the back door or forget the whole thing and go home?

Yesterday she would have gone home and been grateful for the excuse. Today she wanted the diversion of work. She wanted to quit thinking about Kent Grantham. Quit trying to figure out why he did what he did. So she began walking along the sidewalk that would take her to the rear of the church.

"Wait, Tobi! Come back," called a voice.

She turned to see Joshua Moses holding the door open and beckoning for her to return. "I didn't realize how late it was," he explained as she walked past him into the cool dimness of the church. "And I wasn't so sure you'd be back."

She faced him, looking surprised. "I said I'd be back."

"Of course you did. Well, I'm glad you're here. Come right on in and let's get to work." He turned the key in the lock, then pulled it out and put it in his pocket.

As he walked down the hall toward the church offices, Tobi hesitated. She looked at the locked door with a sense of foreboding. Then she muttered to herself, "Get a grip," and followed the big evangelist into the dark hall.

Moses was waiting for Tobi in the secretary's office. He held her chair for her with a gallant flourish, then seated himself nearby. "Well, you missed the excitement last night," he told her smugly.

Tobi, who had experienced enough excitement the previous night to last her several years, said politely, "How's that?"

"We witnessed a dramatic healing!" Moses said exuberantly. "A woman who was crippled ten years ago in a car accident got out of her wheel chair and ran around the sanctuary. Literally ran! Like a teenager! It was one of the most exciting nights of my life!"

Tobi watched the evangelist's expectant face for a few moments, then asked mildly, "And how much did you have to pay her for her performance?"

There was a stunned silence, followed by joyful laughter. "A pretty penny - that's for sure!" Moses said. "And you're a smart cookie to figure it out. Do you know that not one person in the service raised the slightest doubt? They all swallowed it whole!"

Tobi looked horrified. "That's fraud!" she gasped. "And you admit it as if you do it every day."

"Not every day," Moses said. "I never know when she's going to be in a service. And she's a master of disguise. She and her husband too. They have my schedule, and they decide when to show up. That way it's easier for me to pretend it's real."

"But that's fraud," Tobi said again.

"Of course it is," Moses agreed. "And these people - these Christians - are asking for it. They're begging for it. What kind of performer would I be if I didn't give them what they want?"

"Performer?" Tobi asked faintly. "Performer?"

"Come on. Don't give me an act. I already know you're too bright to fall for this God stuff. So tell me - what's your racket?"

"M...my racket?" Tobi felt weak all over.

Suddenly Joshua Moses was on his feet, towering over her. "Yes, your racket." He squatted beside her so they were face to face and his tone became confidential. "You can tell me. We both know God is green." He rubbed his thumb across his fingers to show he was talking about money. "So tell me. What's your game?"

Tobi shook her head and pushed her chair away from him. "I don't know what you're talking about."

"Okay, then I'll tell you." Moses put both his knees on the floor and his face very close to Tobi's. She tried to push away again, but her chair was hard against the desk and wouldn't move. "You were here by yourself all afternoon yesterday," Moses said in a triumphant voice. "You know - and I know you know - that there is a table full of my autobiographies - my finished autobiographies - out in the lobby. So we both know you didn't come back today to work on my autobiography."

He put both his big hands on her face and pulled it toward his face. "And we both know why you did come back today," he added in a tender, exultant tone. And then his mouth was on Tobi's. His tongue was forcing its way into her mouth.

"No!" Tobi tried to scream, but he was too strong for her. She slapped and pushed and finally wrenched her face out of his grasp. "Are you crazy?" she gasped when she finally regained control of her mouth. "Let me go!"

Moses only laughed. He stood and pulled her up into his arms. "Don't play hard to get with me," he urged. "It's not necessary." Then he was kissing her again, and his right hand was exploring her breasts. Next he was fumbling with her buttons!

Tobi kicked and slapped and tried to knee him in the groin. Moses laughed again and spun her around as easily as a child spinning a top. Pulling her close, so that her back was against his chest, he held her in a viselike grip. "You're quite the little wildcat, aren't you?" he asked. And now he was pulling the tail of her blouse free from her skirt. Then his hand was under her shirt, pushing her bra over her breast, out of his way.

"Stop!" Tobi screamed over and over, but her rejection seemed only to fuel his passion. And his body was a rock, impervious to her puny fists and her kicking feet. Suddenly she knew with horrifying clarity that Joshua Moses was going to rape her and she did not have the strength in her body to stop him.

"Lord," she prayed desperately, silently. "Lord, help me."

"Joshua, wait a minute," she said, forcing the terror and the loathing out of her voice. In their place, she was able to manage a cajoling, flirtatious tone. And he responded. The hand that had begun moving toward her skirt paused. "Listen," she said urgently. "I really need to go the bathroom first. Okay?"

To her relief, his grip loosened. He turned her to face him and again his lips sought hers. Instinctively, she knew it was a test, and this time she accepted his caress, allowing his tongue to explore her mouth. She even put one hand on the back of his neck and stroked his face with the other. When, at last, the kiss ended, she whispered coquettishly, "Now, don't you go away. I'll be right back."

To her relief, he didn't object when she picked up her purse, which held Joel's cell phone. But he did follow her into the hall and watch her disappear into the bathroom. As soon as the bathroom door closed behind her, Tobi began to tremble all over. She saw with a sinking heart that the door didn't have a lock.

With legs that threatened to buckle at every step, she went into the farthest stall and punched 911 on the cell phone's key pad. She would have preferred to call Ben direct, but she was afraid her trembling fingers would dial a wrong number and she would lose the opportunity altogether. When the 911 operator answered, Tobi flushed the toilet and said urgently,

"Don't talk; just listen. This is Tobi Kirkland. Tell Police Detective Ben Walling I need him at the Church of the Living Vine. That's Ben Walling. Send him to the Church of the Living Vine. Tell him to hurry."

At that moment Moses pounded on the door so loudly that Tobi almost dropped the phone. Without breaking the connection, she dropped it into her purse. "Who are you talking to in there?" Moses demanded, opening the door and stepping into the restroom.

"Myself," Tobi said. "Who do you think?"

Moses came into the room and crossed to the stall Tobi was in. "Joshua, I'm not finished," she said pleadingly. "Go away. I'll be out in just a minute."

He rattled the door hard, and the flimsy latch gave way. Trembling like a leaf in a hurricane, Tobi faced him. "Who were you talking to?" Moses demanded again.

"The 911 operator," Tobi said defiantly.

Moses snatched her purse from her grasp, found the cell phone and broke the connection. Then he flung the phone across the room. "In that case," he growled, "I guess we'd better take care of our business now."

"I think you should know," Tobi said, trying to steady her voice, "that my brother-in-law is on his way here. He's a homicide detective, and the police chief never allows him anywhere near a rape case for fear he'll kill the perp."

Moses sneered. "Give me a break. What kind of fool do you take me for?"

"His sister was raped when she was in college," Tobi continued hastily. "It destroyed her life - she still lives at home with her parents. And Ben nearly took a rapist apart with his bare hands right after he joined the force. I probably shouldn't have asked for him, but I suddenly had an irresistible desire to see you bloodied up a little." She shrugged and added contemptuously, "Or a lot."

Moses' fist flew toward Tobi's face a second after her cell phone rang. She had already ducked to get past him and retrieve the cell phone, just before his fist slammed into the bathroom stall. He howled in rage and pain.

"Ben?" Tobi cried into the phone.

"Tobi. What happened?"

"Joshua Moses tried to rape me," she said distinctly, wanting to be sure Ben heard the name correctly.

"He tried to or he did?" Ben asked with steel in his voice.

"He tried to," Tobi said.

"Where are you now?" Ben asked.

"In the women's restroom."

"Where is he?"

"He's in here too," Tobi said.

"Oh good," said Ben in a voice that boded no good for Moses. "Let me talk to him."

Tobi held out the phone to Moses, who took it, grunted at it, listened for a moment, then handed it back to Tobi.

"I'm about three minutes away right now," Ben told Tobi. "I told that pig that if you and he aren't both outside the church when I get there, I'll drive in and get you."

Before Tobi could answer, the phone beeped and died. It hadn't been fully charged after the night's interruption and she was unable to get a dial tone again. But it didn't matter. She snatched her purse away from Joshua Moses and marched out of the restroom and down the dark hall to the locked front door.

By the time Ben's pickup roared into sight, Tobi was standing by her car waiting for him. He rammed his gear shift into Park and flung open the door. As soon as he stepped onto the ground, Tobi hurled herself at him and, when those strong, friendly arms closed around her, her tears erupted. Ben said nothing, but merely held her close and prayed God would restore her sense of safety and security.

Moses watched this scene impassively. He was standing by the door of the church, waiting, with a bland expression on his face. As he stood there and Tobi wept in Ben's arms, a police car pulled up, two doors opened, and two officers leaped out with drawn guns. Standing behind their open doors, they trained their weapons on Moses.

Staring down the barrels of two fierce looking firearms, Moses decided it was time to activate his own best weapon - his glib tongue. Half raising his arms in surrender, he said earnestly, "Now look, officers, this was all a big misunderstanding. If you'll put those guns down, I'll be happy to explain."

"Tobi," Ben said urgently. "Do you want me to put a bullet between his eyes? Because if you do, I will."

"No," Tobi said, just as urgently. She wiped her eyes with the back of her hand and turned to glare at Moses. "He's not worth spitting on. Don't waste a perfectly good bullet on him." No one was close enough to see the angry muscle twitch at the corner of Moses' mouth or see the steely change in his eyes. But his laid-back, good-old-boy demeanor vanished and was replaced with an alert, guarded pose. If he had been a cat, the change in his stance would have been betrayed by the twitching at the end of his tail.

Ben nodded and addressed his next remarks to Moses. "It's a good thing they turned up to protect you," he said, motioning with his head toward the police officers who hadn't moved since they trained their guns on Moses, "because if they hadn't..."

"Look here," Moses challenged in a mocking voice, "if you've got the guts to take me on, tell your goons to put down their guns, and we'll see who's the bigger man."

In Ben's arms, Tobi felt his muscles tense like a straining spring, eager to accept the challenge. "Ben Walling," she hissed, pulling away from him. "Don't even think about it. I shouldn't have asked for you, but I was so scared I didn't know what I was doing."

Ben tore his gaze from Moses and tried to focus on Tobi. "What?" he asked.

"Don't do it," she repeated. "Didn't you hear what I said? He's not worth it. If he were lying on the ground there, he wouldn't be good enough for you to wipe your feet on. Don't throw your career away over a piece of garbage!"

He studied her face and finally seemed to comprehend the meaning of her words. His muscles relaxed and a slow, half smile softened his furious expression. "You're right. Thanks. Do you want to press charges?"

"Would it do any good?" she asked. "You know he'll deny everything."

Ben shook his head. "Probably not. But I'll take you to the station and you can make a report. That way we'll have a record of this incident for future reference."

"Okay," Tobi agreed. "What about my car? I'm not going to leave it here. I can meet you there."

"How do you feel?" Ben asked. "Are you up to driving?"

Tobi shook her head. "I feel like mush."

Ben nodded. "I understand. Give me your keys, then, and I'll ask Clay to drive it to the station for you."

Tobi fished her key ring out of her purse and handed it to Ben. He took it to the police car where the waiting officers had returned their guns to their holsters and were waiting to see what would happen next.

He thanked them for showing up and asked them to drive Tobi's car to the police station. Then, as he turned back to his pickup, his eyes fell on two vehicles in the carport between the church's buildings. One was a black limousine. The other was a red convertible.

"Whose cars are those?" he asked Moses, gesturing toward the carport.

Moses glanced toward the cars. "I guess the limo belongs to the church. I rented the convertible to use while I'm here."

"Who drives the limo?" asked Ben.

Moses shrugged elaborately. His defensive posture had receded. "I guess the preacher does."

Ben frowned at the two cars momentarily, making a mental note, then turned to Moses again. "You should know," he told the preacher, "that you can't walk into a small town and take over just because you think the cops are clowns. In some small towns, when you misuse women, their menfolk may shoot first and ask questions later. And the idiots on the police force - like me, for instance - might be inclined to take their word over yours."

He and Tobi climbed into his pickup then and roared away. One of the police officers followed in Tobi's car, and the other in the police cruiser. Moses watched them go through narrowed eyes. Then he went back into the church and locked the door.

Chapter X

At the police station, an officer on duty took Tobi's report while Ben studied the information he had gathered about Lincoln Nix. By the time Tobi was ready to go, Ben was almost asleep at his desk. She shook his shoulder to rouse him and said, "Hey, sleepy head, I'm leaving."

"No! Wait." He sat up straight and yawned. "Listen, you're going to have to stay at our place. For a few nights, anyway. With Grantham on the loose and that maniac Moses angry that you thwarted him... Well, I couldn't sleep unless I knew you were in a safe place."

"Really?" Tobi grinned. "You were sleeping pretty good just now."

"Of course!" he countered. "You're at the police station. You're perfectly safe!"

"Actually," Tobi said, "I'd be grateful if you'll put me up for a few nights. I have a feeling I'm going to be having nightmares about Joshua Moses for awhile."

Ben's face clouded. "I should have blown him away," he muttered, more to himself than Tobi. "The jerk doesn't have any business walking around on the same planet with real people." He looked up into Tobi's eyes, then, "Are you sure you don't want me to arrange a fatal accident for him?"

"Forget him, Ben," Tobi urged. "I keep telling you he's not worth it!"

"And I keep hearing you," Ben said. "But I'm a policeman. I'm supposed to protect the public from gorillas like him."

"Right. But you have to do it legally. That's part of being a police officer, too."

"Yeah, yeah, yeah. Come on. Let's get out of here."

DeeDee was not of a hysterical nature, but when she heard what had happened to Tobi that afternoon, she went ballistic. "That's it!" she stormed. "I'm calling Joel Trent this minute and telling him to come marry you. Somebody has to take care of you before you get yourself killed. Or worse!"

After Tobi recovered from her surprise at this outburst from her big sister, she stormed back. "Don't you dare call Joel," she ordered. "If you do, he'll come rushing back here. And for what? So we can stare at each other? I'm not going to marry him now. And he's not ready to marry me."

"I don't care," DeeDee said stubbornly. "I can't stand it, any more. If something happened to you, Tobi, I couldn't bear it. I love you!"

"I love you, too," Tobi said more gently. "But don't forget - nothing has actually happened to me." She hesitated, remembering Joshua Moses' loathsome touch, then forced herself to continue. "The Lord has taken care of me so far. Just like he takes care of you and Allison and Davy and Ben. Are you saying you don't trust Him any more?"

DeeDee glared at her. "It doesn't mean I don't trust Him just because I want somebody to take care of you."

"DeeDee..." Tobi said with a pleading tone in her voice. "How can you talk like that when Ben has taken such good care of me? I couldn't ask for anybody better."

"I know," DeeDee blubbered. "He's wonderful, but last night was *horrible*. Then this happened. And I'm so scared!"

"Me too," Tobi agreed. "That's why I called for Ben today. I know I shouldn't have. For a minute there, I was afraid he was going to attack Moses. Or shoot him." She gazed earnestly into DeeDee's moist, brown eyes. "I didn't know fear could make me so stupid. Can you forgive me?"

"Oh, Tobi," DeeDee said brokenly, with a look that said as clearly as words there was nothing to forgive. She put her arms around Tobi and they wept together.

Once their tears had cleared the air, the sisters got busy in the kitchen and put together a fried chicken feast. It was partly to nourish their bodies, but mainly to nourish a sense of family togetherness and safety.

After dinner was eaten and the dishes cleared, Ben went to bed. DeeDee and Tobi were both ready to do the same, but Tobi needed a favor first. "DeeDee, would you please call Joel?" she asked. "Tell him about last night and that I'm here because of Kent. I'm afraid if I talk to him I'll cry and upset him."

"You're not going to tell him about Moses?" DeeDee asked, frowning.

"Not yet," said Tobi. "I'm afraid he'll come back home if he knows. I'll tell him later."

"Are you saying you don't want to talk to him, at all?" DeeDee asked.

"Not tonight," said Tobi wearily. "I'm so tired and so emotional, I don't know what I might blurt out if I hear his voice." She stood. "I'm going to go to bed. Tell him I'll talk to him tomorrow." She handed DeeDee a scrap of paper with Joel's cell phone number and his uncle's home phone number on it. Then, with a yawn, she went to Davy's room where she would be sleeping.

DeeDee had begun dialing when Tobi poked her head back in the room. "I forgot," she said. "Tell him I love him." And then she was gone, leaving DeeDee open-mouthed.

———

Tobi had been afraid foul memories of Joshua Moses would keep her awake all night and, under normal circumstances, that might have been the case. But her exhaustion - both physical and emotional - was more compelling than the ugly memories, and she slept long and deep. DeeDee had to send Davy the next morning to wake her in time to get ready for Sunday School.

"Aunt Tobi," he called softly, bouncing the twin bed where he usually slept. "It's time to get up."

Tobi gazed at him sleepily through half open eyes. "Are you sure?" she asked.

"Mom said," he reported.

"Well, in that case...," Tobi sat up and stretched. "So how did you sleep in your sleeping bag in the living room?" she asked her nephew.

"Great!" he said, hopping into the bed with her and snuggling into her arms.

"Wasn't the floor hard?" Tobi asked sympathetically.

"Didn't sleep on the floor," said Davy. "I slept on the sofa."

"And you were comfortable?" she asked. It disturbed her far more than it did Davy that she had displaced him from his room.

"Sure, it was great!" he insisted, having covered this territory before. "You can come live with us if you want to. I don't mind sleeping in the living room all the time!"

Tobi kissed the top of his head. "Thank you, Davy, you're a sweetheart! I guess I'd better roll out and get ready for church, don't you think?"

Sunday was almost always a peaceful, busy day with Sunday School, church and a lazy dinner. This Sunday was no different from most, and it was nearly 3:00 in the afternoon before DeeDee could get her sister alone to interrogate her.

When the kitchen was clean and the dishwasher was humming, DeeDee said to Tobi, "Let's go sit in the back yard. Davy has the dogs with him, so it'll be nice and peaceful out there."

Tobi followed DeeDee outside and strolled around the yard, enjoying the salmon-colored geraniums in the flowerbed and the thickness of the St. Augustine grass under her feet. She examined the progress of the peaches and plums on the trees bordering the lawn and called, "You'll be having some luscious fruit before long."

"If I can keep Davy from pulling it before it's ripe," DeeDee agreed. "And that's not to mention the birds and the wasps."

Tobi joined her sister on the patio and settled into one of the blue and white plaid lawn chairs near DeeDee. "It looks to me like you could share half the crop with the birds and wasps and still have a lot of fruit," she observed.

"And a lot of work," DeeDee agreed. But her mind was elsewhere. She had been planning this tete-a-tete all day. "I have a message for you from Joel," she said.

Tobi looked at her expectantly. "What?" she asked.

"He said to tell you he loves you."

Tobi smiled, but she only said, "That's nice."

"Nice!" DeeDee exploded. "Nice? When did this 'I love you' talk start? And has he asked you to marry him? What's going on?"

"Give me a break, DeeDee! With freaky church services and bombings in the night, not to mention...yesterday..." Tobi paused to gather her composure, as the memory of Joshua Moses loomed large. "When have I had a chance to tell you anything?"

"Okay, okay," DeeDee said. "Tell me now."

So Tobi recounted her conversation with Joel at Cleo's Kitchen the previous Thursday. When she finished, DeeDee said, "And..."

"And what?"

"Well, what's next? Are you going to get married?"

Tobi shrugged. "I don't know. It's too soon to say."

"Oh bother!" said DeeDee impatiently. "I'm ready to plan a wedding. If you love each other, what are you waiting for?"

"You mean besides the fact that he hasn't proposed?" Tobi asked innocently.

"Yes. Besides that," DeeDee said, brushing aside this gnat-sized detail.

Tobi sighed. "I guess, since you've never been divorced, you can't understand."

DeeDee studied Tobi's face for a moment, then she sighed too. "I guess you're right about that."

At that moment the back door flew open and they looked up to see Davy waving a telephone handset. "Aunt Tobi, telephone," he called. "It's Coach Trent."

Tobi gave DeeDee an impish glance, said, "Yummy!" and went to meet Davy. She took the phone into Davy's bedroom and shut the door behind her. Plumping up the pillow under a bedspread decorated with baseballs, footballs, and basketballs, she kicked off her shoes, got comfortable on the little twin bed, and said, "Hi Joel."

It took her five minutes to convince him that she and Deepwater had survived the early morning explosion more or less whole. Then he turned to the topic she was dreading. "So how's the job with the preacher?" he asked. "Are you still working for him?"

"No!" she said, trying to make her voice sound indignant without betraying any other emotion. "That was a farce! I was supposed to be working on his autobiography, but his autobiography has already been written. He had a table full of them for sale in the lobby!"

"Then what was the point of giving you a job?" Joel asked, and she could hear the tension rising in his voice.

"Oh, I guess he thinks he's being cute and clever," Tobi said. "He probably does it in every town he preaches in." She shuddered at the thought. "Listen, Joel, I'll tell you all about it when you get back, but let's not talk about that jerk now. I want to hear about you. Have you met the professor yet?"

"Yes, yesterday afternoon," said Joel eagerly. "His name is Caleb Hancock - Dr. Caleb Hancock - and he's a little guy with salt and pepper hair. He has bright black eyes that are about as sharp as knives. After we introduced ourselves, the first thing he said was, 'Now tell me, when you got involved in the Charismatic movement, how much time did you spend with your Bible, studying those doctrines?'

"I didn't want to sound like a complete fool by telling him the truth, so I finally said, 'Do you see that button over there on the wall? If I push it, the floor will open up and swallow me. If you don't mind, I'll stroll over there now and push it.' "

Tobi laughed, but she was feeling grateful that she hadn't been the one facing Dr. Caleb Hancock when he asked that question. "What did he say, then?" she asked.

"He said, 'You're not much of a Berean, are you?' Of course, I didn't know what he was talking about, and he had to explain that when Paul preached in Berea, the people studied the scriptures before they accepted what he said."

"What else did he say?" Tobi asked.

"Well he says that the biggest problem with Charismatics is that they let someone else tell them what the Bible says and what it means. And he believes the biggest problem Charismatic *teachers* have is that they don't rightly divide the Word of God. So even if a scripture belongs to a certain dispensation, they'll try to appropriate it for their lives today."

"Like what?"

"Well, one example, of course, is tongues." Joel was silent for a long moment. Then he continued with a sigh. "I have a feeling the spectacle we witnessed Thursday night at the Church of the Living Vine will haunt me the rest of my life. But, Tobi, that may have been one of the most important nights of my life."

"Why?" she asked, amazed.

"Well, it was a living demonstration of what's wrong with tongues, with any claim that God is still providing new revelation through tongues or prophecies or words of knowledge or whatever else you want to call it. As soon as we accept the premise that God is still putting forth new revelation, we become vulnerable to a snake like Joshua Moses."

"Speaking of that snake," Tobi said, "Moses admitted to me that he pays a woman to pretend she has been healed in his services. She was there Friday night, and he said everyone in the congregation believed her. No one even questioned whether her health problems were legitimate."

"You're talking about fraud," Joel said slowly.

"Yes!" exclaimed Tobi. "Exactly. That's what I said, and he laughed. He said Christians are asking for it - they're begging for it - so he has to give them what they want."

"You're not still working for him, are you, Tobi?" Joel asked.

"I told you I'm not!" she insisted, beginning to feel defensive. "Anyway, how could I? There is no job! I hope I never see him again."

"Good!" Joel said. "Listen, Tobi, I need to think about this for awhile. Maybe I should call Emory - Pastor Morel - and tell him what Moses said to you."

"Moses will deny it," Tobi said. "He's a slick liar."

"He's pretty slick in a lot of ways," Joel said soberly.

At bedtime, Tobi worried again that she would have nightmares about Joshua Moses. But she knelt beside the bed and cast this care upon the Lord. Then she crawled into Davy's little twin bed and immediately fell into a deep, sweet sleep. The next morning, DeeDee wakened her at 9:00 to tell her she had a phone call.

"Who is it?" Tobi asked, stretching.

"What's the difference? Just take the call," DeeDee urged.

Tobi, who had been struggling to overcome sleep, was jerked awake by this strange response from DeeDee. "Who is it?" she demanded.

DeeDee hesitated so long Tobi thought she wasn't going to answer, but she finally said, "Clayton Archer."

"Clayton Archer? The publisher of the *City Crier*? The jerk who believed I killed Hugh Mansett and proclaimed it to the whole town?" Tobi exclaimed disbelievingly.

"That's the one," said DeeDee.

"Forget it!" said Tobi, burying back into the covers.

"No!" DeeDee said. "I already told him you're here."

"Good! Now tell him I don't want to talk to him," Tobi said peremptorily.

DeeDee disappeared, but soon returned with the phone, her hand covering the mouth piece. "Tell him yourself," she said, depositing the phone on Tobi's pillow.

With a sigh, Tobi picked it up. "Hello," she said, trying to sound awake.

"Tobi. It's Clayton Archer here. How have you been?"

Just ducky! she wanted to reply. "Fine," she said.

"Look, I know I'm not your favorite person and I can't blame you. But maybe today I'll be able to make up for some of the grief I inadvertently caused you."

Tobi was grateful later that she restrained herself from saying what she was thinking. Instead, she remained silent, waiting for him to go on.

"You know about the *E Pluribus Unum* Fourth of July Parade, don't you?" he asked.

"Know what about it?" she asked.

"Well, that it's going to be held on the Fourth, followed by fireworks."

"I've heard that," she said. Why in creation was he bothering her about a parade?

Out of Darkness

"Do you know the story behind it?" Clayton asked, continuing doggedly on, in spite of Tobi's obvious disinterest.

"Well, some billionaire is financing it, I think," Tobi said, trying to remember what she'd heard.

"Yes. His son was accused of possessing drugs and imprisoned in a Middle Eastern country several years ago. Late last year the boy died in prison. The father was never able to get satisfactory information about the whole situation. He's not even sure his son wasn't executed when he was convicted. Anyway, the father is so grateful for the United States - for our freedoms, our judicial system, and so forth, that he decided to sponsor a huge parade, with 50 floats to honor all the states."

Tobi was nodding to herself. She did remember hearing the story. "What does that have to do with me?" she asked.

"Well, the sponsor, Dalton Granville, has been organizing the parade. But he had a heart attack last week. He asked me to find someone to take over for him, and I thought of you. Of course, if you already have a job..."

"At the moment I'm between jobs," Tobi said, "but I can't imagine why you think I would want to organize a parade!"

"To tell the truth," Clayton said, "I feel like I owe you. Dalton has already done most of the work, but he's going to pay someone $5,000 to finish the job for him."

"5,000!" Tobi gasped. "For what? Less than two weeks of work?"

"That's right," said Clayton.

"What's the catch?" asked Tobi.

"No catch."

"Okay. Let's put it this way. Why didn't you take two weeks' vacation from the paper and take the job yourself?" she asked.

Clayton chuckled. "I thought of that, but Dalton doesn't want me. He says I'm too cuss-ed. He wants someone with an iron-velvet touch, so the job gets done quickly and smoothly. And he wants a person of absolute integrity. It was when he said 'integrity' that I thought of you. I believe you're the ideal person for the job. So are you interested?"

Tobi's heart melted upon hearing such high praise and she spoke with warmth for the first time. "Oh, Clayton, thank you for thinking of me. Of course, I'm interested, but I don't know why you think I'm the person for the job. I don't know anything about parades."

"Tell you what," Clayton said, "you go to the hospital and meet Dalton. He can tell you what still needs to be done, and the two of you can decide together whether you're the right person for the job."

"The hospital?" Tobi repeated. "I would feel terrible going to him with a business matter while he's in the hospital."

"I had a feeling you would say that," Clayton told her, "so I called his doctor this morning. The doctor said that finding the right person to take over the parade would be the best medicine Dalton could get right now. I promise you, Tobi, you'll be doing him a favor if you'll go to the hospital and talk to him about it."

Tobi showered and dressed, then went to the kitchen to find her sister. DeeDee was standing at the sink, gazing out the window at the back yard. Her kitchen, like the rest of her house was decorated in shades of blue, shades of brown, and creamy white. Tobi particularly liked the blue-and-cream gingham swag that framed the sink window. It reminded her of a blue-and-white gingham dress DeeDee had worn when they were small. When she wore it, Tobi would gaze at her adoringly, thinking DeeDee was the most beautiful girl in the world. She was still beautiful and still a hero to little sister Tobi.

"What's out there?" she asked, joining DeeDee at the sink.

DeeDee laughed. "Just some sparrows splashing around in a puddle the sprinklers leave. What did Mr. Archer want?"

"It was a job offer," Tobi said. She poured herself a cup of coffee and told DeeDee about the parade and Dalton Granville's sad story. "The job sounds too good to be true - $5000 and it's less than two weeks until the Fourth," she said in conclusion. "I'd like to know what the catch is."

"Go to the hospital and find out," DeeDee advised. "Have you prayed about it?"

"Sure, while I was in the shower. Well, ever since Clayton hung up, actually."

"And?" DeeDee asked.

Tobi looked troubled. "I finally decided I would talk to Mr. Granville, tell *him* I know nothing about parades, then let him make the decision.

"I think that's a good plan," DeeDee said. "Why do you look so worried?"

"I'm afraid I'm getting into something I won't be able to handle and I'll mess it up for everybody."

"Then tell him how you feel and ask him what happens if you want to bail out in a day or two or a week," DeeDee said.

Tobi poured some cereal into a bowl. "Okay," she said looking happier. "Do you have any more suggestions? What do you know about parades?"

DeeDee laughed. "Less than you. But I'm sure we can find somebody, somewhere who knows all there is to know about parades."

"And when all else fails," Tobi said, "there's always the internet."

———

At Carlyle Memorial Hospital, Tobi was directed to a room on the third floor. "Mr. Granville is expecting you," the receptionist told her with a smile.

Tobi knocked softly on the door of Room 301 then, hearing no response, she rapped louder. Still no response. Shyly she pushed on the door and peeked in. Dalton Granville's hospital room was a luxurious suite, decorated in tones of green and blue, and supplied with every modern medical machine known to man. It was also dark and gloomy.

"Mr. Granville?" she said.

"What is it?" came a querulous voice. "Don't hang on the door. Either come in or go out."

Tobi went in. Dalton Granville was a tall, gaunt man with curly white hair - now mashed flat after days in the hospital - and intense blue eyes. He wore a Mark Twain mustache and was dressed from head to toe in sorrow.

"Mr. Granville, I'm Tobi Kirkland. Clayton Archer sent me to talk to you about the Fourth of July parade."

Dalton Granville's eyes came alive. "Ms. Kirkland! At last!" He tried to sit up, but only floundered in the big hospital bed.

"Wait!" Tobi put a restraining hand on his shoulder and touched the button that would raise the head of his bed.

He relaxed, then, and gazed companionably at her. "I apologize for snapping at you. I assumed you were somebody in a white uniform, coming to torture me."

Tobi smiled. "Has that been happening to you a lot?"

"Constantly. But never mind. Clayton says you're the only person in town who can do justice to my parade, so sit down and tell me about yourself."

Tobi pulled a chair close to the bed and said, "Well, the main thing you need to know is that I know nothing about parades. I don't know why Clayton recommended me."

"Are you saying you don't want the job?" Granville demanded.

"Not at all," Tobi said. She surprised herself by not being intimidated by this blunt, cranky billionaire. Her intuition told her that his bluster was a cover for a frightened little boy - a Davy-sized little boy - hiding somewhere inside his tired, old body. "What I'm telling you is that I don't know anything about parades."

He scowled at her. "Look, girl. I did a lot of work on this parade. I'd like to think my replacement has a little backbone. A little grit in her craw."

"I have a little," Tobi said mildly, favoring him with a sparkling smile.

He scowled at her a few moments longer, then laughed. It was a wheezy, gravelly laugh, but Tobi thought it was among the loveliest sounds she had ever heard. "Okay, then," she said, "how about a little light in this place? Are you allergic to sunshine, Mr. Granville?" She went to the window and waited for his okay before she drew the drapes.

"No allergies," he said, trying to regain his scowl, "and call me Dalton."

"Okay, Dalton. And I'm Tobi. What else do you want to know about me?"

"I want to know if you want this job."

"Yes," she said, suddenly realizing it was true. "I want it very much."

"Well, now we're getting somewhere," said Dalton. "And you should know that you don't need to know anything about parades. I've taken care of all the major details - like music and bands and permits." He waved a frail, wrinkled hand. "All that stuff is done."

"And what do I need to do?" Tobi asked.

"Two things," said Dalton. "First, keep checking on the floats in progress. Make sure they're going well and the builders have everything they need. Second, you'll have to find someone to do the floats for Connecticut, Maine, and Wisconsin. Those three states haven't been claimed yet."

"Not at all?" Tobi gasped. "But it's less than two weeks until the parade.

"Yes, I know," said Dalton. "Why do you think I had a heart attack?" Then he asked anxiously, "You don't have a weak heart, do you?"

"Not that I know of," said Tobi.

"Good. Okay, here's what you need to remember." He paused and thought for a few moments. "I want every state to be represented by somebody who loves the state, someone whose heart is in the task. Because that's what it's all about - loving our nation. And our states. And our people. I want the love and respect to be obvious in every float."

Tobi nodded. "That's beautiful! Clayton said this parade was your idea. You must be a really special person to have such an exciting idea!"

Dalton smiled sadly. "I had to do something constructive to keep myself from dying of bitterness." He looked into Tobi's eyes with his own sad gaze. "I guess a lot of people have been treated unjustly in this country over the years but, at least, we're a country that believes in justice. We keep trying to improve our justice system. And I'm grateful for that. I'm grateful for my country. It's a beautiful country full of beautiful people. One short parade isn't much of a thank you to a country where I've been so blessed, but it's something. And it's better than wallowing in bitterness and grief."

His voice broke and Tobi gave him a few minutes to regain his composure. Then she said softly, "Would you tell me about your son?"

Dalton looked self-conscious. "Oh, you don't want to hear an old man rattle on about his...his..."

"Please," said Tobi.

Dalton looked at her searchingly, then seemed to conclude she was sincere for he began haltingly, "Gabe...Gabriel, actually...for the angel Gabriel. My wife and I tried for a long time to have a child. And when Gabe finally came along and the nurse put him in Lettie's arms, she said, 'My beautiful little angel!' So we named him Gabriel."

Dalton paused to savor the memory of his wife holding their newborn son, and Tobi waited for him to continue. "It was *so* hard not to spoil him. We were old enough to be grandparents - that age where you're supposed to be able to give your grandkids anything they want. But Gabe wasn't our grandson. He was our son. And he turned out pretty good, all things considered. He had a heart as big as Texas - warm and affectionate. But he had a weakness for cocaine. Maybe he never got over it. I sent him to manage my affairs in the Middle East, hoping he wouldn't be able to get his hands on drugs over there. But it was a mistake - he was arrested for possessing cocaine and died in jail."

Dalton's voice broke again and Tobi waited again. "Lettie died five years ago," he continued after a long moment. "Gabe and I missed her like the dickens! I'm probably making excuses - but I think Gabe would have done better if she had lived longer."

He sighed deeply, then studied Tobi's face. "I'm all alone now, wondering, 'Why? Why did I bother?' I've got more money than I can spend and no one to leave it to."

"Oh Dalton," Tobi cried impulsively, the words springing from her mouth before she could stop them, "I hope you'll do something with your money that will make Gabe proud of you. And Lettie too."

"Like what?"

"Well...," Tobi hesitated, thinking, "...well, like feeding children in third world countries. Or sending them medicines and doctors... I don't know - something like that."

"If I did that, would you manage the estate for me?" Dalton asked. "Would you make sure the money went for food instead of lining some rich man's pocket?"

"Oh no!" cried Tobi in dismay. "Please don't ask me to do that. I work with words. When it comes to money, I'm a dummy!"

"You're no dummy," Dalton said, "and I like your idea. So would Gabe and Lettie." His face suddenly looked bright with hope. "I do believe when this parade is over I'll do some traveling - find a few hungry children to feed. I believe I'll manage the estate myself before I die! " His eyes were brimming with tears. "Thank you, Tobi. It's like a beam of light walked into the room when you came in."

"Oh, that's not me," she said softly. "That's Jesus."

Dalton squinted at her. "Jesus?"

She nodded.

He gave her a quizzical look. "Please tell me why you would say such a thing."

Tobi smiled and recited, "The people walking in darkness have seen a great light. On those living in the land of the shadow of death a light has dawned."

"What does *that* mean?"

"It's Isaiah 9:2 in the NIV Bible. It's a prophecy about the coming of Jesus. He's the only spiritual Light in this world," Tobi said. "If there's any light in me, it's because Jesus is in me."

"In you? Jesus is in you?" Dalton's face was a picture of confusion.

"Yes," Tobi said excitedly. "That's what Jesus does. He came into this world because He wants to live in us and through us. He wants to use us to shed His light and love abroad in the world."

"I never heard such a thing," Dalton said. "If I'd known that... Well, if I'd known that, I might have tried it myself. I'd like to bring light to people the way you brought light to me."

"It's not too late," Tobi said. "It's never too late."

He looked dubious. "I'm sure you're wrong about that. Do you know how old I am?"

Tobi shrugged. "It doesn't matter. If you're still breathing, it's not too late."

"How...how would I do it?"

"Tell Him," Tobi said simply. "Tell Him you want to quit living for yourself and start living for Him."

"And you think He'll hear me?"

"If you mean it, I know He will."

Dalton didn't bow his head or close his eyes. Instead, he continued to stare straight into Tobi's eyes as he said, "Jesus, I'm tired of living for myself. I want to live for You. I want You to use me to bring light to people the way this little girl does. If You'll do that, I'll be grateful to You for the rest of my life."

By this time, his face was wet with tears. Tobi bent over and kissed a wet cheek. "Did He hear you?" she asked.

"He heard me," said Dalton, wonderingly. "He heard me."

Tobi took one of his bony, calloused old hands and held it while Dalton lay quietly with his eyes closed, savoring the wonder he had just experienced. At last, he said, "Well, on to the business at hand. I apologize for taking up so much of your time, Tobi."

"Don't apologize!" Tobi cried. "Telling you about my Jesus is more important than anything else I could be doing. I'll never forget this wonderful morning, Dalton. Do you know that you're my brother now?"

He shook his head. "Do you mean it? Because if you do, I'm not alone any more."

Tobi tightened her grip on his hand and said earnestly, "You'll never be alone again. Never, never, never! When Jesus lives in us, we're all family."

Dalton squeezed her hand, then pulled his own hand away from hers so he could push himself further up in the bed. The shroud of sorrow no longer encased him as he said jubilantly, "I can't wait to get out of this hospital and see the *E Pluribus Unum* parade, so I can get on with the rest of my life!"

"Then tell me what else I need to know so I can get out of here and you can rest and heal," Tobi said, taking a pad and pen out of her purse.

"Let's see," Dalton mused, trying to get his mind back on the business at hand. "The goal is to show each state's greatest contribution to America's strength and unity - either at the present time or historically. For example, Alabama's float is first - I decided to have them go in alphabetic order because I don't want to insinuate any kind of preference. The Alabama float will be a still-life depiction of Rosa Parks refusing to give her bus seat to a white man." His eyes were shining. "What a courageous woman she must have been and what a glorious moment that was in our history! It's a perfect way to begin a parade honoring the American spirit."

He had grown so excited that Tobi feared for his heart, so she spoke as softly and soothingly as she could even though she felt her own pulse quickening and her heart expanding. "Oh I agree. I wish I had half the courage she did!"

"And New York!" Dalton continued, his excitement growing. "Tobi, don't go see that one until you've prepared yourself. On the New York float they've constructed a small-scale New York City skyline. And in the place where the twin towers used to stand there'll be a policeman and a fireman, standing shoulder to shoulder... American heroes..."

His voice faded away and he brushed a hand across his eyes. He and Tobi avoided each other's eyes for a long minute. Finally Tobi said, "Will we ever be able to remember that day without weeping?"

"No," Dalton said. "I never will."

As it turned out, Tobi didn't take many notes. When she started to write, Dalton stopped her. "Just ask my secretary. She has all the information you need." He gave Tobi the name of his secretary - Judith - and the address of his office. "Now," he said, at last, glancing around as if checking for spies, "here's a deep, dark secret. Each group will have up to $50,000 to spend on their float. But only dole it out $5,000 at a time."

"Me?" Tobi gasped.

"Of course you! Who else? Why do you think I was looking for a person with integrity?" asked Dalton. "And the money grants are a secret because I don't want gold diggers in my parade. I want people who truly love each state creating the floats. But *then* I want money not to be an issue. I want each group to have all the money it needs to create the float exactly as they have dreamed it."

He paused with shining eyes. "It's going to be a glorious parade, Tobi. This Fourth of July may be one of the greatest days in the history of Deepwater."

"If it is, it's only because of you," Tobi said. "I feel honored to know you."

"Aw, never mind the kissing up," said Dalton with a wave of his hand. "You better get out of here. You have a lot of work to do."

Chapter XI

Dalton Granville's secretary Judith Carson was a plump woman in her thirties. She had a friendly smile and a no-nonsense manner. When Tobi appeared in her office, she greeted her warmly. "Come in," she said, beckoning. "I just got off the phone with Dalton. He's so thrilled about you I've about decided you bewitched him."

"Well then, the bewitching was mutual," Tobi said. "I'm crazy about him."

Judith nodded. "I am too. I wouldn't want to work for anyone else. Come on into Dalton's office. All the paperwork is in here, so I'm going to put you in here, too. He's not going to be using the office for awhile."

Tobi followed Judith into Dalton's office. The deep carpet was gold, and the furniture was dark cherry wood. And although it was a large corner office with four windows, it was simple and practical, giving little evidence of Dalton's vast wealth. "It's a beautiful office," Tobi said admiringly.

"It's a lot more beautiful now than when the Dalton is here," Judith said. "He tends to be a slob, but I've had a few days to clean up and straighten up. He'll be furious when he gets back - all his papers will be 'lost' because I've filed them."

Judith pointed out the neatly stacked piles of paper on Dalton's huge desk. "This pile is ledgers, itemizing the costs for every float. The next pile is contracts - each builder had to sign a contract, agreeing to use Dalton's money on their floats. Here's a pile of how-to instructions, including internet addresses; they're almost gone now that we only have three unclaimed floats. The last pile includes detailed descriptions of every float under construction. Last and most important right now," Judith said, picking up a single sheet of paper, "is a list of contacts who might be willing to make the floats for Connecticut, Maine, and Wisconsin."

Tobi took this last sheet of paper and glanced at it. "Where did the names come from?" she asked.

"Well, that first group includes peopled who have lived in Connecticut or who have family in Connecticut or have visited Connecticut. I compiled the lists from courthouse records, newspaper records, newcomer information, the internet, word-of-mouth contacts - anywhere I could think of."

"You and Dalton have already worked so hard," Tobi said. "I feel guilty coming along at the last minute and taking advantage of all your work."

Judith gave a short laugh. "You won't feel guilty long. There's still plenty to do." She opened a drawer and took out a leather-bound spiral checkbook, which she handed to Tobi. "The first thing you need to do is go to the bank and sign the signature card for the Dalton Granville Parade Account. There should still be about a quarter of a million dollars available, which is more than enough to finish paying for the parade."

Tobi swallowed hard and carefully set the checkbook on the desk. "A quarter of a million dollars?" she repeated, staring at the checkbook as if it might spring at her and bite her. "Are you sure this is what Dalton wants? I can't even imagine so much money."

"You don't have to imagine it, just use it," Judith said unsympathetically. She looked at Tobi's stricken expression and added, "It goes with the territory; get used to it."

And so Tobi drove to a big steel and glass building and signed on to the Dalton Granville Parade Account. Then she went home and ate a peanut butter and jelly sandwich. While she ate, she looked over the list of contacts who might be interested in the last three floats. Since her main task for the day would be making phone calls, she had decided to work from home that afternoon. She paused in mid-chew when she came to an entry at the bottom of the list: "Paul Hudson, formerly lived in Wisconsin."

"No way!" she laughed. What a great piece of luck - a name she recognized! She would call him first. Surely he could be persuaded to spearhead this worthwhile project. He seemed like such a nice man. But she would definitely call him at his office; she didn't want to call his house in case Rachel might answer the phone.

In fact... Tobi tossed the last section of her sandwich onto the saucer and picked up her phone. Consulting her list, she punched in the phone number for Paul's office.

To her surprise an answering machine informed her that the office was closed for lunch and the dentist was out of the office for a few days. If she would leave her name and number, someone would return her call as soon as possible.

"What do you mean out of the office for a few days?" she muttered, hanging up. "I need you now, not a few days from now."

She sighed and consulted her list. There were several contacts who had some connection to Maine and Connecticut and, after several hours of fancy talking, she had found her float builders. She'd had to promise she would drive all over the state, if necessary, to procure the materials they needed. But they had agreed to build the floats.

It was nearly 5:00 o'clock when Tobi dialed Paul's office again and learned that a family emergency was keeping him away from the office. "When will he be back?" she asked pleadingly. "I need to talk to him in the worst way."

"He didn't say," she was told.

"Is he at home? Could I reach him there?" she persisted.

"Ma'am, I can't give out that information," replied the receptionist.

Tobi sighed as she dialed Paul's home phone number, which was also listed on her sheet of contacts. "Please, please, don't let Rachel answer," she whispered as the phone rang. But the answering machine took her call. She hesitated, then broke the connection. She couldn't bring herself to leave a message that Rachel might pick up and answer.

She sat staring at the phone for awhile - then dialed Joel's cell number. Maybe he would know how to reach Paul.

The phone rang one and a half times before Joel's excited voice said, "Tobi! I'm so glad you called! I've just figured it out! It's like stumbling out of darkness into light."

"What is?" she asked, catching his enthusiasm and completely forgetting why she had called him.

"Well, theologians say that Paul prophesied the gift of tongues would cease, based on the passage in I Corinthians 13...um...just a sec...verses 8-12. I could never accept that - it sounded to me like Paul was talking about being in Heaven. I thought 'that which is perfect' referred to Jesus. But it refers to the Bible, the completed canon of Scripture. So I was doing the same thing all the Pentecostal types do."

"What's that?" Tobi asked, hanging on his every word. She had struggled with the same issue herself.

"They take things out of context. Paul is talking about spiritual gifts all through chapters 12, 13, and 14. He's not talking about Heaven. He's trying to get the Corinthian church to quit misusing tongues. And quit inflating the importance of tongues. But you know what we've done with that passage."

"Yes," said Tobi soberly. "We - at least when we accepted the Pentecostal position - used those same chapters to *justify* our belief in tongues."

"Right!" exclaimed Joel. "We acted like Paul was *inflating* the importance of tongues. He's not. He's trying to show what a minor issue it is. It *was*."

"And," Tobi added, "it's like you said last night - all of those references to tongues don't apply to the church today because tongues have ceased. So it's not rightly dividing the Word of God to use those passages to explain how we should use tongues today. That's just...just backward!"

Joel laughed. "Yes! Yes! I finally get it! I am so excited I could dance a jig."

"Aw, save that," Tobi said. "That's something I'd like to see!"

"Don't hold your breath," Joel warned. "I'm not much of a jigger!"

"So how does it work?" Tobi asked. "Did Dr. Hancock explain all this to you?"

"No! That's the beauty of it. He just put me in his library, gave me access to all his references and the internet, made a few suggestions about what I might want to consider, and left. He'll be back soon to discuss some scriptures with me, but he understands that it's something I need to work out for myself."

"He sounds like a perceptive man," observed Tobi.

"And an humble man," said Joel. "He could have used this opportunity to clone himself, cram all his beliefs into my head. Like Rachel does. And Emory."

"And me?" asked Tobi.

"Not at all," Joel said. "I've never heard you preach at anyone for hours on end. Or try to manipulate them into agreeing with you by using guilt. Or screaming. Or threats."

Tobi gave a soft sigh of relief, then she remembered why she had dialed Joel. "Oh, wait! I haven't told you why I called," she said eagerly. "I have a job!"

"Oh, no!" Joel moaned. "Another one? Why won't you just let me give you as much money as you want?"

"And why won't you," Tobi asked, "let me tell you about my wonderful new job?"

"Does it involve any disappearing babies or predatory preachers?"

"None of the above," said Tobi cheerfully. Then she launched into a description of Dalton Granville, his secretary Judith, and the *E Pluribus Unum* Fourth of July Parade.

When she finished, Joel whistled softly. "Hey! That sounds exciting," he said. "I was thinking maybe you would join us in Dallas for the Fourth, but it sounds like Deepwater is the place to be this 4th of July."

"It is!" cried Tobi. "Oh, I hope you can be here for the parade."

"I wouldn't miss it for a million dollars," Joel assured her. "Listen, Caleb's back. I'll call you later."

"Wait, Joel," said Tobi urgently. "I still haven't told you why I called."

"Why?"

"I need to reach Paul Hudson to see if he'll be in charge of the Wisconsin float, but he's out of the office for a few days because of a family emergency. Do you know where he is? Or what the emergency is? I don't want to disturb him if something terrible has happened, but I'd like him to do the float. He seems trustworthy."

"Absolutely," said Joel. "Gloria and Gracie will know. I'll ask them as soon as I see them and call you back."

The instant Tobi broke the connection, her phone rang. It was DeeDee sounding worried and angry. "Tobi Kirkland, what are you doing besides trying to starve my family to death and terrify me out of my mind!"

"DeeDee, chill! What are you talking about?"

"I'm talking about dinner getting cold. And your phone being busy for hours on end. What's going on? What was Archer's job? Why didn't you call me?" Suddenly DeeDee sounded close to tears.

"Deedee, I'm so sorry," Tobi said contritely. "I'm on my way right now, and I'll tell you all about it. It's a wonderful job - wait til you hear!"

"Just hurry," DeeDee said, sounding calmer.

"Don't wait for me," Tobi said. "Go ahead and eat."

"Hmph! I guess you and I didn't have the same mother, after all," DeeDee observed before she punched the button that broke the connection.

Tobi laughed and made for the door. In her childhood, there had been rare occasions when the Kirklands had waited impatiently for a tardy family member to arrive before Margo Kirkland would consider serving dinner. When the delinquent hurried guiltily into the house, be it her husband or her child, Margo would be waiting with a tight-lipped frown and blazing eyes. The culprit wasn't likely to be late again any time soon. Tobi laughed again. Mom was such a fraud - all bark and no bite! But her family had adored her and all were eager to please her, so they did their best to be on time for dinner every night of the world.

When Tobi reached the Walling home, she found that her sister had exaggerated a bit. Dinner wasn't quite ready, and no one except DeeDee was upset by her absence.

It was nearly an hour before they were seated at the table, enjoying DeeDee's spaghetti and hearing about Tobi's job. When the phone began jangling in the kitchen, Ben held up a hand to his children, who were both halfway out of their seats. "I'll get it," he said firmly. "You eat."

The telephone wasn't a lifeline to Davy, so he merely plopped back into his chair and scooped up his next bite of spaghetti. Alison, on the other hand, listened intently as her father took the call. Almost immediately he retreated into the small room off the kitchen that he used for an office. Tobi and DeeDee exchanged glances. It must be business.

"I hope he doesn't have to go out," DeeDee said. "He's still tired from Friday night."

"Are they getting anywhere with the investigation?" Tobi asked. "Do they know who blew up the houses on Tomlin Street?"

DeeDee shook her head. "Ben is certain it has something to do with that group of Kent Grantham's, but he can't find a shred of evidence. And that Lynx character - Lincoln Nix - is a complete mystery."

Tobi looked up in surprise. "Who? I never heard of him."

"Not much to hear," said DeeDee. "His house was in the middle of the explosions - Ben is certain he or his house was the target. But none of his neighbors seem to know anything about him."

When everyone, except Ben, had finished eating, Tobi began clearing the table and DeeDee went to find her husband. He was sitting in his office, gazing blankly into space.

"What's wrong?" DeeDee asked.

Ben started, then said hoarsely, "Get Tobi."

The two women joined him in his small, cramped office. By stacking books and papers onto his small desk, DeeDee and Tobi were able to make room to sit. Ben shut the door, settled himself in his chair, and said, "The phone call was from Joel."

Blood rushed into Tobi's face. "What's wrong? Is he hurt?"

"No, no. Nothing like that," Ben said. "It was about the case."

"What case?" asked Tobi, and, "What about it?" asked DeeDee at the same time.

"The little boy - the toddler, you know? - is Paul Hudson's niece's child. The child's name is Trevor; the niece is Patrice. Patrice Lacey."

"Why didn't he tell you sooner?" asked DeeDee indignantly.

"He didn't know. He called Paul in Green Bay, Wisconsin, this evening, and Paul just told him."

"Why did Patrice put Trevor in the police station Wednesday night?" asked Tobi.

Ben paused, then said quietly, "She didn't. It seems that Trevor's father was murdered that night. Apparently the murderer delivered Trevor to the police station."

"No!" exclaimed Tobi. And, "Why?"

"Who?" was DeeDee's question. "Who was his father?"

Ben stared at the women for a long moment, seeing nothing. Then he said with a deep sigh. "Lincoln Nix. Lynx was Trevor's father."

Tobi and DeeDee stared at him open-mouthed until Tobi finally said, "You mean...? You're saying...?"

Ben nodded. "He was already dead when his house exploded."

After more moments of stunned silence, digesting this item, DeeDee said, "You'd better start at the beginning. Where was Patrice Wednesday night? Was she the one who killed Lynx? Was he her husband?"

"No, they never married. It seems Nix wasn't the marrying kind, but he did take an interest in his son. And Patrice was rather protective of Lynx - guarding his privacy as if he were a state secret and allowing him to see Trevor anytime he asked."

"And Patrice left Trevor with Lynx Wednesday night?" DeeDee asked.

Ben was nodding. "Yes. Rachel and Patrice wanted to spend the evening passing out flyers about the big revival at their church, starting Thursday night. So Lynx was going to keep the child that evening and Patrice would pick him up the next morning before work and take him to his day care. But when she got to Nix's house Thursday morning, Lynx was dead and Trevor was gone."

"She must have been frantic," DeeDee murmured.

"To say the least," agreed Ben. "She went straight to Rachel, and Rachel advised her not to call the police. She was afraid Patrice would be accused of Lynx's murder..."

"How did he die?" Tobi interrupted. "Lynx, I mean."

"Patrice wasn't sure. She didn't want to handle him because she was afraid of getting his blood on her shoes or clothes. She did try to feel for a pulse, but his body was so cold she knew she wouldn't find one. She said his shirt was torn and bloody, so she guessed he had been stabbed in the chest."

"There's no way of knowing now, is there?" asked DeeDee.

"No," said Ben. "There's nothing left to examine."

"So what happened next?" asked Tobi. "What did Rachel and Patrice do when they *didn't* go to the police?"

"They went to the courthouse and watched for Trevor. Joel had told Rachel the child would be taken to Children's Services that morning. When Flossie showed up with him, they waited for her to leave and followed her home. They peeked in windows until they saw Flossie putting Trevor down for a nap. Then Rachel was going to knock on the back door and try to get Flossie occupied in the back yard while Patrice broke in and got Trevor. But before she got to the back door, Flossie came out with a load of trash, heading for the alley. So they broke in, got Trevor, and ran. They 'ran' all the way to Green Bay, Wisconsin, where Paul's family lives."

Tobi shivered. "That means I was at Flossie's house when they were there," she said. "They must have been taking Trevor while we were talking in the back yard."

DeeDee squeezed her sister's hand. "I'm glad you and Flossie didn't meet up with those two. It sounds like they were desperate enough to hurt you if you got in their way."

Tobi nodded. "Still, I can't imagine Rachel Hudson breaking into houses and running off to Wisconsin with a murder suspect. She's supposed to be a Christian."

"And an adult," added DeeDee drily.

Tobi turned to Ben. "Now what?"

"Now, I'm going to call Paul and ask some questions of my own."

"What about Patrice?" asked DeeDee. "She sounds like the person you've been looking for. Someone who can tell you about Lynx."

"She disappeared," said Ben. "She, Trevor, and Rachel were at Paul's parents' home when he arrived Friday night. Saturday morning when the family woke up, she and Trevor were gone."

"Gone where?" asked DeeDee.

"Nobody knows," said Ben. "Or nobody's telling."

"Are the Green Bay police looking for her?" asked Tobi.

Ben looked grim. "The Green Bay police haven't been called."

Ben had told DeeDee and Tobi everything he had learned from Joel, so they returned to the kitchen, and he returned to the telephone. He was about to punch in the number Joel had given him to reach Paul Hudson in Wisconsin, when he had another thought. Instead, he called the police department and got a number for Flossie Bobbsey in San Diego. It could only do her good to know that Trevor was safe with his mother.

Flossie's son answered the phone and told Ben that Flossie and his wife had taken the children to the beach for the day. Ben quickly relayed the information he had about Trevor's abduction by his own mother. "I just wanted Flossie to know the child is safe and happy," he finished.

"Thank you for calling," said the young man. "I can't wait to tell Mom. Maybe she'll quit having nightmares now."

"I hope so," said Ben fervently. "We all love her at the Deepwater P.D."

He hung up, feeling rejuvenated in knowing Flossie would be sleeping easier that night. "And now for Green Bay," he muttered.

Paul Hudson was anxious to help. Paul Hudson was generally anxious. He had been horrified at his niece's behavior and appalled that his wife had aided and abetted her. But he had little to add to the information Joel had already given Ben.

"What about your niece?" Ben asked. "I need to talk to her in the worst way."

"I wish I could help you," Paul said, "but I've turned over every rock I can find, looking for a trace of her, and not a sign."

"Every rock?" asked Ben. "You make her sound like a spider."

Paul sighed. "Not Patrice. All things considered, she turned out fairly well. But her parents are both lowlifes. Even my brother, I'm sorry to say."

"And you think one of them is hiding her?" asked Ben.

"My brother is in jail at the moment," said Paul sadly. "So I'm guessing her mother is helping her."

"I'm going to have to call the Green Bay Police Department and ask them for help finding your niece," Ben said.

"Good," said Paul. "If I called them, Rachel would never forgive me.

"I'll let you go now, but I'm sure the Green Bay P.D. will be calling you for more information about Patrice and her parents. They'll want pictures. Will that be a problem?"

"I may have to do a little detective work of my own," Paul said, "but I'll see what I can do. Pictures of Patrice and Phillip - he's her father - will be no problem. Finding a picture of her mother will be harder...unless..."

"Unless what?"

"Well, Patrice has a framed picture of her mother holding Trevor. It's at her apartment in Deepwater, hanging in the hall."

"Okay," said Ben. "Thank you for your help."

"Wait!" Paul said. "Joel mentioned a parade. He said Tobi Kirkland was trying to reach me. Is she your sister?"

"My wife's sister," said Ben.

"I'm afraid we got sidetracked when I started explaining why I suddenly took off for Wisconsin. But I am interested in hearing more about the parade. She needs someone to build a float honoring Wisconsin in time for the Fourth of July - is that it?"

"In a nutshell," said Ben.

"Listen, would you tell her to sign me up? My whole family is in the den right now making drawings and fighting about the relative importance of cheese and the Packers."

Ben grinned. "You're Dad is voting for the Packers, right?"

"Right. He played for the team seven years. A linebacker. When he retired, he opened a sports shop that's practically a shrine to the Packers."

"And your Mom is voting for cheese?" Ben guessed.

"She puts cheese in everything she cooks," Paul laughed.

"Thanks, Dr. Hudson. Tobi will be excited to hear you're taking on the float. May I have her call you about it tomorrow?'

"No, tell her I'm flying home tomorrow. I've only stayed to look for Patrice. If the police are taking over the search, I'm coming home. I'll call Tobi tomorrow evening."

Ben gave Paul Tobi's phone number and his home phone, too, even though Tobi had announced she was moving back to her own place the next day. She needed lots of room to spread out, and both Kent Grantham and Joshua Moses had faded into distant memories since she met Dalton Granville. Of course, DeeDee had objected. She was certain Tobi's house was going to be bombed any day. Ben grinned. The two women were probably arguing about Tobi's move right now. He might as well go put in his two cents' worth.

Chapter XII

That night, at 2:23 A.M., according to Ben's bedside clock, his eyes shot open, and he relived the nightmare that had awakened him. It had been about Tyson Banning, Lincoln Nix's teenage neighbor. The boy had been riding a bicycle around town, randomly tossing grenades at houses. Ben had been chasing him frantically on foot and hadn't been able to prevent the destruction of the homes. He woke up in a sweat.

He stared at the ceiling, trying to decide what, if anything, to do about the dream. It would be foolish to tie up manpower following a boy on a bicycle. But his instinct told him it would be more foolish to ignore the intuition that had produced the dream.

Finally, he stole out of bed and tiptoed out of the bedroom. In his office, he called the police department and requested a tail be put on Tyson Banning for a period of two days. He would re-evaluate the situation in 48 hours.

"You couldn't wait until morning?" Nancy Montgomery asked.

"He's a night owl," Ben explained.

She asked a few more questions, learned that Ben knew little about their quarry's nighttime activities, and said, "I'm on it. Go back to bed." The dial tone buzzed in his ear.

Ben grinned admiringly, as he often did after dealing with Nancy. He yawned and went gratefully back to his soft bed and sleeping wife.

When he arrived at his desk the next morning, a report was waiting for him. According to Miguel Padilla, who had been assigned to follow the boy, Tyson Banning, dressed in black, had left his home at 3:10 A.M. and ridden his bicycle to a rundown apartment building about two miles from his house. Leaving his bike chained to a pole in front of the building, Tyson had entered the building and gone into apartment 12A.

Hoping to find a window where he would be able to hear something, Padilla had retraced his steps. Once outside, he had gone to the back of the apartment building and located the window of apartment 12A. He could see neither lights nor movement in the apartment so, after watching half an hour, he approached and found the window open and the screen unhooked. The silence within convinced him no one was inside, so he entered through the window. It was a one-room efficiency apartment. One sweep of his flashlight revealed that no one was asleep in the bed and the apartment did not appear lived in.

Climbing back out through the window, he waited in the alley behind the apartment building, thinking he would learn which direction Tyson would return from. But Tyson never returned. When Padilla finally left, he saw that Tyson's bicycle was gone. Obviously, Tyson had considered the subterfuge of passing through the apartment unnecessary on the return trip.

Padilla had driven to the Banning's home and found the bicycle chained to a post on the front porch. Tyson had not left the house again until he went to school at 7:30 A.M. The report ended with a question. Did Ben want Padilla's replacement to watch the school?

"School?" Ben muttered to himself. "What? Summer school?" He would call the high school and make arrangements with the principal himself. If Tyson left the building early, school personnel could notify the department. With Tyson traveling by bicycle, it shouldn't be hard to pick up his trail.

In 20 minutes, arrangements had been made at the school and the P.D. to continue surveillance on Tyson. Then Ben picked up Padilla's report again. There was an apartment manager he wanted to talk to. He noted the address, and headed for the door.

The manager of the Sunflower Apartments wasn't much help. He wasn't much interested either. "You wantta' see the place? Sure, here's the key." He tossed a small object at Ben's head. Ben caught the key and put it in his pocket. "Just lock up when you're through and bring the key back to me," the manager instructed.

He was a grizzled old man, clad in blue jeans and a tee shirt. He had been eating cereal when Ben arrived and hadn't let Ben cut his meal short. But he had stopped eating long enough to introduce himself as Willard Duffy and to locate a key to apartment 12A.

"What can you tell me about the tenant?" Ben asked.

"A fellow name o' Jonas Jackson," Duffy said after a long, satisfying slurp. "He paid for a year in advance - eight months ago. I ain't seen him since."

"What did he look like?"

Duffy squinted at Ben. "You kiddin'? I don't remember what I look like. How'm I gonna' remember a stranger I saw eight months ago?"

Ben shrugged. "Good question."

Apartment 12A's furnishings were threadbare. They didn't look comfortable but, judging from the accumulation of dust on them, no one was using them anyway. Only the outside door and one window were free of dust. The room was nothing but a passageway from the street in front of the Sunflower to the alley in back.

Tobi had wakened that morning feeling excited and expectant. Now that all the states were spoken for, she would read the plans for all 50 floats, make phone calls and visits, and try to resolve any problems that might have arisen. It was a daunting project and an eye-opening one. As she read, she could see that Dalton had been able to communicate his vision to each of the participants, for their plans revealed their thoughtfulness and their love for the states they were to represent. She loved Texas because she was a Texan, but she had given little thought to the idea that other Americans might feel a similar allegiance to their states. Realizing that Sooners loved Oklahoma and Cornhuskers loved Nebraska and Hoosiers loved Indiana warmed her heart.

"Dalton Granville, you are quite the visionary," she whispered. Then she closed her eyes and prayed, "Dear Lord, please help me find a way to express to Dalton how special and wonderful he is."

She was still brimming with excitement that afternoon when she stepped off the elevator onto the third floor of the hospital. She could hardly wait to tell Dalton how well things were going. And then, turning a corner into the corridor where his room was, she halted and went into reverse before she even knew what she was doing. Joshua Moses was carefully closing the door to Dalton's room. In two seconds he would turn and see her.

She dived into the nurses' station. There was nowhere else to go.

"What are you doing?" gasped the charge nurse, gazing at Tobi who was crouching at her feet.

"Please, please, please, don't look at me," Tobi begged. "Don't say anything."

The nurse tried to look away, but her gaze was immediately drawn back to Tobi.

"Please," Tobi mouthed, putting a finger in front of her lips. She closed her eyes and prayed Moses wouldn't see her.

It seemed like a lifetime had passed before she dared to ask, "Is he gone?"

"Who?" the nurse asked.

"The big man. Rev. Moses," Tobi whispered.

"Oh. Yes, he's long gone."

"Did he see me?" Tobi asked.

"Don't see how he could," the nurse assured her. "Why, child, look at you - you're shaking like a leaf. What did that man do to you?"

Tobi just shook her head, fighting off the tears. "I can't...I can't...say...," she stammered. "I can't...can't..."

"Never mind," the nurse said. "You run along now. Do you need some help?"

Tobi shook her head violently and hurried down the hall to Room 301. Forgetting to knock, she burst into the room, shut the door behind her, and leaned against it hard, as if she were holding back an army.

"Tobi!" Dalton Granville's face creased into a deep frown. "What's wrong, Tobi?"

She put her hand over her mouth and shook her head, unable to speak, still straining against the closed door.

"Should I ring for a nurse?" Dalton asked.

"No!" Tobi shook her head vigorously. "No!"

"Well, then, I'll come over there myself," Dalton said, throwing aside the covers.

"No, don't." Taking a deep breath, Tobi hurried to his side and pulled the covers over him again. "What...what...was...that...horrible man...doing here?"

Dalton looked perplexed. "What horrible man?"

"Joshua Moses."

"The preacher?" Dalton asked.

Tobi shuddered. "That's what he calls himself."

Dalton studied her. "What do you call him?"

Tobi had to think a moment before she whispered, "A monster."

Gazing at the pale, trembling woman before him, Dalton understood that tact was required. "Do you want to tell me about it?" he asked gently.

"No," Tobi said pitifully. "But I will. He...he...tried to...to...rape me."

In all the decades of his life, Dalton Granville had never been so quickly and intensely drawn to anyone as he had to Tobi Kirkland. She had walked into his dark room and his dark life, full of joy and energy, and splattered light all over the suffocating darkness that plagued him. Now she stood before him as limp as a rag doll, trembling and weak. He wanted to find Joshua Moses and strangle the man with his bare hands.

"Why was he here?" Tobi asked again.

"Money. He wanted me to contribute to his evangelistic association."

Tobi's emerald eyes were huge in her white face as she asked urgently, "You didn't do it, did you?"

"No, of course not. Tobi, sit down. Can you pull that big recliner over here by the bed and get comfortable? You're trembling like an earthquake about to split open."

Tobi did as she was told with ease, because the big chair was equipped with rollers. She collapsed into it and took some deep breaths. Slowly her color began to return and the trembling receded.

"There, that's better," Dalton said, beginning to relax himself. "Now, tell me. When did this happen?

"Saturday afternoon," Tobi said.

"Then why is he still walking around on the streets?" Dalton asked indignantly.

"I couldn't prove it," Tobi said. "It was my word against his."

"And that's it? He's free to go out and attack some other woman. Or even you again? Tobi, did he see you just now?"

Tobi giggled, remembering her undignified dive to safety. "No, I hid under a nurse's desk."

Dalton grinned. "That must have been a sight to see."

Tobi nodded. "The nurse thought so."

"Okay, then, why don't you tell me everything you know about Monster Moses?"

Tobi leaned forward with an earnest expression on her face. "Oh, Dalton, I shouldn't. My Mother always said, 'If you can't say something good about a person, then don't say anything at all.' And I don't know one good thing I can say about him."

Dalton looked stern. "With all due respect to your Mother, please tell me anyway."

Tobi sighed. It had been such a beautiful day until that horrible man came along and ruined it. She took a deep breath and launched into the story of Joshua Moses. It surprised her how much she knew about him but, as she concluded, she cautioned Dalton, "I don't know if you can believe anything in his autobiography. He's a monstrous liar."

Dalton nodded thoughtfully. "I understand that."

"I'm so glad you didn't give him any money," Tobi said. "Could you tell just by meeting him that he was rotten to the core?"

"Not at all," Dalton said. "I never hand out money without checking on the person making the request. And this time I'll double check. Or triple check. And now," he changed the subject, "tell me about my parade."

Light came into Tobi's eyes and her face glowed. "Everything is wonderful, Dalton. I've found sponsors for the last three states. So I was looking over the plans this morning - you know - for all the floats. And they're going to be beautiful! I love my country. And I love it that we Americans can love our states, and still love our country too. I think you're a genius for dreaming up the whole idea and then making it happen!"

"You give me too much credit," he said modestly. "Besides, I didn't exactly make it happen, did I? You're the one who's making it happen."

"You did all the hard work," Tobi said. "I'm just riding the momentum you already had going." She paused, searching for words. "And every time I think about it I feel this desperate need to tell you how much I admire you for what you've done. And how grateful I am to be a part of it."

Dalton lifted his hand. Tobi took it and held it.

"I wish my Lettie could have known you," he said. Then he added brokenly, "And Gabe, too. You're a treasure who came into my life so late, and I ache to share you with my loved ones..."

His voice trailed off, and they were silent for several minutes. Then Dalton squeezed Tobi's hand and released it. "Now, tell me about the new ones - Connecticut, Maine, and Wisconsin. Cold country - all three."

"Yes," Tobi agreed, "but beautiful."

She told him about the contacts she had made and the deals she had closed. "I'll be talking to Paul Hudson tonight about Wisconsin," she said. "When he signs on the dotted line, we'll have our 50th float spoken for."

"You're doing a good job, Tobi," Dalton said. "I'll have to take Clayton Archer out to dinner for sending you to me. He did what I couldn't have done - found the perfect person for the job."

Tobi blushed with pleasure. "Thank you, but I'm having so much fun it's not even like a job!"

He smiled wearily. "And that's probably why you're the ideal person to do it."

"You're tired," Tobi said. "I'm going to leave so you can rest." She took his hand for a moment, then asked, "Dalton, would it be all right if I ask my pastor to visit you? He's real, not like Joshua Moses."

Dalton's weary eyes brightened. "Please do, Tobi. I'd like to talk to him."

"I'll call him today," she promised. "His name is Dan Brighton." Rising, she leaned over and kissed his cheek. "Please take good care of yourself."

He smiled. "I will if you will."

Dalton rested for 30 minutes after Tobi left. Then he picked up his telephone and asked the hospital operator to connect him with the Deepwater Police Department.

When Ben's phone rang, he considered ignoring it. He'd been trying to get away from his desk for an hour. But the ringing annoyed him, so he snatched up the receiver. "Homicide. Ben Walling."

"Detective Walling, this is Dalton Granville. Do you have a few minutes to talk?"

"Mr. Granville!" Ben said in his most respectful voice. Almost everyone in town knew the name Dalton Granville, but Ben had never met him. "Of course I can give you a few minutes. How can I help you?"

"Look," Dalton began, sounding defensive, "I know that on television police officers always hate private detectives. I don't know whether it's the same in real life or not, but I called to tell you that I'm going to have Joshua Moses investigated. I'd like for your department to cooperate with my investigator."

"Joshua Moses?" Ben asked. "Why?"

"He came to my hospital room today, begging for money. Your sister-in-law Tobi Kirkland saw him here, and he scared her to death."

Ben was on his feet. "What happened? What did he do? Why didn't she call me?"

"Nothing happened," Dalton said. "Tobi saw him first and hid under a nurse's desk. But she came to my room looking like she'd seen a ghost. When she told me what he'd done to her, I promised myself I'd find a way to get him off the streets."

"She told you?" Ben asked in amazement, sinking back into his chair. "She told you...everything?"

"She told me he howls like a wolf in church! She told me he's a blooming freak! She told me his entire autobiography. And she told me he tried to rape her and would have succeeded if you hadn't intervened."

Ben whistled. "She must think a lot of you. I would have sworn she'd never tell a soul outside the family about that day."

"Perhaps she did it to protect me," said Dalton. "She was afraid I might give the man's organization some money."

"Mr. Granville, there's nothing I'd like better than to see Moses behind bars," Ben said. "If cooperating with your investigator will make that happen, all he has to do is ask."

It was 7:00 o'clock that evening when Paul Hudson called Tobi. "I just walked in the door," he told her, "but I had to call you first thing to make sure you didn't give Wisconsin to someone else."

Tobi laughed. "Not a chance. I've been saving it for you. Did your parents ever agree about Wisconsin's most important contribution to the Union?"

"No, and they never will," Paul said. "But Dad knows we're not going to put a football team on a float that represents the whole state of Wisconsin. Especially not down here in Dallas Cowboy country."

Tobi breathed a sigh of relief. She had been hoping Paul's mother was going to win that debate. She arranged to meet Paul at 8:30 the following morning in his office so she could fill him in on details.

Two hours later, Tobi carefully folded back the quilt her Grandmother Kirkland had made for her when she was ten. She loved its fields of pink and yellow tulips, their lush green foliage, and the quilt's snow-white background. She never failed to think of her grandmother's tender love and nimble fingers when she looked at the quilt. And, in winter, when she pulled it up to her neck, she imagined herself in her grandmother's strong, old arms, receiving a bear hug that would have to "last until I come again!"

She sank into bed with a contented sigh and picked up her Bible. She turned to I Corinthians and read chapters 12-14 slowly and carefully. Then she focused her attention on the last half of chapter 13, thinking about Joel's excitement the previous day. Was the apostle Paul really prophesying an end to the supernatural gift of tongues in the first century? Or was he talking about the fact that the gifts of tongues, prophecy, and knowledge would be unnecessary in Heaven?

Why was Joel so sure? Of course, it should be obvious that these gifts wouldn't be needed in Heaven where Jesus, the Author of all wisdom and knowledge, was present. So why would Paul bother to mention the fact here? Didn't it make more sense to believe that Paul wanted the Corinthian church to understand that these gifts were temporary?

Tobi consulted her bedside clock. It was 9:30. She picked up the handset of her portable telephone and dialed Joel's number. His voice, warm and welcoming as always when he took her calls, sent her heart into double time. Tobi leaned against the headboard of her bed with a goofy smile on her face, as they exchanged news about their day. Then, when the conversation lagged, her expression sobered. She sat up, bent over her Bible again, and said earnestly, "I've been reading I Corinthians 13, Joel, and I don't understand how you can be so sure the last half of the chapter isn't referring to Heaven."

"Which verses are you talking about?" he asked.

"Verses 8-12, but verse 12, especially. It says 'For now we see through a glass darkly; but then face to face: now I know in part; but then shall I know even as also I am known.' How can that be talking about any earthly situation?"

"That's how I saw it at first, too," Joel admitted. "It seemed to me that it was an example Paul was giving to strengthen his case. First he says that tongues, prophecies, and words of knowledge will cease. Then he explains why they'll cease - they're incomplete. Once the Holy Spirit had given the full understanding of God's new covenant, it would be "perfect" or complete. Then it would be foolish, even dangerous, to continue accepting new revelations as being from God."

"Why dangerous?" Tobi asked.

"Because it's so easy for wolves to lead the sheep astray. Look at Joshua Moses."

"You're right about that," Tobi said thoughtfully.

"Next," Joel continued, "I figured Paul was giving two examples of how something incomplete or imperfect is replaced by something more mature or more complete. In one case, a grown man puts off childish behavior. In the other case, we Christians here on Earth reach Heaven, where we move from partial vision to complete vision."

"Oh, I see what you mean!" Tobi said excitedly. "But what did Caleb say?"

Joel laughed, "The man is a prince! He never says, 'You're wrong.' Instead, he says, 'That's certainly a possibility, but why don't you consider...?' And then he gives an explanation so simple and clear, I can't understand how I missed it."

"Don't keep me in suspense," Tobi begged. "What did he say about this passage?"

"Okay, you have to keep two things in mind," Joel said. "First, put yourself back in New Testament times. They couldn't go to the shelf and choose between 10 versions of the Bible. They had no versions. Zero. In other words, God's new plan, His new covenant for the church, which was different from His old covenant with Israel, was still mysterious to them. It was incomplete."

"That *is* hard to remember when I have a Bible in every room of my house," Tobi said. "What's the other thing I have to remember?"

"Well, the mirrors they used in those days weren't like our mirrors. They were often polished metal. Have you ever tried to use a spoon to put on lipstick?"

Tobi grinned, "How did you know?"

"It's not the same, is it?"

"Not at all," she agreed.

"Okay then. *Now* look at these verses. Verses 9 and 10 explain that, in Paul's day, they had only partial knowledge because prophecy was only partial at any given church. But when all of it was gathered together in the canon of the New Testament, knowledge would be complete. And once the Holy Spirit had given the entire New Testament, He would stop giving prophetic knowledge. That's what it means when it says 'that which is in part shall be done away.' Prophecy was extremely inadequate but, fortunately, it would no longer be needed."

Tobi was nodding as she listened. "Okay, I'm with you."

"In verse 11, Paul is comparing prophecy, which includes tongues and their interpretation, to childish things. Studying and meditating on the completed Word of God is a mature behavior, while relying on scraps of prophecy is inadequate and immature."

He paused dramatically before he continued, "Okay, now for verse 12. Hang on a minute and let me read it one more time." There was a pause while he found his place, then he read slowly, " 'For now we see through a glass darkly; but then face to face: now I know in part; but then shall I know even as also I am known'."

He paused again, then said, "Look at it this way, and this may be a quantum leap, but what if the phrase, 'then shall I know even as also I am known,' does *not* refer to God at all? Paul is *not* in Heaven; he's *not* talking about God knowing him." Joel paused again. "Are you still with me?"

"Go slow," Tobi said. "You're about to lose me."

"I understand," said Joel, "but this is the key. You've got to quit thinking that Paul is referring to God knowing him in Heaven. When you understand that fact, you're practically home."

"Go on," Tobi said.

"Now watch this," Joel said. " 'Seeing through a glass darkly represents having to rely on inadequate prophecy.' 'Face to face' represents being able to study and rely on the completed New Testament. Paul says '*now* I know in part' because he has only the incomplete Word of God, namely prophecy, tongues, and interpretation of tongues. But when the scripture is completed, he says, he will be able to see the whole plan of God clearly. And he makes a comparison between looking into one of those imperfect mirrors - or looking glasses - and actually looking at a person face to face. When all of the scripture has been given, he says, 'I will be able to see God's whole plan as clearly as the person looking at me face to face is seeing me - then shall I know even as also I am known'."

"I will be able to see God's whole plan as clearly as the person looking at me face to face is seeing me," Tobi repeated, staring at her Bible. " 'Then shall I know even as also I am known'."

A full minute of silence passed, as she read the passage again, applying Joel's interpretation to it. Finally she said musingly, "It's a picture. Paul is creating a word picture to show them how much better it will be to have God's whole plan for the church than it is to have just the bits and pieces they get from prophecy."

"You do get it!" Joel cried eagerly.

"Wait," Tobi said, "let me read it one more time." And as she prayerfully meditated over those five verses, the passage became so clear it was as if it had come alive! "Oh Joel," she cried at last. "I see it. I really see it! But why has it taken me so long to get it?"

"I think," Joel said, "that we had the same problem. We had accepted the Charismatic interpretation so long that our vision was blocked. That darkness kept hiding the truth from us."

"But now...now we're out of the darkness!" Tobi cried. "Oh Joel, I'm so grateful for you. It has been a struggle for me these last few years to understand why the Lord didn't tell us clearly that tongues were going to cease, so that thousands of people wouldn't be led astray. But he did tell us clearly. We just have to be willing to see it."

Her eyes were full of tears. They spilled over her lashes and rolled down her cheeks. A few minutes later when she put down the phone and knelt beside her bed, her eyes were still full of tears and her heart was bursting with longing for Joel. "Thank you, Lord, for that wonderful man!" was all she could say. So she whispered it over and over, loving both Jesus and Joel more with every word.

Chapter XIII

Tobi arrived at Paul Hudson's office the next morning at 8:15. They discussed contracts and finances and Wisconsin. "Have you decided what you'll put on your float?" Tobi asked, eager to hear Paul's vision of his home state.

"Not all the details," Paul said, "but we've decided to use the theme America's Dairy Land. And the float will be a dairy farm."

"Are you going to have plenty of help?" Tobi asked. "I've dumped a huge assignment on you at the last minute."

"Not to worry," Paul assured her. "My folks are rounding up a caravan of family and friends. They're leaving today. Mom says they'll bat around ideas all the way South and, by the time they get to the Red River, they'll know exactly what they want to do."

"What about your niece and her little boy?" Tobi asked. "Have they turned up yet?"

Paul shook his head. "Not a sign of them." Suddenly, he snapped his fingers. "Hey! Here's an idea. Your brother-in-law, Ben...Ben Walling, isn't it?'

"That's right."

"He wanted a picture of Patrice's mother to email to the Green Bay police. I stopped by her place just now and got one. I don't have a scanner here, so he's going to have to pick it up. If you would take it to him, it would save some time."

"I can do that," Tobi said. "I'd like to stop by and see what's new in the case."

Paul picked up the framed photograph and handed it to Tobi. Studying it, she saw a willowy, middle-age woman holding a robust child with dark curls. "Trevor?" she asked.

Paul smiled. "The one and only." His expression was both sad and proud.

"I'm sure they'll find him and his Mom soon, " Tobi said. "Try not to worry."

He nodded forlornly, as he returned to his desk and picked up a patient's chart. Praying earnestly for Paul, Patrice, and Trevor, Tobi returned to her car and drove to the police station.

Ben had hurried to his desk that morning, eager to see what Miguel Padilla would have to report on Tyson Banning. The boy had proved to be a tedious quarry the previous day. After leaving school, he had gone straight home and stayed there. "Never mind," Ben had muttered to himself. "His business - whatever it is - takes place after dark."

Padilla's report was short. Tyson Banning hadn't left the house all night.

Ben scowled and scooped up another report he had received late the previous afternoon. He was poring over it when Tobi approached. She watched him a few minutes, then said, "That must be fascinating reading."

Ben looked up, startled. Seeing Tobi he smiled wearily. "Actually, 'disturbing' would be a better word for it," he told her.

"Why?"

"It's about the fingerprints we found on that diaper bag. What was the kid's name?"

"Trevor," Tobi supplied.

"Right. From Trevor's diaper bag." Ben was frowning and studying the report again.

"Well, what does it say?" Tobi asked. "Whose fingerprints were on the bag?"

"We don't know," he said. "We can match one print to a couple of unsolved murders around the country. But, since the crimes are unsolved, it doesn't help us much."

"Murders?" Tobi repeated.

"Murders," Ben said grimly. Then he forced himself to brighten up. "But that's not your problem. What can I do for you today?"

"I just left Paul Hudson," Tobi said. She held out the photograph.

Ben recognized its significance as soon as he saw it. "Patrice's mother?" he asked.

"And Trevor," Tobi added. "Paul said you want to email the picture to the Green Bay Police."

Ben nodded. "What I really want to do is hop a plane and go find Patrice myself. Short of that, I may turn Rachel Hudson upside down and shake her until I jar some information loose." He picked up his telephone receiver and began punching in numbers.

Seeing he was preoccupied with his case, Tobi headed for the door. Just before she was out of earshot, he yelled after her. "Where is she?"

Tobi looked back. "Who?"

"Rachel Hudson. She doesn't answer at home."

Tobi shrugged and shook her head. Ben scowled and began jabbing numbers again. Tobi tarried long enough to hear him ask for Dr. Hudson. Then she stepped outside into blinding sunshine and, a few minutes later, was on her way to Dalton Granville's office.

"Rachel didn't come home with me," Paul Hudson told Ben. "She says she won't leave Green Bay until she knows where Patrice and Trevor are."

"Look Dr. Hudson, I don't want to call your wife a liar, but do you think there's any possibility Rachel already knows where Patrice is?"

Paul's answer was slow in coming. "I'm afraid to second guess her. I would have sworn she'd never do what she did last week - running off to Wisconsin with Patrice instead of reporting Lynx's murder. Last week I would have said, 'Of course, she'd tell you if she knew.' This week...this week, I think she's a liar and a...criminal."

"I have to find Patrice," Ben said urgently. "I can't solve this case without her."

Again Paul hesitated. Finally he asked, "What do you want me to do?"

"Tell *me* what to do," said Ben. "Tell me how I can get your wife to cooperate."

"I've already tried everything I can think of," Paul told him. "Let me mull it over some more. Maybe something will come to me."

"Is she going to disappear again, too?" Ben asked. "I'll tell you the truth - if I thought she might, I would fly to Green Bay and put handcuffs on her myself."

Paul sounded defeated when he replied honestly, "I don't know."

Ben shuffled papers like a madman for 30 minutes after his call to Paul Hudson. He had reports from the fire department, reports from the lab, reports from the P.D.'s crisis unit. Reports. Reports. Reports. And none of them said anything useful! He picked up and put down his telephone ten times, thinking of some witness or expert who might help, then concluding he was beating a dead horse. He had just decided to drive to 1809 Tomlin

Out of Darkness

Street and kick some rubble around before he exploded, when his phone rang.

"Yeah? Walling, homicide," he growled into the receiver.

"Detective Walling," said a crisp, masculine voice, "my name is Mac Bolton and I'm located in Houston. Dalton Granville hired me to investigate a preacher by the name of Joshua Moses. He led me to understand that you might give me some help."

"If you'll keep me informed about your findings, I'll do what I can to help," Ben said. "Of course, I'll have to ask Mr. Granville about you before I pass on any information."

"Of course," said Bolton, his voice still as crisp and businesslike as a corporate vice president. "So far, my information is sketchy, except for one small detail."

Ben smiled. Bolton had a gleam in his eye - Ben could hear it in his voice. "What is your one small detail?" he asked.

"Joshua Moses is an assumed name. Our preacher was born Jess Hurley. His mother is deceased. His father - Jethro - is a drunk. Jethro Hurley lives in a nursing home now - what's left of him - and no one, including his son, ever visits him. What I'd like from you, of course, is a background check on both names: Joshua Moses and Jess Hurley."

"I've already run a check on Joshua Moses," Ben said. "It was a blank. But I'm grateful to you for providing his real identity. Any indication why he changed his name?"

"Yes. His father said it's not spiritual enough. It seems that when he got the 'call' to preach, he decided he needed a biblical name."

Ben snorted. "Well, he could hardly get more biblical than Joshua Moses."

The call from Mac Bolton and the sense that he wasn't alone in his quest for information calmed Ben. He phoned Dalton Granville's office and spoke to his secretary Judith Carson. Judith confirmed that Mac Bolton was working for Dalton. Ben then returned to his reports and read them again. Buried in a fire report he found the following notation: "Unidentified personnel encountered in the basement of 1809 Tomlin. White male in full garb seemed to be searching for something."

"Unidentified personnel?" he muttered. "What unidentified personnel?"

It took him an hour to contact the fireman who had reported the unidentified personnel. It was a novice named Nick Lyon who had come upon the stranger in the cellar of the gutted home.

"There was a safe down there," Lyon told Ben, "and this guy seemed to be looking for something in it."

"You mean the safe was unlocked?" Ben interrupted.

"Right," said Lyon. "It was wide open and there was nothing in it. I asked the guy what he was looking for, but he just shrugged and moved on. I never got a look at his name tag, but he wasn't familiar. I don't think he was one of us."

"How can you be sure he didn't find something in the safe and hide it under all those fireproof trappings you fellows wear?"

"I was already in the basement when he came down. I didn't pay much attention to him at first, but I would have noticed if he'd taken something out of the safe and put it under his coat," Lyon explained.

"Was there anything unusual about him?" Ben asked. "How tall was he?"

"He was covered head to toe - I wouldn't know him if I met him in the street today," Lyon said. "But I did get a glimpse of his face and I'm pretty sure he was white. He was about my height, 5'10". Why? Do you think he had something to do with the explosion?"

"You bet I do!" said Ben. "If he wasn't one of you, what was he doing there? And how did he happen to have firefighter's garb available at just the right moment?"

"Man! Am I in trouble for not tackling him?" Lyon asked. "I didn't think about it until later that I didn't recognize him."

"No, no, you did just right," Ben assured him. "I'm grateful you reported the incident. It helps me to know someone was nosing around down there, looking in the safe."

"I'm sorry I couldn't be more help," Lyon said.

"You just let me know if you remember anything else," Ben told him. He hung up feeling more optimistic. Somebody was looking for something they didn't find. Now how could he use that information to flush out his bombers?

He leaned back in his chair, closed his eyes, and studied on it. When he had first become a detective, it had been impossible for him to think deeply at the police station in the midst of the noise and activity. Now, a decade later, he could tune out a tornado if he needed to contemplate a case.

He was certain the bombing of Lincoln Nix's house at 1809 Tomlin had something to do with the secret organization to which Kent Grantham belonged - kooks who thought they were going to take over the world! Kent had murdered his stepfather, Hugh Mansett, to protect this organization. So what Ben needed was the file on the Mansett case.

The file was still easily accessible because Kent's trial was pending. Ben located it and began reading. Almost immediately he sat up straight in his chair. The red sports car! Kent had rented a farm house south of town where he could hide his own red car after he framed Tobi for Mansett's murder. What if...?

He slumped again. They wouldn't be stupid enough to use the same farm house. Unless...unless they still believed he was stupid. Too stupid to think of looking there. They had framed Tobi for Mansett's murder, believing the Deepwater police were idiots. What if they thought his catching Kent Grantham was a lucky fluke? What if they figured they could use that farm house for their headquarters and no one would be the wiser?

He did some more thinking. Should he take a couple of uniformed officers with him to investigate? Did he want them to know he was watching them? No. This organization wouldn't scare off. Instead they would quietly kill anyone who got in their way.

Ben took a deep breath. He would need a disguise. He would wear a wire so a couple of backup officers would be able to hear if he got into trouble. And he would NOT tell DeeDee what he was doing until he came out of it, alive and well. He picked up his telephone receiver, then put it down again. First he would cruise past the farm house and see if it was inhabited now. If so, he intended to find out who was living there.

Tobi felt like she was on a flying carpet the rest of the day. Judith had a list of items that needed to be picked up in the Dallas-Fort Worth metroplex for various float builders. It would take a trailer or small truck to haul everything back to Deepwater. Did Tobi want to make the trip or should Judith find someone else?

When Tobi's face lighted up, Judith began punching in phone numbers. She arranged for Tobi to fly to Dallas that afternoon. "Do you want to pick up the U-Haul truck and come back tomorrow or would you like to spend some time in Dallas?" she asked.

"I'd love to spend a day," Tobi said hesitantly. "Would that be a problem for anyone? How soon do they need the supplies?"

"Not until the weekend. If you'll load up Friday morning and head back after lunch, we'll have plenty of time to distribute all the supplies," Judith said.

"That would be wonderful!" Tobi exclaimed.

And so, that evening she walked out of the belly of a commercial airliner into Joel's waiting arms. "The girls have tomorrow scheduled," he told her, "but tonight you're mine."

They ate some of the best Mexican food Tobi had ever tasted. Then, when Joel asked her what she wanted to do next, Tobi said, "Can we go somewhere and talk?"

Joel looked alarmed. "What's wrong?"

"Nothing now," Tobi assured him. "But I think I should tell you what happened last Saturday." She would say no more until Joel had driven to a park near his uncle's house and they were strolling hand-in-hand through the gathering dusk.

They stopped at a fenced-off area, where owners were allowed to take the leashes off their dogs. Three dog owners were throwing Frisbees for their pets. The animals raced and leaped and twisted their bodies into amazing contortions in order to catch the flying discs. "I've never seen dogs having so much fun!" Tobi said with shining eyes.

"Almost as much fun as their owners," Joel agreed.

When they began walking again, Tobi asked, "Joel, did you ever tell Rev. Morel about Joshua Moses hiring a woman to pretend she was healed in his service?"

"No," Joel said. "I never did. I know Moses actually did it because I know you. But Emory doesn't know you. I could never figure out how to convince him you're telling the truth and his precious guest evangelist is a lying fraud!"

Tobi nodded sympathetically, then took a deep breath. "Something bad happened Saturday. I hope you won't be too angry at me for not telling you then, but I was afraid you'd drop your studies and come right home." She paused and gulped in another deep breath. "I didn't want you to do that because I believe what you're doing here is important."

Joel had stopped walking. He took her shoulders and turned her to face him. "Tobi! Quit stalling and tell me what happened."

She had been determined to keep up a brave front for him, but her face crumpled in spite of her best efforts. "Joshua Moses...he...he...tried to rape me," she told him brokenly. "I called 911 on your cell phone, and Ben came in time to stop him."

Joel's face was ashen, and his hands began to tremble. He didn't trust himself to speak, so he enfolded Tobi in his arms and held her for many minutes. She had promised herself she wasn't going to cry, but she did. She wept as if her heart would break. But Joel's arms were strong and he prayed desperately that God would give her comfort and give him wisdom. When she lifted her face to him, she said sorrowfully, "I should have listened to you. It's my own fault for going there. I'm so sorry I was so..."

But Joel put a finger over her lips. "No!" His voice was stern, but she could still feel him trembling. "It's not your fault," he said. "Don't you think that. Not even for a second!"

"How can I stop thinking it?" she asked brokenly. "You told me not to go, not to have anything to do with that evil man!"

"It's not your fault. It's not your fault. It's not your fault," Joel almost chanted. "Don't you dare tell yourself it is."

Tobi nodded, but she seemed to have run out of words.

"So what happened?" asked Joel. "Did Ben lock him up and throw away the key?"

"How could he? I didn't have any proof."

Joel stared at her in disbelief. "Do you mean he's still walking the streets and pretending to be an evangelist?"

Tobi nodded.

"I'll kill him," Joel said. "I'll go back to Deepwater tonight and kill him." Suddenly his voice broke, and Tobi thought he was going to cry, but he paused and regained control.

"What you need to do," she said, and now her voice was soft and calm, "is call Rev. Morel. Even if he doesn't believe me, he should be told."

Joel nodded. "Yes. I need to do that." He looked around the park, which was crowded with joggers, lovers, and dog walkers. "But not here."

"No, not here," Tobi agreed.

Joel looked at his watch. "Are services still going on at the Vine?"

Tobi nodded. "They were scheduled to end Sunday, but there's so much barking and howling and roaring going on they've decided God wants services extended for another week."

"What about clucking?" Joel asked with a straight face. "Is anybody clucking?"

"Oh!" Tobi's eyes widened. "I'm sure there are whole *boatloads* of cluckers!"

They grinned at each other, enjoying their small joke, then returned to their walk. "He won't get away with this, Tobi," Joel said, his voice heavy with menace. Seeing her look of alarm, he hastened to add, "I won't do anything stupid. I'll talk to Ben. But Joshua Moses isn't going to get away scot free."

That evening Ben Walling kept an appointment with a cosmetologist the police department hired from time to time. He was wearing sneakers, a T-shirt, and faded blue jeans. The beautician darkened his blonde hair and gave him a scruffy mustache. After she finished, he looked in the mirror and grinned. "Who is that bum?" he asked.

She grinned back. "Not a policeman - that's for sure!"

At dusk he was walking into the yard of the old farm house south of town. He had driven past the house earlier in the day and observed two cars parked in the driveway.

Once he knew someone was using the house, he had driven to the nursing home where the owner of the property was living and tried to find out who was renting her home. But Mrs. Mavis Gum, the widow of long-time farmer Clyde Gum, shrugged. "My daughter handles all my business now," she told him. "My mind tends to wander, and I forget important things. So I turned everything over to Lannie. Lannie Newcomb her name is."

Unfortunately, Lannie was unavailable. On vacation. No cell phone. "She calls in every other day to check on her Mother," Mrs. Gum's nurse told him. "But she called today, so we won't hear from her again until day after tomorrow."

"She didn't leave a phone number where she's staying?" Ben had asked.

"Not this time. They're on the move, going to the Painted Desert, the Grand Canyon, maybe Yellowstone..."

And so Ben had left his card and asked them to have Lannie call him ASAP. In the meantime, he would have to find out what he could about her new renters without arousing their suspicion. Now, standing in the front yard, he observed the house, baffled. It was dark, but a pickup and a motorcycle had joined the two cars in the driveway.

Without much expectation, he knocked on the weathered front door. Receiving no answer, he banged loudly, then walked around to the back of the house. Immediately, he saw why he'd received no answer at the house. The barn was ablaze with lights. Keeping an eye on the barn, he stopped in the driveway and read off the license plate and make of each of the vehicles. Then he strolled toward the barn.

The barn, once red, had lost most of its paint and much of its posture. It slouched before him with its big double doors propped open. Ben paused just beyond the pool of light spilling out of the doors and studied the activity within. Four men were gathered around a trailer, building something on it. Obviously, they were getting ready for the Fourth of July parade, and this trailer was being transformed into a parade float.

He studied the four men. The one who seemed to be in charge was big - big enough to be a professional wrestler. Another one was small, dark, and agile. The other two were of average height and weight.

"Hello," he yelled, stepping into the barn. The activity ceased abruptly and four pairs of eyes turned on Ben. "Hey!" he greeted them. "I'm Lance Reynolds, and I broke down on the highway. Could I borrow a phone?"

The big man stepped forward with his hand out. "Hi, Lance. I'm Matt Tatum. These three goons are Harry, Ike, and Zorro." He motioned toward the other three men who had gone back to work. Then he pointed toward the door. "Phone's on the wall over there."

"Thanks," Ben said. He dialed the number of one of his buddies who was parked in a patrol car around the bend. Although none of the float builders seemed to be listening, he threw in a few swear words, gave his location and said, "Get a move on! We've got another 100 miles to travel tonight."

After he hung up, he walked back to the trailer. "Here take this five," he said, holding out a bill. "I had to call a cell phone, and there's probably going to be a charge."

"No charge for a local cell call," Matt said.

"I'm not local. I'm helping a friend move from Amarillo to San Antonio," Ben explained. Then he waved toward the trailer as Matt pocketed the five-dollar bill. "What is all this, anyway?"

"Arkansas," said Matt. "We're representing Hot Springs, Arkansas, for the big Fourth of July parade next week."

Ben whistled. "You're doing a great job. Are you guys from Arkansas?"

"Harry is," Matt said. "The rest of us are helping poor ole' Harry out because he's so *pitiful*." Matt yelled this last sentence in Harry's direction, and Harry pitched a chunk of wood at Matt's head.

Matt ducked, picked up the wood, and pitched it back at Harry.

"You've got to tell me one thing...," Ben said. "How did four men get a job building a parade float? Usually there are a few women around to supervise."

"You got that right," said Ike, hopping down from the trailer. "We got tired of being supervised and sent them to the mall."

"Ah malls!" said Matt blissfully. "The greatest invention in the world."

"Listen," Ike said, "can we give you a hand with your car, Lance?"

"Thanks," said Ben. "It's a pickup actually. Don't bother. You've got better things to do, and I'll have help in a few minutes. It serves Dick right for going off and leaving me."

He started for the barn door, then turned back to ask. "Oh by the way. Where are you gonna' put Bill Clinton on your float?" All four men had stopped working to watch him leave and Ben was almost certain Matt, with his eyes on Zorro, had jerked his head in Ben's direction.

"Bill who?" Ike asked with a chortle.

"We're not putting Clinton on our float," Matt said with a smirk. "We can't agree whether he contributed anything to the nation or not. So we decided to leave him off."

"Yeah, we'll find an old geezer with a wheel chair to put in our hot spring," Harry said. "Who knows? Maybe he'll get healed during the parade."

Ben grinned, waved, and walked out into the darkness. As soon as he passed the farm house, he paused in a shadow and watched the barn. Sure enough, Zorro was coming after him, walking fast.

"I'm being followed," he said in a loud whisper to the hidden microphone, as he ran lightly along the highway. "Let's go with Plan B."

According to Plan B, the patrol car was waiting for Ben at his pickup, now loaded with household furniture. Pretending they had found something suspicious in the pickup, the uniformed officers called for backup. When another patrol car arrived, they put Ben in it and waited for a tow truck to come for his pickup.

When they rendezvoused at the police station and compared notes, they agreed no one had seen Zorro in the vicinity. "Are you sure he was following you?" Don Rawls asked.

Ben nodded. "Like a black cat in a dark alley." Picking up a telephone, he punched in Tobi's number. When she didn't answer, he called DeeDee. "Where's Tobi?" he asked.

DeeDee had spent most of the evening praying and worrying about Ben. He had refused to tell her what he would be doing, but she could tell from his manner at supper that he was planning something that was making him nervous. When she heard his voice, she was so relieved, she could barely speak. "Huh?" was the best she could do.

"Is Tobi there? She doesn't answer at home."

"She's in Dallas," DeeDee said. "Why? What's wrong?"

"Call her," Ben said. "Tell her to stay away from Arkansas until I see her."

"Arkansas?" DeeDee frowned. Had her husband lost his senses.

"The Arkansas float," Ben said. "Tell her not to go near it. I'll explain later."

Blessing Joel and his cell phone, DeeDee punched in the number and waited.

"Hello," said Tobi, sounding tired.

"How was the flight?" DeeDee asked.

"Perfect. How's Deepwater?" Tobi asked.

"A little bit scary, but I don't know why," DeeDee said. "Ben says for you to stay away from the Arkansas float until you talk to him."

"Why?"

"I don't know. He was gone most of the evening, and I've been scared to death because he wouldn't tell me what he was going to do. Just about the time I figure he's dead and his buddies don't have the heart to come tell me, he calls and says, 'Where's Tobi?' If I could have reached him, I would have punched his lights out!"

Tobi laughed sympathetically. "I'm sorry you had such a miserable evening. Mine wasn't so great either. I told Joel about last Saturday."

"What did he say?"

"Something about going to Deepwater tonight and killing Joshua Moses," Tobi said.

"What's he really going to do?" DeeDee asked.

"Call Rev. Morel and give him an earful about his evangelist. I told you about his fraud, didn't I?"

"You mean the woman who pretended she couldn't walk and then claimed she was healed?" DeeDee asked.

"Right. Joel hadn't told Rev. Morel about it because he didn't think Rev. Morel would believe him. Now he's going to call him and tell him everything."

"Are you with Joel now?" DeeDee asked.

"No. We spent the evening together, but he just left me at the motel and went back to his uncle's house."

"Have you met his uncle?"

"Tomorrow," Tobi said. "Tomorrow we're going to spend the whole day with Gloria and Gracie, then have dinner with Joel's aunt and uncle in the evening."

"Sounds like you need to get your rest," DeeDee said. "But listen, Tobi, you know I love you, don't you?"

"Sure, sis, I love you too."

"While I was praying and worrying about Ben all evening," DeeDee confessed, "I decided I need to say 'I love you' more often to my family and friends."

"I'm sorry you had such a tough evening," Tobi said. "I wish I'd been there for you."

"No, no. You're right where you should be. Kiss Joel for me tomorrow and tell him I love him."

"It will be a pleasure," Tobi said, smiling. "Good night, sis. You know I pray for you and Ben and the kids every day, don't you?"

"Yeah, but on a night like this one, it's nice to hear it. Good night, Tobi."

Chapter XIV

The next morning Joel knocked on Tobi's motel door at 8:00 o'clock. When she opened it, she was surprised to see that he was alone. "Where are the girls?" she asked.

"Gloria's sleepy; Gracie has to wash her hair. They want to go to a water park this afternoon, but they plan to go shopping this morning, and Gracie's hair *has* to look *GOOD* for shopping! So it's just you and me for breakfast," he said, grinning broadly. Then he took her into his arms for a lingering good morning kiss that left Tobi weak and breathless.

"Well, maybe we can manage without them for one more meal," she said, clinging to him while she waited for her knees to quit wobbling. But she was gazing at him so adoringly that he found it necessary to kiss her again.

"Joel, stop!" she gasped when he released her for the second time. "You're addicting, and I can't afford to get addicted."

"Why not?" he asked. "I'm already addicted to you."

She blushed. "Don't tell me that."

They ate a light breakfast in the motel dining room where Joel told Tobi about his phone call to Emory Morel. "He was furious," Joel told her. "I've never heard him so angry. He yelled, 'Rachel's right! That woman is ruining you. First she makes you leave the church. Now she's slandering our evangelist'."

"I suppose I must be '*that woman*'," Tobi said.

"I suppose you must," Joel agreed.

"What about Rachel? How did she get into the conversation?"

Joel shook his head. "It seems she has been calling him every day since we started dating. I'm a bad example for the girls. I'm sending the wrong message to the community by leaving the church. What if I start filling the girls' young, impressionable minds with lies about Charismatic doctrine?"

Tobi winced. "Poor man. What does she want him to do about it?"

"Get me back, of course. Theirs is a name-it-and-claim-it theology, remember. She can't understand why Emory is being so lazy in his pastoral duties. He should have had me back in the fold within a week after I left."

"She's not really so naive, is she?" Tobi asked.

"What she is, is spoiled," he said. "She believes hers is the only viewpoint, and God and everybody ought to know it by now."

Tobi sighed. "So Rev. Morel doesn't believe the healing of the lame woman was a fraud or that Moses tried to rape me?"

Joel shook his head. "No. He believes you're an evil vixen who has her claws in me and is determined to destroy his church."

"Why does he think I would want to do that?" she asked.

Joel gave her a wry smile. "I couldn't get him to admit it, but I expect he believes you're under satanic delusion."

"Oh, well," Tobi said. "That would certainly explain it."

Conversation languished as they finished their breakfasts. Both of them were lost in troubling thoughts about Joshua Moses, Emory Morel, Rachel Hudson, and the Church of the Living Vine. It was a relief to step out of the motel restaurant into cheerful sunshine.

"Now what?" Tobi asked.

"Well, I'm not 'into' shopping," Joel said. "So I'm going to Caleb's while you ladies hit the malls. I thought you might like to meet Caleb, though, so we'll go to his house now and Uncle William will bring the girls there when they're ready for the day.

Tobi's eyes lighted up. "Oh, I'm so glad. I'd love to meet him."

Caleb Hancock was exactly as Joel had described him - small and spare with intelligent dark eyes. "So you are the famous Tobi Kirkland!" he said, beaming at her.

Tobi look questioningly at Joel, but he shrugged.

"Why am I famous?" she asked.

"Perhaps it's only in the Trent family that your fame is spread abroad," he said, "but Adele Trent believes you're the most amazing woman who ever walked on this planet."

Tobi looked at Joel again. "Your mother?" She could see from his face that understanding had dawned.

"Yes, my mother," he said. "You saved me from that evil church - a feat no one else had been able to accomplish. I'm surprised she hasn't recommended you for knighthood."

"Let's not be hasty," Caleb cautioned. "I'm not so sure she hasn't."

They laughed, then Tobi sighed. "Well, that settles it - I'm either the most amazing woman alive or an evil vixen under satanic delusion. What could be simpler?"

"Satanic delusion?" Caleb asked. So they seated themselves in his big office with floor-to-ceiling book shelves on three walls and Joel and Tobi gave him a brief history of their relationship. When they finished, Caleb said, "I congratulate you both. You escaped from a very alluring heresy without losing your faith altogether. I admire your determination to study the Word for yourself and get back in the mainstream of true Christian doctrine."

"You're very gracious, Dr. Hancock," said Tobi, "and I appreciate your desire for us to find truth for ourselves, but would you explain one passage for me?"

"Madame, if you will kindly call me Caleb instead of Dr. Hancock, I will gladly do anything you ask of me," said the professor.

She smiled. "Thank you. Caleb."

"Ah, what music," he enthused, "to hear my own name on the lips of a beautiful woman! Now, Tobi, name your passage."

"It's in I Corinthians 14," she said, where Paul says he prays with the spirit and with the understanding. And he sings with the spirit and with the understanding. Was he instructing the Corinthians to practice a private 'prayer language' in unknown tongues, as well as praying in their own language?"

"Not at all," Caleb said. "I know the verse to which you refer, but I must tell you, first, that 'tongues' were never practiced in a private setting. The gift of tongues was always used very publicly because it had a public purpose."

Tobi nodded. "Yes, that's what I thought, and that's why I'm confused."

"Context," said Caleb. "Always, always, put it in context. Right Joel?"

Joel nodded. "Seems like I've heard that somewhere before."

Caleb winked at Joel before he asked Tobi, "Now, what is Paul saying before he comes to that verse."

"Well." Her forehead wrinkled as she strained to remember the chapter. "There's something about a harp, I think, and a trumpet."

"Very good," said Caleb. "What about them?"

"Well, if the instruments just squeak and squawk, there will be no music for the listeners to enjoy," said Tobi.

"And the trumpet," said Caleb. "What if all the telephones are out and the king needs to gather his troops for war?"

Tobi smiled. "The trumpet must make a clear sound that the army will recognize as a call to arms."

"Absolutely!" cried Caleb. "Paul is saying that a message in tongues and its interpretation must be given *together*. Now, what is Paul saying in your verse, Tobi?"

She smiled. "Oh, of course! He's saying that if he prays in tongues, he will also pray an interpretation. If he sings in tongues, he will also sing an interpretation."

Caleb beamed at her. "Bravo! You're a Bible scholar!"

Tobi beamed back at him. "But he's not talking about a so-called private prayer language," she added. "He's explaining how they should conduct their *public* services."

"That's how I see it," Caleb agreed.

"Knock, knock," said a voice at the door of Caleb's study. The little group looked up to see Gloria and Grace escorted by Mrs. Hancock. Both girls looked fresh and young, with their long dark hair shining. "Are you ready to go, Tobi?" Grace asked.

With goodbyes and thank you's, Tobi followed Gloria and Grace out of the Hancock's home. Joel walked with them to his SUV and asked, "Do you want to drive, Tobi, or do you trust this adorable 16-year-old child with your life?"

"Dad!" Gloria objected. "I'm not a child."

"Do *you* trust her?" Tobi asked Joel.

He nodded. "Yes, but I have no choice."

"Dad, don't be lame!" Gloria chided. Suddenly her hand darted into his pocket and extracted his keys.

Joel let her capture the keys, but he put her in a headlock and turned to Tobi again. "It's your choice. Who drives?"

"If you trust her, let Gloria drive," Tobi said. "I hate driving in big cities."

"Thank you!" Gloria said, as Joel released her. She gave her father a severe glare, then pranced around the SUV to the driver's side.

As the girls were fastening their seat belts, Joel took the opportunity to steal one more kiss from Tobi. "Have I mentioned lately how much I love you?" he asked.

"Not in the last few minutes," she said, and then she remembered her conversation with DeeDee the previous night. "That reminds me - DeeDee sent you a message."

"DeeDee?" he asked in surprise. "What's the message?"

"She said to kiss you," Tobi replied, planting a gentle kiss on his lips, "and tell you that she loves you."

"*She* loves me?" he asked, obviously touched. "Why?"

The vehicle's horn blared and Grace yelled, "Hey love birds, it's hot in here."

"I'll tell you later," Tobi promised. "It's a long story. Well, too long for now."

Reluctantly Joel opened the door for her and let her get in. Then he addressed his daughter. "You be careful, Gloria. If you start acting like a teenager, Tobi is going to take the keys and do the driving herself. You got that?"

"Dad, have you ever seen me driving like a teenager?" she asked indignantly.

"No, I guess not," he admitted. "But it makes me nervous for you to be driving in Dallas without me along to keep an eye on you."

"I be good, Daddy," she said in a little girl voice.

He sighed and gave Tobi an abashed look. "She will, too. Why do I *always* have to act like a parent?" Suddenly he grinned, kissed Tobi one more time, and slammed the passenger door. "Get lost!" he yelled. "And have fun!"

"Were your parents ever that lame?" Gloria asked Tobi, as she pulled into the street.

Tobi smiled wistfully. "It's too late to ask me," she said. "All I can remember about my parents is how wonderful they were."

"You mean they're...dead?" gasped Grace. "How sad!"

"They died in a car wreck," Tobi said, fighting the tears that always welled in her eyes when she thought of that dreadful night.

"Were they in Dallas when they died?" Gloria asked, checking the traffic anxiously.

"No, they were on the highway, probably driving 70 miles an hour," Tobi said. "They were in a head-on collision. The highway patrol officers thought the other driver might have fallen asleep at the wheel."

A gloom had settled over the little group, and Tobi hastily changed the subject. "So where are we going?" she asked Gloria. "Do you have a particular mall in mind?"

"Yep, Aunt Jen told me how to get to this awesome place..."

"They have quality merchandise at discount prices," Grace interrupted. "Aunt Jen says they have beautiful clothes, and they sell all kinds of other stuff, too."

"Well, that sounds perfect," Tobi said. Her voice was light, but she was keeping a close eye on the traffic, trying to do it without giving Gloria the impression that she was nervous. "Have you talked to your Mother since you got to Dallas?" she asked.

"Finally," Grace said. "She's in Green Bay, Wisconsin, with Paul's parents."

"Was she angry with you for coming to Dallas with your Dad?" Tobi asked curiously.

After a pause, Gloria answered, sounding surprised. "I guess not. She never acted angry, and she *always* let's us know when she's mad."

"She's right about you, isn't she?" Grace asked unexpectedly.

"What do you mean?" Tobi asked.

"Well, that you're trying to get Dad to leave the Vine and go with you to some dead church," Grace said.

"Not exactly," Tobi said. "I think some of the doctrines at the Church of the Living Vine are terribly wrong, and I hope he won't stay there. But I don't want either of us to go to a dead church."

"Mom says the Vine is the only church in town that's *not* dead," Grace told her.

"I'm afraid I don't agree with her," Tobi said patiently. "But let's not discuss church doctrine. That's a subject you should discuss with your parents."

"Okay," said Gloria. "Are you going to marry Dad?"

Tobi tried not to blush as she replied, "I...don't...know."

"Put it this way," Grace said, "if he asked you today, would you say yes?"

Tobi laughed. "I would say, 'I don't know'."

"So how come you and Dad aren't sleeping together?" Gloria asked.

"Gloria! Why don't you girls ask your Dad these questions?" Tobi stalled.

"We do," said Grace coolly, "and he says to mind our own business."

Tobi took a deep breath. She would like to take Joel's way out but, at the same time, she wanted the girls to know her answer. "Well, your Dad and I believe people shouldn't sleep together unless they're married," she said.

"Oh come on!" Gloria hooted. "Quit living in the Dark Ages."

Tobi frowned. "I thought you girls believed in the Bible," she said carefully. "Are you telling me you think the Bible was only for the Dark Ages?"

"No, of course not," Gloria explained patronizingly, "but some parts of it are outdated. I mean, do you think it's a sin for women to cut their hair?"

"Well, no," Tobi admitted. "You're right, some commandments *are* cultural, but most of God's laws are for all times because they describe the best way to have a happy life."

"Like, no sex without marriage?" Grace asked.

"Right," said Tobi.

"So you're saying men ought to do what Jacob and David and Solomon did? Marry more than one woman?" asked Gloria.

"I didn't say that!" Tobi objected.

"Well, you said God's laws are for all ages. And it was all right for Jacob to have four wives, so why can't Dad?"

Tobi laughed out loud. "Have you girls ever told your Dad he should have four wives?"

They looked at each other, then agreed. "Nope."

"I think you should run the idea past him and let me know what he says."

"Sure," Gloria said cheerfully. "That'll be fun. But you didn't answer our question."

"Well, in the first place, I'm not so sure polygamy was ever pleasing to God," Tobi said. "But the main thing is that the New Testament tells us it's wrong."

"Oh." Gloria looked defeated. "Well, never mind polygamy. Let's get back to sex outside marriage. Everybody else does it so why shouldn't we?"

"That's easy," Tobi said. " 'Everybody else' isn't our standard. God's Word is our standard. We do what He says to do, no matter what '*everybody else*' is doing."

"But if we do what the Bible says, everybody thinks we're freaks," Gloria objected.

Before Tobi could address the freak issue, Grace shrieked, "There it is! There it is!" She was pointing at a huge store in the midst of a vast parking lot. "See, it's white brick and two-stories tall, just like Aunt Jen said."

The conversation was forgotten as Gloria began maneuvering across three lanes of traffic. And Tobi, instead of helping her watch the traffic, closed her eyes and thanked God that the interrogation was over.

Inside the store, Tobi, Gloria and Grace soon decided to split up. Tobi wanted to find gifts to take to her family. Gloria and Grace were only interested in clothes.

Tobi was trying to choose among boxes of imported chocolates for Ben when she heard a familiar voice. Although it was familiar, she couldn't place it. Looking about she spied Audrey Mansett, Kent Grantham's mother. "Audrey!" she said, more to herself than to Audrey.

But Audrey heard her and hurried over. "Tobi! What are you doing in town?"

The two women hugged and Tobi said, "I'm playing today - tomorrow, business." She explained briefly about her new job, then turned the conversation to Kent.

"You know Kent escaped, don't you?" she asked.

Audrey nodded and her shoulders drooped. "I can barely stand to think about him," she confessed in a whisper. "I don't know how he turned out so bad..." She would have said more, but her voice failed her.

"Audrey, you mustn't blame yourself," Tobi said urgently. "Some kids turn out bad no matter how they're raised."

Audrey simply stood there, shaking her head, her eyes closed, looking old and gaunt. She had been a beautiful woman once, but now she seemed to be aging a year for every day that passed.

"I saw him the day before he escaped," Tobi said.

Audrey's eyes flew open. "You didn't! Why?"

"He called and asked me to visit him," Tobi said. "Ben... Do you remember my brother-in-law Ben Walling?"

Audrey nodded.

"Ben thought he wanted to see me one more time, as a kind of farewell."

"How did he look?" Audrey asked.

"Thinner and sadder," Tobi said. "But, Audrey, he apologized to me. He said he was glad I wasn't in that hole. That's what he called the jail, a hole."

"Oh, Tobi, I'm so glad." Audrey took both of Tobi's hands and squeezed them. "It's not much, considering what he did. But it's something. What else did he say?"

Tobi repeated as much of the conversation as she could remember. When she got to Kent's admission that he'd had a first love named April who had resembled Tobi, Audrey listened intently. "I'd forgotten about April," she said, "but Kent never did, did he?"

Tobi shook her head. "No. I think he still has very tender feelings for her."

"He was furious about her death," Audrey said thoughtfully. "In fact, I think that's when he began to change. First he lost his father. A few years later he lost April. And then I married Hugh a few months later." She gazed into Tobi's eyes with a look of agonizing vulnerability on her face. "He was never the same after that."

"Audrey," Tobi said, stepping closer and putting her arms around Audrey's frail shoulders, "it's okay to love him. He was your precious little boy. You'll love him forever no matter what he does, and that's okay. In fact, it's normal and wonderful. He'll always be special to me, too."

Tobi's words loosed a dam, and Audrey wept in her arms for several minutes. When the tears stopped, she was desperately ashamed. "I have to get out of here," she said. "I'm so embarrassed. But I'll never forget what you said."

Tobi watched her walk away, trying in vain to regain the air of dignity she had worn all her life.

Chapter XV

Back in Deepwater, Ben was having a busy morning. The first thing he saw when he sat down at his desk was a report from Miguel Padilla. Tyson Banning had been on the move the preceding night and Padilla hadn't lost him at the Sunflower Apartments this time. At Ben's request, he had been driving an unmarked car, rather than a police cruiser. As soon as he was certain Tyson was pedaling toward the Sunflower, Padilla drove there and parked near the alley.

He had watched Tyson crawl out of the window of apartment 12A and hit the alley running. He had raced a block and a half to a used car lot where he took a key out of his pocket, mounted a motorcycle, and buzzed off the car lot.

Tyson had driven around town for half an hour and finally taken a highway heading north. Five miles out of Deepwater he had turned off the highway and followed a couple of dirt roads. He stopped in the middle of nowhere, opened a barbed wire gate, drove the motorcycle through, and closed the gate. Then he headed off across a pasture.

Padilla had had no choice but to drive on past the gate, knowing Tyson would be suspicious if he stopped by the side of the road. So he drove to the next farm house, pulled in, and parked. Returning on foot, he had marked the location by wrapping his belt around the fifth fence post from the gate.

Since he had no intention of strolling across that pasture in the dark and didn't dare use a flashlight, which Tyson might see, he had returned to his car, gotten in and waited for Tyson to return. Over an hour passed before the motorcycle reappeared. Padilla watched Tyson take the gate down, drive the motorcycle through, and secure the gate again. Then he waited five minutes more before he drove slowly toward town.

Out of Darkness

The motorcycle was back at the used car lot, still warm to the touch. Tyson's bicycle was chained to the post on his porch at home. It was 3:00 A.M., the time Tyson had *begun* his errand two night before. Included in Padilla's report was a map to Tyson's pasture.

"Ridiculous," Ben muttered to himself. "This is the most ridiculous case I ever heard of." But he found Don Rawls, told him to dress for hiking, and went home to find some hiking boots himself. They weren't likely to cross paths with any rattlesnakes in the heat of the day. But during the cooler morning hours... Well, he wasn't taking any chances.

Even though Padilla had drawn the map in semi-darkness, Ben had no trouble following it to the pasture Tyson had entered the previous night. While Rawls examined the gate, Ben unwrapped Padilla's belt and tossed it into the cab of his pickup. "What's the holdup?" he asked.

"It's locked," Rawls reported, holding up a chain. "Unless you want to take some target practice at this lock, I'd say we're afoot."

"Mighta' known," Ben muttered.

They crawled through the barbed wire fence and followed the motorcycle tracks over a hill to another fence. "Looks like he left the motorcycle here," Rawls observed.

Looking back the way they had come, Ben nodded. "It's hidden from the road here. He could have left it all day and nobody would be the wiser."

They crawled through the second fence and looked around. "There's nothing here," growled Rawls. "What's he coming here for?"

Ben shrugged. "Search me. Come on - we might as well look around."

The ground sloped sharply downward into a limestone draw. Tyson's tracks, which were faint enough in the dry earth, were absent in the rocky gulch. The men walked from one end of the draw to the other and found nothing that might indicate Tyson's presence the night before.

"That's it!" Ben suddenly exclaimed, pushing back his hair, which was plastered to his forehead with sweat. "I'll bring the kid in and let him tell me about it. One way or the other, I'm going to make him talk."

"Oh right," Rawls grumbled, "*now* you decide."

―――

When Ben plucked Tyson Banning out of his summer school class, he asked where to find Mrs. Banning so she could be present when he questioned Tyson. Tyson's face hardened. "Leave my mother out of it," he said, "or you're gettin' nuthin' from me."

"You think she's never going to find out?" Ben asked, incredulous.

141

"After I tell you, then you can tell her what you have to - that's all. Do you promise?"

The two men - one a teenager, the other a 45-year old homicide detective - glared at each other. Neither blinked.

Finally Ben shrugged, "Have it your way." He led the way to his pickup. "What are you doing in summer school?" he asked as they drove. "Are you trying to get ahead?"

"No," Tyson said sullenly. "I'm trying to make up classes I failed, so I can graduate."

"You mean you'll graduate this summer?"

Tyson nodded.

"Why did you fail the classes in the first place?" Ben asked, trying to keep his voice neutral. If he sounded judgmental, he was certain he would get a non-answer from Tyson.

"I kept falling asleep in class," Tyson said.

"Because you spend so much time running around at night?" Ben asked.

"If you call working 'running around,' sure," Tyson growled.

Ben thought about this answer for a few minutes before he responded in a gentler tone than he had been using. "Do you *have* to work so late?"

"Sure, if I go to school all day."

"But *why* do you have to work? You don't seem to have a car to support."

Tyson shrugged. "I'm trying to help my Mom support both of us. As soon as we get her car paid off, I'm going to get one."

Ben nodded. "That's good, Tyson. I admire your gumption."

Tyson shrugged. He was still hostile and defensive but, at the police station, facing Ben across his desk, his bravado vanished. "What do you wanta' know?" he asked.

"A police officer followed you to an empty pasture last night," Ben said. "What were you doing there?"

Tyson's face registered understanding. "I thought that car was acting funny!"

"What were you doing there?" Ben asked in the same no-nonsense tone.

Tyson slumped resignedly in his chair and said, "Picking up mail."

"Picking...up...mail?"

Tyson shrugged. "You asked."

Ben drew a deep, calming breath before he spoke. "Okay, Tyson, here's the deal. We can sit here all day with me trying to guess the right questions to ask you. Or you can start at the beginning and tell me everything you know. Start with the first time you ever saw or heard of Lincoln Nix."

Tyson looked up startled. "Who?"

"Lynx," Ben said.

"That was his name? Lincoln Nix?" Tyson asked.

"Let's try this again," Ben said sternly. "You've known ever since Saturday that this moment was going to come. You've had plenty of time to decide how you want to tell the story. So quit stalling and tell it."

Tyson hung his head. "I had time, but I couldn't decide how to tell it."

"Good," Ben said. "I'm glad you haven't rearranged the facts - I need to know the exact truth. When was the first time you ever heard of or met Lynx - Lincoln Nix?"

"Nearly a year ago. I was coming home from work about 2:00 A.M. one night and, when I got to his house, he yelled at me from the porch, 'What are you up to at this hour? No good, that's for sure.' When I told him I'd been working, he offered me a better job. He said he needed a courier and a security guard and both jobs paid good."

"Which were you - a courier or a security guard?" Ben asked.

"Both."

"How much did he pay you?"

"It was never the same amount," Tyson answered. "He paid me when I brought his mail. It was always big envelopes or little boxes, and they never had his true name on them. Some of them were addressed to J.J. Johnson, some to Mary Johnson or M. Johnson, and some to R.R. Johnson. He would open one, pull out some hundred dollar bills and give them to me."

At that point it took all of Ben's self-control to keep from firing questions at Tyson. Instead he nodded and waited.

"Lynx gave me a fancy camera that takes photos in the dark. He said it was mine to keep, but I had to patrol the neighborhood regularly. Whenever I saw someone I didn't know, I had to take a picture of them. But not so they knew. Real sneaky like, you know?"

"How often did you take a picture for him?" Ben asked.

"Maybe twice a month until lately. Lately I saw a lot of strangers hanging around. Lynx didn't like it. He said he was going to have to move on or else take care of them. I don't think he wanted to leave Deepwater because of his son."

"What did he mean by 'take care of them'?" Ben asked.

Tyson shrugged. "He never said."

"Where are the pictures?" Ben asked.

"I gave them to Lynx," Tyson said.

"And now they've been blown to kingdom come," Ben lamented. "Do you have any undeveloped pictures in the camera?"

Tyson hesitated. "A couple. There was a little, dark guy on a bicycle. I took four or five pictures of him this month and gave them to Lynx. But the guy came back this week. I saw him twice." Tyson studied Ben's face for a clue. "I didn't know if I was supposed to take any more pictures or not. I mean, Lynx is dead, but..."

"But?" Ben prodded.

"I dunno'. Maybe Lynx was rubbing off on me, but I took the guy's picture both times."

"Yes!" Ben exulted. "Now we're getting somewhere. Tell me about the pasture. How did you get mail out of a pasture?"

"Well, if you go to the other side of the pasture, and crawl through a fence, there's this rocky ditch. If you climb the back wall of the ditch, you'll find a cave. It's mostly covered up from the outside, but inside it's like a cavern. It opens out again in a big ravine maybe half a mile from the first one. When I come out on the other side, I walk another half mile to a farm. I stop in the shed to make sure I'm not being followed. Then I go in the back door of the farm house."

"And Lynx received mail at that farm house?" Ben asked.

Tyson nodded. "I would get the mail from the box out front and put it in a safe in a secret cellar - it had a trap door under a rug."

"Did anyone ever try to follow you to the farmhouse?"

Tyson shook his head. "I don't think so. I was suspicious once or twice, but nobody ever got closer than the first pasture."

"So what about his mail?" Ben asked. "Was it always money?"

Tyson shrugged. "Every package I saw him open had money in it."

"Where did it come from?"

"Everywhere. I didn't notice the return addresses. I didn't want to know where it was coming from," Tyson said.

Ben studied him. "You were afraid of him?"

Tyson nodded and shivered involuntarily. "He would have killed me if I'd betrayed him. And my mother too."

"Then why did you keep working for him?"

"I was afraid to stop," Tyson said. "But I've been saving my money. Mom and I have to move before my Dad gets out of prison, anyway."

"Why is your Dad in prison?"

"For beating my Mom and me, and for dealing drugs." Tyson said in a monotone. He had apparently trained himself to detach his emotions from thoughts of his father.

Ben was suddenly looking at the scrawny teenager through new eyes. The boy should be wearing a cape and an "S" for "super" on his chest. He was a young hero standing between his battered mother and a hostile world.

"Hey, we've missed lunch," Ben said, glancing at his watch. "Let's go find some food. What do you like? Hamburgers? Pizza? You name it and we'll eat it."

"Not hamburgers or pizza," Tyson said. "I've had too many of those already."

"Why is that?" Ben asked in surprise.

"I've worked at two hamburger joints and a pizza place. I loved it at first, eating hamburgers or pizzas every day, but it got old after a few years."

"I'm sure," Ben said. "Well, then, how about Cleo's Kitchen?"

Ben was on his feet and ready to head for the door, but Tyson was still seated. "I'll have to go home and get some more money if we're going to eat at a nice place like that," he said, looking embarrassed.

Ben sat back down. "Tyson, you've given me more information about Lincoln Nix than I've been able to round up in days. So here's the deal. We'll go to Cleo's Kitchen and you can order everything on the menu if you want to. The information you've given me this morning has more than paid for it."

"Thanks," Tyson said, and his eyes looked bright and eager for the first time that day. But his happy expression didn't last long. "Look, Mr. or Officer Walling, I have to know one thing before I'm going to be able to eat anything."

"What's that?" Ben asked gently.

"Have I broken any laws?" He studied Ben's face earnestly.

"Not intentionally," Ben said. "As far as I'm concerned, you're a hero."

Tyson seemed to brush the praise aside, as he stood. "I don't care so much for myself," he said. "But my Mom...well, I'm all she has."

"In that case," Ben said, thumping Tyson on the back and starting him toward the door, "I'd say your Mom is richer than most folks."

Tyson looked up, surprise showing in his face. "That's what *she* always says."

Ben and Tyson spent the rest of the afternoon, trying to squeeze Tyson's memory dry of every idea, impression or notion he'd ever had about Lincoln Nix. Tyson had no idea why people all over the country were sending Lynx money. He recognized Patrice and Trevor when he saw them, but he had never met them. He had never been inside Lynx's house - as far as he knew, Patrice and Trevor were the only people allowed inside.

"He never did the same thing at the same time," Tyson said. "He once told me that being unpredictable was the key to staying alive. 'Remember that,' he said, as if I was in some kind of danger. So I never got his mail two nights in a row. And I changed the times when I would go."

"Is he still getting mail?" Ben asked.

Tyson nodded. "Same as ever." He looked uncomfortable then. "I had to bring some back with me last night. The safe is crammed full."

Ben perked up. "Are you saying all those packages are in the safe just like they arrived? With return addresses and post marks?"

"Sure."

Ben shook his head. "Am I an idiot or what? Why didn't I pull you in three days ago?" He picked up his phone and began dialing.

After Ben had made arrangements for the crime scene unit to examine the farm house, Tyson said, "I'm glad you *didn't* pick me up three days ago."

"Why is that?" Ben asked.

"I was still too scared to talk. I didn't know who killed Lynx. I didn't know what was going to happen next. I didn't know who I could trust." Tyson shrugged.

"And what changed?" Ben asked.

"When I brought those packages to my house - I don't want them there. Lynx is dead, but I don't know how to get free from him."

"We're working on it. Before this thing is over we'll make sure you're free of him forever," Ben said. "Come on, we'll go by your house and get those extra packages and your camera before we take the crew to Lynx's farm house."

Tobi loved water parks. But that afternoon, standing in front of a mirror in the women's dressing room, clad in an emerald green swimsuit with her red-gold hair floating around her shoulders, she wasn't sure she wanted to go outside. She didn't want to see Joel in a swimsuit. It was already hard enough to keep her thoughts about him pure. And she wasn't so sure it was a good idea for Joel to see her, either.

"Come on, Tobi," said Gloria. "We're ready." She was wearing a one-piece, turquoise swimsuit. And Grace had chosen a hot pink two-piece.

"Dad's going to be tired of waiting," Grace added.

Out of Darkness

With a sinking feeling in the pit of her stomach, Tobi followed them into the blinding sunlight. By the time her eyes adjusted to the brightness, Joel had seen them and was walking toward them. His body was as magnificent as she had known it would be, and Tobi suddenly felt breathless.

Then he was there and they went into each other's arms like a pair of magnets. After one brief kiss, they clung to each other, lost to the world in a sea of sensations. And then Gloria was pulling on Joel's arm and Grace was pulling on Tobi's.

"Okay, you two," Gloria said. "Break it up. Remember, you don't believe in sex before marriage."

"Gloria!" Joel was aghast. "We weren't...weren't..."

"Of course, you weren't," Gloria laughed. "But what were you *thinking*?"

"That's right," Grace chimed in. "You know what Jesus said - if you think it, you might as well be doing it."

"That's not what...," Joel began. Then he caught himself. "What's wrong with you two - don't you know better than to talk...like that?"

"We're just trying to help," Gloria said. "Tobi told us you don't believe people should have sex unless they're married."

When Joel turned his gaze on her, Tobi blushed and looked away.

"Don't blame her, Dad," Grace said. "We asked her."

"You didn't!" Joel was too horrified even to imagine such a scene.

"Tobi, I'm so sorry," he told her. "I had no idea they might..."

"Hey! I know!" Grace interrupted. "You could buy T-shirts over in the gift shop, Dad. Tobi says she sunburns easy. It would be like, you know, killing two birds with one stone."

"Or maybe, saving two birds with one T-shirt," Gloria grinned.

"No, they'd have to have *two* T-shirts," Grace said judiciously. "So you'd be saving two birds with *two* T-shirts," she told Joel impishly.

"I have never wished so much for a bottomless pit to sink into," Joel told Tobi.

But Tobi was nodding excitedly. "I think it's a good idea, Joel. I'll pay for them."

She was about to go back to her rented locker for money when Joel caught her hand and pulled her to himself. He enclosed her again in a long, tight embrace. When he released her, he said, "All of you stay right here. I'll get the T-shirts. What about you, Gloria and Gracie? Shall I get shirts for you, too?"

"No way!" said Grace, striking a pose in her hot pink swim suit. Her young body was firm and rounded, her dark hair framed a face that was as beautiful as her mother's.

"You're right," Joel growled. "T-shirts all around."

In high spirits, Gloria and Grace giggled as they watched him walk away. Then Gloria said to Tobi, "I hope we didn't embarrass you. We didn't mean to."

"Yes, you did," Tobi said. "That's exactly what you meant to do."

The two girls looked at each other and giggled again. "Yes, I guess we did," said Gloria. "But we were just having fun."

"Well, whatever you did it for, I'm grateful to you, Gracie, for thinking of T-shirts. It's a splendid idea," Tobi said, smiling radiantly at Grace. "With your Dad wearing a T-shirt, it will be much easier for me to keep my thoughts under control."

"Why? Do you think Dad is *hot*?" Gloria asked.

"Oh, *yeah*!" Tobi said emphatically. "Don't you?"

"Oooooooo!" both girls said, as one, making faces to express their disgust.

Gloria and Grace were good swimmers. Joel had seen to it as soon as they were old enough to know what, "Hold your breath," meant. And the afternoon slipped past in a happy whirl of splashes, water slides, and dunkings.

The little group arrived at William and Jen Trent's home at 7:30 that evening, sunburned and wet-headed. After introductions were made, Tobi opened her mouth to apologize for her appearance, but Jen spoke first. "Joel Trent, I thought you said you were never going to date a beautiful woman again as long as you live!"

Joel smiled ruefully and looked into Tobi's eyes. "Yep, I said that, but it was before I found out a beautiful woman could have a beautiful spirit, too."

Tobi smiled at his kind words, still gazing into his admiring eyes.

"Oh no! There they go - all googly-eyed again!" Grace said. "Break 'em up or they'll start kissing."

Red-faced, Tobi insisted on helping Jen with something in the kitchen. Gloria and Grace went to shower. And William took his nephew into the den to tell him he'd found a mighty fine woman this time. Mighty fine!

After a sumptuous meal and a pleasant evening, Joel drove Tobi to her motel. They sat in his SUV a few minutes to talk before he went back to his uncle's home. "I wish you weren't leaving tomorrow," he told her. "When I'm with you, I always feel like I have sunshine in my heart. After you leave, it's going to be all rainy in my heart."

Tobi laughed. "I don't want to go off and leave you with a rainy heart, but I do have to go." She stretched up to kiss him tenderly. He held her then, for a long time and, as she thought about her imminent departure, she realized her heart was feeling a little rainy too. So were her eyes.

"Don't cry," he whispered when a tear fell on his arm. "We'll be back next week in time for the parade."

"I know, but I'll miss you until then," she told him. "And that reminds me - I never told you what DeeDee said last night." She explained how DeeDee had worried and prayed all evening for Ben. "Sometime during the evening, she decided she didn't say 'I love you' often enough to the people she cares about. So she told me to kiss you and tell you she loves you."

Joel tightened his embrace. "Well, you hug her for me and tell her I love her too."

"Okay," Tobi said. "And Joel?"

"Yes?"

"I love you, too."

"And I love you."

Ben Walling was wrangling around his office like a wounded bear. Watching from the kitchen, DeeDee thought once she even heard a low roar. She had been annoyed with him for breaking her # 1 rule of family life by missing dinner. So when he arrived home after Davy was in bed and Alison had gone out with friends, she had greeted him coolly. Now she was annoyed with herself for being annoyed with Ben.

As she watched, she prayed for wisdom - should she go apologize or leave him alone to work on his mystery? Finally she walked softly to the open door of his office and waited. When he saw her, she would be guided by his reaction.

It only took a moment. Ben saw her and covered the distance between them in an instant. "DeeDee! Thank God you're here! Please sit down and tell me what you think."

He led her to his swivel chair and held it for her. "Look, honey, I'm really sorry I missed dinner," he said, as she sat down. "I lost track of time."

"It's okay," she said. "I'm sorry I got mad at you. Now, tell me what's wrong."

He summarized the information he had gotten about Lynx from Tyson Banning. "Okay, now here's the thing I'm trying to figure out," he continued. "At this farm house, there was a fingerprint that matches a fingerprint on that toddler's diaper bag. You know, Lynx's son Trevor."

DeeDee nodded. "Yes, I know who you mean."

"Well, we had been hoping the finger print would be a clue to Lynx's murderer. And that made sense because it matched prints in several murder cases around the country. But if that's the case, then Lynx's murderer was at that farm house..."

His voice trailed off. DeeDee looked up and saw that he was lost in thought. "And?" she prompted.

"Well, what would the murderer have been doing at the farm house? How did he even know about the farm house? I don't think Lynx ever went there, so he couldn't have followed him there."

"Maybe he followed Tyson Banning there."

"Maybe. But I don't see how he could without Tyson realizing he was being followed. Besides, how would he know about Tyson? Tyson and Lynx didn't make contact often and, when they did, they were very careful about it..."

When his voice trailed off again, DeeDee asked, "Like what?"

Ben looked up, almost startled at the sound of her voice. "Well, Lynx had his house and back yard protected with burglar alarms. But when he expected Tyson, he turned the system off for five minutes. Tyson had to ride his bike somewhere, sneak out the back door of the house or store he was in, and run back to Tomlin Street. If he was sure he wasn't being followed, he would walk up the alley and go through the back yard gate during the five minute window when the burglar alarm was off. If he didn't make it in time, he knew to come again the next night one hour later. Other than those occasions, they communicated by telephone."

"Who was Lynx afraid of?" DeeDee asked.

"I don't know," Ben said, "and I have to find Patrice Lacey or I'll never know."

He studied his wife. "So what do you think?"

"You mean, where do I think Patrice is?" she asked.

"No. The fingerprint. Does it belong to the person who murdered Lynx? Or does it belong to Lynx?"

DeeDee shrugged. "I should think it belongs to Lynx. He owned the farm house didn't he?"

"He leased it," said Ben, "and it makes sense that it was his fingerprint."

DeeDee nodded. "Sure. Why does that bother you?"

"It doesn't bother me," Ben corrected. "But it changes the direction of my thinking. It means Lynx himself was a murderer. So maybe the motive for *his* murder was revenge. Or could it have been mob related? Or..."

When he paused, DeeDee said, "I get the idea. Is there any way I can help?"

He gave her a pitiful look. "Yes, feed me."

She smiled. "I'll feed you if you'll kiss me."

"I'll kiss you if you'll forgive me."

"I'll forgive *you* if you'll forgive *me*."

It was a good deal. They kissed on it. Then DeeDee fed her husband.

Chapter XVI

The next morning Joel drove Tobi around the Dallas/Fort Worth metroplex in the truck Judith had reserved, picking up materials for five or six floats. It felt strange to Tobi to be so high in the air, looking down on the other traffic. She enjoyed the sensation as a passenger, but was grateful that Joel was the one maneuvering the unwieldy truck through the busy streets of Dallas and Fort Worth.

As they waited at one store for some merchandise to be loaded, Tobi told Joel about meeting Audrey Mansett the day before. "She's dying of a broken heart," Tobi said. "I'd like to find Kent Grantham and slap him around for giving his Mother so much grief."

"Being a parent isn't easy," Joel said. "I worry almost every day about things I've done wrong. Or things I haven't done at all."

"Is it worth it?" Tobi asked.

Joel answered without hesitation. "Totally." Then he paused before he added, "At least, so far. I hope I feel the same way when they're Kent's age."

"Do you think God ever feels like slapping *us* around?" Tobi asked

"I expect He was about to slap me *down* yesterday when I saw you in that green swim suit," Joel admitted in a husky voice.

Tobi blushed. "Let's not go there," she said with a coquettish glance. "I've been working like crazy to get that image of you out of my mind."

"Really?" Joel looked pleased as he pulled her into his arms and kissed her. "I'm not going to ask what you were thinking. It would not be a good thing for me to know."

Tobi agreed. "That's for sure!"

At that moment the salesman appeared with a charge slip for Tobi to sign and they were soon on their way again.

"Listen," Joel said, as he drove, "Did Gloria and Gracie give you a hard time yesterday when you went shopping? It sounds like they got pretty nosy."

Tobi nodded. "Oh yeah, they were nosy all right." She recounted some of their conversation for him, and he apologized repeatedly.

"Joel! You don't have to apologize for them," Tobi said finally. "I don't mind their questions - it just means they care about you and want to know what's going on in your life. But I was concerned about their approach to the Bible. They seem to think they can pick and choose what they want to believe."

Joel nodded soberly. "I've been concerned too. They won't listen to any criticism of the Vine or its doctrines. And Gracie is still unhappy with me for taking them out of the service the other night."

"Have you told them about Joshua Moses?" Tobi asked.

"I've tried, but they're not willing to listen. And when Rachel gets back, it's going to be worse. According to the girls she was beside herself with excitement when she heard an evangelist was bringing the Toronto so-called Blessing to town."

Tobi frowned anxiously. "What are you going to do, Joel?"

"Pray," he said. "What else can I do?"

She shrugged. "Not much. But do keep trying to talk to them. I would hate for them to have to learn from experience what's wrong with Charismatic doctrine."

He already knew about her experiences, which included an ex-husband who had been praying earnestly for her to die so he could marry his new love without committing the sin of divorce. And the worst blow of all had been the death of her beloved parents on the highway after they had attended a healing service to which she'd sent them in Abilene. The guilt of their death had plagued her ever since.

Most of the talk was light-hearted for the rest of the morning, and Tobi noted how easy it was to talk to Joel or just be quiet with him. It was an important point.

The last stop of the morning was in Fort Worth. Gloria and Gracc met them for lunch on the west side of the city. After they ate, Tobi would start for Deepwater while Joel and his daughters returned to Dallas.

They were almost through with their meal when Gloria said, "So, Dad, you believe the Bible is true from start to finish. Right?"

"Of course," he said.

"Okay. Here's what we want to know. Tobi was telling us yesterday that God's laws are for all ages. So if it was all right for the Patriarch

Jacob to have four wives, it should be all right for you, too. So why don't you?"

Joel looked at Tobi; Tobi nearly choked; and Gloria and Grace gazed at their father.

Joel took a drink of his iced tea while he considered the question. Finally he asked, "Is this your way of telling me you want four more mothers, just like Rachel?"

The girls' eyes widened. "Uh!" Gloria said.

"Not like Mom," Grace said. "But we wouldn't mind four more like Tobi."

Tobi smiled gratefully at her, but said nothing. She had no intention of getting involved in this exchange.

"Don't get us wrong, we love Mom," Gloria said quickly. "But we don't want *four* more of her around."

Joel shrugged. "Well, it's taken me all my life to find one Tobi. I don't have much hope of finding three more of her."

He smiled at her affectionately, and she said softly, "I should hope not."

Since they had an audience present, Joel and Tobi kept their parting brief. "It's only for a few days," they reminded each other, as they kissed and hugged. Then Gloria and Grace hugged Tobi, and Joel helped her up into the cab of the truck. "Are you sure you don't want me to come along and drive?" he asked. "I could fly back tomorrow."

"Of course not," she said, waving him off. "I can't thank you enough for doing the driving this morning. But I'll be okay on the highway."

She had barely left the outskirts of Fort Worth when her cell phone rang. It was Ben. "Where are you?" he asked.

"Just leaving Fort Worth," she said.

"Oh good, you're practically home," he said. "You remember about not going to check on the Arkansas float, don't you?"

"Ben, I won't see *any* floats today. It's going to take all afternoon to get home."

"I know, but I had to remind you. Listen, what do you remember about the guys building that float?"

"Nothing. Why?"

"Well, one of them was hanging around Lincoln Nix's house before it was bombed, and afterward, too. I have a picture of him in the area. I want all the information you have on those guys."

"It's at Dalton's office," Tobi said. "Go over there and tell Judith, his secretary, that you need it. I'll phone her now and ask her to make copies for you."

There was a pause on the other end of the line before Ben said, "You call the richest man in town 'Dalton'?"

"Sure," Tobi said. "That's his name."

Ben whistled and hung up.

Tobi punched in Judith's number and asked her to make the copies Ben wanted. She told Judith she expected to be in Deepwater around 4:00, and Judith said she would have a couple of men waiting to deliver the materials Tobi had picked up. "It's good timing," she said, sounding pleased, "right at the end of the day. And the float builders will have their supplies for the weekend."

It was 4:30 when Judith left Tobi at her own doorstep with overnight bag and packages in tow. "You'll go see Dalton tomorrow, won't you?" Judith asked. "He says he doesn't want to be a nuisance, but he misses you."

"Of course," Tobi promised. "I can't wait to see for myself how he's doing."

Inside the house, on her answering machine, she found a message from DeeDee: "Dinner will be at 6:30. We'll expect you by 6:00 - no excuses. I want to hear about Joel. Don't go near the Arkansas float!"

Tobi shook her head, but she was smiling. "Thanks, Sis, I needed that," she whispered. She didn't want to spend the entire evening mooning over Joel and reminding herself how much she missed him.

―――

When Tobi walked into DeeDee's kitchen an hour later, DeeDee threw her arms around her. "You're back! I'm so glad. Did you have any trouble? How's Joel?"

"No trouble. Joel's good," Tobi said. "He said to tell you that he loves you too."

DeeDee put Tobi to work chopping vegetables and then they caught each other up on the events of the past two days. Tobi was understandably concerned about the men building the Arkansas float. "Did Ben say they were doing a good job on it, or is it just a front for some kind of criminal activity?" she asked.

"He didn't say. You'll have to ask him yourself," said DeeDee. "He's been so preoccupied with this case that I don't ask questions. I just listen when he needs to talk."

Tobi nodded. "Is he making progress?"

"Some. He found a teenager named Tyson Banning who worked for Lynx. Tyson gave him a lot of information, and now Ben's trying to sort it all out."

"Aunt Tobi!" Davy yelled, banging in from the back yard with two dogs, Pogo and Jasper, at his heels. "What did you bring me from Dallas?"

"Aunt Tobi!" Ben said, appearing in the kitchen door. "What did you bring me from Dallas?"

"How about giving her a hug before you start looking for presents?" DeeDee said reproachfully. Then she added, "Of course, I've already hugged her. So, Sis, what did you bring me from Dallas?"

Tobi collected her hugs and greeted the two dogs. Pogo was a ten-year-old mutt and long-time family pet. Jasper was a German Shepherd puppy Kent Grantham had given to Tobi and Tobi had given to Davy. Both animals greeted her as a long-lost love with wagging tails and sloppy doggy kisses.

Then Tobi passed out chocolates to Ben, a video game to Davy, and a blouse to DeeDee. As they were giving her thank you hugs, Alison sailed in, breathless and excited to see Tobi. She squealed with delight over the sun dress Tobi had brought her. "Thank you so much! I'm going to go put it on right now!" she said, dashing out of the kitchen.

Davy had already gone to his room to play with his new game, so Tobi turned to Ben. "What's the problem with the Arkansas float? Why do you and DeeDee keep telling me to stay away from it?"

"Tobi," he said with an undertone of excitement in his voice, "do you know what farm house they're using to build that float?"

"No clue."

"The one Kent Grantham rented to hide his red sports car when he framed you for his stepfather's murder."

"You don't mean...?"

"It's beginning to look that way," he said. "The farm belongs to a Mavis Gum, but Mrs. Gum is in a nursing home, and she recently turned over all her business to her daughter Lannie Newcomb, who lives in Oklahoma City. I wasn't able to speak to Mrs. Newcomb until today."

"And she said it's still rented to Kent?" Tobi asked with a worried frown.

"He's the last one Mrs. Gum rented it to. I spoke to her in May after Don Rawls followed Kent to the farm. Do you remember that?"

Tobi nodded. She remembered it vividly.

"But Kent paid for six months in advance, and Mrs. Newcomb had no way of knowing he's incarcerated."

"What does it mean? I don't get it," Tobi said with a little shiver.

"I think it means Kent passed the house keys on to his buddies, so they would have a place to stay in Deepwater. And they took on the Arkansas float as cover - you know, to explain why they're here."

"But why are they *really* here?" Tobi asked.

Ben didn't answer for a few moments. Finally, he said, "Well, I can only speculate, but it obviously has something to do with Lincoln Nix."

"But Lynx is dead. Why are they still here? Are they going to go off and leave the Arkansas float half finished? What does it look like? Is it a real float or just an excuse for a float?" she asked, growing more upset with every question.

"Calm down," Ben said. "They're doing an excellent job. They're building a spring for Hot Springs, Arkansas. I think they're trying to represent it as a place of healing and recuperation for the nation."

"That's right," Tobi said, "I remember now. And it looks good?"

Ben nodded. "They're doing some serious work on it."

"So why are they hanging around now that Lynx is dead?" she asked.

"Just speculation," he cautioned her again, "but I think he had something they want."

"Something like what?"

"I don't know, Tobi. That's why this case is making me old before my time. I can't get a firm grip on anything about it."

His frustration was obvious in his voice, and she looked at him, surprised. "I'm sorry I asked," she said. "I didn't mean to upset you."

He shook his head and brought his voice back to its normal tone. "You don't upset me. The case upsets me."

DeeDee and Tobi exchanged glances, then DeeDee opened her mouth to change the subject. But Ben spoke first. "Patrice Lacey. I have to find Patrice Lacey." He went off to his study, muttering to himself.

Tobi watched him go, then said, "Does he do that often?"

"What?" DeeDee asked, glancing after Ben.

"Mutter."

"No. Only when he's really frustrated."

Alison returned, then, modeling her new dress. She twirled and the full skirt floated gracefully around her in shades of green on a white background. "How do I look?"

"Beautiful!" said DeeDee.

"Gorgeous!" said Tobi.

"Aunt Tobi, you should go to Dallas more often," Alison said giving Tobi a hug. "I can't wait to wear it somewhere."

"Gloria and Gracie helped me pick it out," Tobi told her.

Alison looked interested. "Did you spend much time with them?"

"We went shopping yesterday morning and to a water park in the afternoon."

"So what do you think," Alison asked, "am I going to like having them for cousins?"

Tobi gave her a severe look. "Well, I can say this - the three of you are all cut out of the same cloth. They kept asking me embarrassing questions, too."

"Like what?" Alison asked.

"Like whether I'm going to marry their father."

"Are you?" Alison asked with a wicked gleam in her eye.

"I don't know."

"Is that what you told them?"

"Word for word," Tobi said.

"Has he asked you to marry him?" Alison asked.

At the sink, DeeDee cocked her head to listen. "No, DeeDee, he hasn't asked," Tobi told her sister's back.

Tobi went to see Dalton Granville the first thing Saturday morning. He was sitting in a chair and seemed stronger. His beautiful white hair had been washed and styled. His mustache had been trimmed. And his blue eyes were bright and clear. "You look wonderful!" she told him.

"I'm starting to feel wonderful," he said. "And how are you?"

Tobi told him about her trip to Dallas and how much she had enjoyed seeing Joel. "You paid for all of it," she said, dropping a light kiss on his cheek. "Thank you so much."

He touched his cheek and smiled at her. "You just paid me back for every bit of it. Now! What are you up to today?"

"I'm going to visit as many of the floats as I can. Time is getting short, you know."

"Less than a week," he agreed. "Well, you run on and take care of business."

"When are you going home?" Tobi asked.

"The doctor says if I'm really, really good, maybe Monday. Tuesday for sure."

"I'm so glad," Tobi said. "Please be really, really good."

He grinned. "I'm going to try really, really hard."

Tobi's next stop was the police station where Ben met her and fitted her with the same listening device he had worn earlier that week. "You're sure you want to do this?" he asked her.

She shrugged. "I don't think you would let me if there were any danger."

"*Probably* not," he said with an mischievous grin. "Now remember, don't try to pry any incriminating information out of them or act suspicious in any way. But you might notice whether you see any signs of women around. When I talked to them, they said their wives were at the mall. I'd like to know if they really have wives with them or not."

Tobi consulted her clipboard. "Let's see, Harry and Myra Marcum are in charge of the project. So a Mrs. Marcum should be around somewhere." She looked up with a frown, trying to remember what Ben had told her earlier. "Where did you say those guys are from? Are any of them local?"

Ben took out his notebook and found the notations he'd made about the owners of the vehicles he'd seen at the farm house. "There was a pickup - it belongs to Matt Tatum of Austin. A motorcycle registered to Lyndon Deatherage of Waco. And the two cars belong to Harry Marcum and Isaac Simmons, both of Houston."

"What did Judith tell you yesterday?" Tobi asked. "When she was looking for parade participants, where did she find the Marcums?"

"She didn't find them," Ben said. "There was a writeup in the newspaper a month ago. One of the Granville Industry phone numbers was given in the article, so that anyone who read the article and wanted to build a float could call Judith. Harry called her."

Tobi shivered. "So these guys have been here awhile. Did they come here to help Kent escape? Or to destroy Lincoln Nix's world?"

"That's a question I'd like to ask them," Ben said.

Tobi nodded. "Well, let's get on with it, then."

"Okay," Ben said. "Remember, you're just doing your job. I've got you wired to make sure you're safe, not because I want you to ask nosy questions."

"Right, chief," Tobi said. "I'm no hero."

But her visit to the Arkansas float required no heroics, just nerves of steel. When Tobi arrived, only Matt and Harry were on the premises. "It's beautiful!" she told them, as she gazed at the hot tub they were disguising as a hot spring from the mountains of Arkansas. "It's wonderful of you to come here and do all this work."

"No problem," Harry told her. "Mr. Granville said he was looking for somebody who loves Arkansas and wants the whole world to know why he's proud of his state. I told him I was his man."

"And your wife - is she from Arkansas, too?" Tobi asked.

"Nope, Myra's a Texan. That's why we live in Texas," he said.

"Is she around? I'd love to meet her." Tobi let her gaze roam around the rickety, old barn. Other than the float and float materials, it was empty. Under the hay mow, which held nothing but dust and cobwebs, a door opened into another section of the barn. She could see a couple of empty stalls beyond the door.

"Nope, she's checking on the artist who's painting our banner," Harry said.

Tobi nodded. "What's the banner going to say?"

Harry frowned. "The ladies have been handling that. Do you remember, Matt?"

"Hot Springs, Arkansas..." Matt said, then paused. "Well, something like '...where Americans bathe away all their cares'."

"It's going to be wonderful, and we do appreciate your hard work," Tobi told them sincerely. "Is there anything, at all, I can do to help?"

"Well," Matt said, "we were thinking we'd have an actual person in the spring, and a wheel chair next to the spring. If you run across anybody who looks like they have some cares they need to bathe away and they want to be in the parade, you might send them our way. Otherwise, I'll have to hogtie Harry and Myra and toss them on the float."

Tobi smiled and made a note to herself. "Okay, if you think of anything else, give me a call. You still have the number, don't you?"

They assured her they did, and Tobi started toward the door.

"Oh by the way," Matt called after her, "if you should run across Kent, tell him Matt and Harry say hello."

Tobi froze for a moment. Then she turned and gave him a puzzled look. "Who?"

"Kent," Matt repeated. "What was his last name, Harry?"

Harry shrugged. "I forget."

"Well, never mind, then," Matt said with a careless wave of his hand. "Catch you later." And he went back to his hammering.

Tobi knew there must be a correct response to Matt's strange request, which she took to be a veiled threat, but she couldn't begin to think what it was. Her mind felt scrambled. She didn't dare pursue the matter. So she turned automatically, walked to her car, and drove away, passing Ben without a glance in his direction. When they met at the police station, she asked, "What was I supposed to say to *that*?" Her hands were trembling. She wanted to cry. She wanted to scream. She wanted to make Kent Grantham cry and scream.

Ben gave her a quick hug. "You handled it fine, Tobi. Don't give it another thought."

"Right! Of course, Kent's not waiting outside so he can follow me wherever I go. Or hiding in the alley behind my house so he can sneak in after dark. Or..."

"Tobi, stop!" Ben ordered. "You're just making yourself crazy. Is Kent stupid?"

"Of course not!"

"Then he's left the country. He would have to be stupid to be hanging around now."

"He's not stupid," Tobi said, "but he does think he's invincible - that he can do whatever he wants to and use either his wits or his money to get out of any problem."

When Ben didn't reply, Tobi looked at him. He had a worried expression on his face. "Maybe you should move in with us again," he said.

"Maybe I should get my gun back again," she said, glaring at him. "Where is it, anyway?"

"It's here at the department - it's evidence."

"Right. Evidence for a case that's never going to trial because the defendant escaped."

"Look, Tobi, if you want a gun, we'll get you a gun," Ben said seriously.

She buried her face in her hands. "There's a good idea - he'd take it away from me and shoot me with it. Look, I'm sorry, Ben. Why do those guys keep hanging around here? It's not loyalty to the state of Arkansas - I'm sure of that."

"They're here because of Lincoln Nix."

"Because they want something he had?" Tobi asked.

"That's the way it looks," Ben said.

"Then why aren't they looking for it instead of building a float?" Tobi asked.

"I told you, the float is their cover. And they're not looking because there's no place to look. At least not at the moment."

"Ben quit talking in riddles," Tobi said. "What are they doing?"

Ben studied her a moment before he said, "If I tell you, you have to promise me two things - that you'll pray about it and that you won't tell anyone else what I'm going to say."

It was an unusual request, but Tobi was happy to comply. "Sure," she said.

"They're waiting for Patrice Lacey to return," Ben said. "Pray that I get to her before they do."

Chapter XVII

By Sunday morning, Ben had reached the end of his patience with Rachel Hudson and Patrice Lacey. "I'm going to Green Bay," he told DeeDee, thumbing through the phone book to find the numbers of airlines or travel agents, whichever he came to first.

"When?" DeeDee asked.

"Now. Right now!"

DeeDee took the book away from him and fixed a stern gaze on him. "No! You're going to rest today. Relax and forget the case. Tomorrow you can go to Green Bay."

Ben stared back at her for only a moment before he collapsed onto the bed. "You're right. I've got to relax or I'll go nuts."

That afternoon, Ben called Paul Hudson to see if Paul would make the trip to Green Bay with him and help him convince Rachel to tell them where Patrice was. "I have patients scheduled all day," Paul said regretfully, "but I can make the arrangements for you. I know a travel agent who can do magic. Tell me when you want to go and return."

"Hey, good deal!" Ben said. "But I need you to do something more important for me - don't tell Rachel I'm coming. If you do, she may disappear too."

It was just before 10:30 Monday morning when Ben parked a budget rental car in front of an attractive brick home in a quiet residential section of Green Bay, Wisconsin. Paul Hudson had given Ben the address and phone number for his parents' home and, from the internet, he had printed out a map with detailed directions for getting to the house.

He consulted the map and address one more time before he got out. Satisfied that he was at the right place, he walked up the sidewalk and rang the front doorbell. When no one answered, he knocked loudly. Still no answer. So he pulled out his notepad, checked the phone number, and called it. Inside, the phone rang and rang, but no one picked it up.

Ben rang the doorbell again and waited. Nothing. So he hammered on the door and yelled, "Mrs. Hudson. I'm Ben Walling from the Deepwater Police Department. I must speak to you."

When he still got no response, he sat down on the top step of the porch to wait five minutes. Maybe she was in the shower. After waiting the longest five minutes of his life, he repeated the doorbell, the knocking, and the phone call. Nothing.

He sat down again and called Paul Hudson at his dental office in Deepwater. "I could use your help," he told Paul. "No one answers the door. Do you think she's out? Would you give me her cell phone number?"

"I'm sure she's there," Paul said. "Where are you now?"

"I'm sitting on your parents' porch," Ben said.

"Good. Sit tight," Paul said. "Let me try. She doesn't know who you are, and she's pretty jumpy. If she doesn't open the door in five minutes, call me back."

Ben consulted his watch and prepared to wait another endless five minutes, but the door opened in less than two minutes. "Detective Walling?"

Ben stood and turned, expecting to see the beautiful woman Tobi had described to DeeDee. Instead, Rachel's platinum blond hair was flat and uncombed. She had dark circles under her eyes and wore no makeup.

"Mrs. Hudson?" he asked.

"That's right," she said. "Paul says I have to talk to you, but you're wasting your time. I have nothing to say."

She led Ben into a gloomy den, which he thought must be a favorite hangout of Paul's father, judging by the massive, dark furniture and the green and gold decor. A large fireplace undoubtedly made this the coziest room in the house in winter. But in summer it offered a dreary contrast to sunshine, blue skies, and lush grass.

The furniture, upholstered in expensive leather, was deep and comfortable; but Ben perched on the edge of a chair and Rachel perched on the edge of the sofa. They faced each other with tense, grim expressions on their faces. What followed was one of the most difficult interviews of Ben's career. Rachel insisted she had absolutely nothing to tell him and, to every question Ben asked, she gave a shrug or a sulky, "I don't know."

Finally he got up, placed a small ottoman in front of his chair, then sank back into the depths of the chair with his legs extended. "I'm not leaving until you tell me what you know," he said. "You can start when you're ready."

She gave him a resentful look, then said through gritted teeth, "I don't know any specifics, but Lincoln Nix earned his living by blackmail."

Ben frowned. "What?"

"Blackmail! You know - you give me money or I'll rat you out to the police. Or to your wife. Or to your boss. Or to your whoever."

"For example?"

"I told you, I don't know specifics. Whatever Patrice knew - and it wasn't much - she didn't want me to know."

"Because?"

"She was terrified of Lynx."

"Afraid he would do what?" Ben asked.

"Kill her, I assume," Rachel said.

"Did she know for a fact he was a murderer?" Ben asked, remembering Tyson Banning's belief that Lynx might kill him and his mother.

"I don't know," Rachel said.

"Mrs. Hudson," Ben said, almost too angry to hide the fact any longer, "you have to tell me where Patrice is. It's the only way to clear her name."

"Detective Walling, I don't know where she is," Rachel snapped, and her fury was not concealed as well as his. "Do you think I would be perched here like a sitting duck if I knew where she is?"

"Where would you be?" Ben asked.

Rachel tightened her lips, but gave no answer.

"Mrs. Hudson," Ben said in his best bad-cop voice, "contrary to popular opinion, small town cops aren't idiots. If your niece hasn't done anything wrong, she has nothing to fear from cops."

Rachel spat her next words at him. "Cops? She's not afraid of cops!"

Ben went absolutely still. Maybe he was about to get some information from her, at last. "Then who is she afraid of?"

"Whoever killed him, of course."

"And who does she think that is?"

"One of his blackmail victims."

"She knows who they are, doesn't she?" he asked quietly.

"She didn't," Rachel said defensively.

"But?"

"When she found his body, she took all his notes and hid them. They were in a safe in the basement of his house, and he had told her to get them out of there if anything happened to him."

"What was in the notes?"

"Everything about his blackmail victims. Names. Dates. Payments."

"But you don't know any specifics?"

"I do not. For my own protection, Patrice said."

"Does she have these notes with her now?" Ben asked.

Rachel shook her head.

Ben frowned. "No?"

Rachel shook her head again.

"You mean they're in Deepwater?"

"I don't know."

"For your own protection?" he asked.

"That's right."

With a frustrated sigh, Ben took out his cell phone and called the Deepwater P.D. "Get a search warrant and search Patrice Lacey's apartment," he told Don Rawls. Then he looked at Rachel, "What's the address?"

"4312 Wheeling, # 18."

Ben gave Rawls the address and explained the what and why for the search, then put his phone away. "I'd like for you to come back to Deepwater with me," he told Rachel.

"No," she said flatly.

He sighed and rose. Out of his wallet he took a business card and handed it to her. "If you decide you want to tell me anything else, please call."

She took the card and set it on a coffee table without so much as glancing at it.

Ben walked to the door, thanking God he didn't have to deal with this woman every day. At the door he stopped and asked a question he hadn't asked anybody else since the case began. And, other than divine intervention, he couldn't explain why he asked Rachel Hudson. "You wouldn't happen to know a Jess Hurley, would you?" he asked over his shoulder.

He almost walked out the door, because he was so sure he would hear a surly "No" hurled at his back. But he heard nothing. When he turned around to look at Rachel, her pale face had blanched. Then the blood rushed to her cheeks in a fury beyond her previous anger. "Why would you ask me that?" she asked through clenched teeth.

"Because I want to know," he said.

"Don't play games with me!" she snapped. "Why did you ask about Jess Hurley?"

"He's preaching at your church. He goes by the name Joshua Moses now."

The horror in her expression was unmistakable. "I'm going back to Deepwater," she said. "Would you be kind enough to see if you can get me on a flight today?"

Ben pulled a ticket out of his shirt pocket. "We fly out at 2:00 P.M.," he said.

Rachel glanced at her watch, snatched the ticket, and disappeared into the back of the house. "I'll get packed," she called.

When Rachel returned, both her appearance and demeanor had changed. Her fair hair was curled and combed and her makeup was flawless. She was dressed in an expensive light blue suit. But, more important to Ben, she had become meek. And talkative. During the flight, in quiet tones, she told Ben what she knew about Jess Hurley. "Jess Hurley," she said, "is the father of Lincoln Nix."

Before Ben could begin to react to this thunderbolt, she added another to it, through tears. "And I am his mother."

Rachel and Jess had met in Austin, Texas, as high school juniors. He was a football player on a team that won the state championship that year. Rachel's school was also playing for the championship and, because she was a cheerleader, she was in Austin, too.

"We spent every minute we could together," Rachel said. "And when our weekend together was over, I was pregnant, although I didn't know it for three months."

"Was the sex mutual or did he...force you?" Ben asked.

Rachel, resisting tears, hesitated. Finally, with obvious effort, she said, "He forced me at first. But he said he loved me and...and I liked it, so it was mutual after that."

They had written to each other after returning home, but Jess had written only twice. And the letters were perfunctory, not love letters. Even to an immature teenager, it was obvious that he had lost interest in her. And after she found out she was pregnant, she never wrote again - she never heard from him again.

"And you put the baby up for adoption?" Ben asked.

Rachel nodded. "I had a small crush on my Sunday School teacher, so I begged him and his wife to adopt the baby. It seemed like a romantic notion to me at the time. My parents and I moved to Deepwater later, but I knew where Lincoln was and the Nixes must have told him about me. I wasn't surprised when he showed up in Deepwater several years ago. He didn't stay at first but, after Trevor was born, he moved to Deepwater. I think he really cared about Patrice and Trevor."

"I thought you said Patrice was afraid of him."

"She was," Rachel said wearily, "but she was attached to him through Trevor. And maybe she understood that, in his own way, he cared about her."

As Ben tried to digest the information she had just fed him, Rachel said, "Detective Walling, would you mind if I take a nap? I haven't been sleeping well."

The dark circles under her eyes supported her statement, and Ben told her to rest. She didn't waken until the airplane touched down in Dallas. For the rest of the journey - first on another airliner to Midland/Odessa, then in Ben's pickup to Deepwater - she seemed refreshed and tried to answer any questions that occurred to Ben. When they passed the Deepwater city limits, she straightened in her seat and said firmly, "Would you please take me to the Church of the Living Vine?"

He glanced at the dashboard clock. "Services will be over by now, don't you think?"

"You don't know much about Charismatics, do you?" she asked.

"Mr. Hudson will be expecting you," Ben said.

"Detective Walling, it's either yes or no," Rachel said impatiently. "Which is it?"

"I presume you plan to speak to Joshua Moses?" he asked.

"You presume correctly."

"And you think he's still at the Church?"

She smiled sweetly at him. "I can absolutely guarantee it."

Ben didn't say it, but he would be interested to hear what Rachel Hudson had to say to the Rev. Joshua Moses, a.k.a. Jess Hurley. "Sure, why not?" he decided.

He was amazed when they arrived at 9:35 and found the church parking lot crowded with vehicles. He parked on the street and followed Rachel into the sanctuary. What he observed there was so bizarre that he completely forgot Rachel. At first, he thought the congregation was playing "zoo," for he heard wailing, whining and baying; barking, howling, and roaring. Some people were shaking like leaves in a strong wind. The floor was littered with people doing... Well, Ben didn't know what they were doing, including the ones who were lying as still as death.

Rachel drew his attention again when he heard an unearthly screech from the front of the church. Looking for the source of the scream, he saw that Rachel had attacked Joshua Moses. "You killed him!" she was shrieking. "You killed your own son, the father of your own grandson."

She was clawing, scratching, and hitting, but he shoved her aside like a giant, batting away a gnat. So she attached herself to his arm and began kicking. By the time Ben got there, several ushers were holding Rachel away from Moses.

"Get her out of here!" Moses bellowed, his face purple with fury.

"I believe the lady would like to speak to you," Ben said before the ushers could follow his order.

Moses glared at him. "I'm trying to conduct a service here."

Ben glanced around contemptuously. "This is not a service; it's a zoo." He took out his police shield and showed it to Moses.

Moses glanced at it, then stared at Ben. "We've met before, haven't we?" he asked.

"That's right," Ben said, "the day you tried to rape my sister-in-law."

Rachel gasped. "You haven't changed, at all," she screamed. She struggled to loose herself from the hands holding her, but their grip tightened, so she contented herself with shrieking, "You're a monster."

"Perhaps the pastor would be kind enough to let us use his office?" Ben asked, directing his question at Rev. Morel, who was watching in dismay.

"Of course," he stammered, "but...what? Rachel?"

"If you'll kindly move to the back and wait for services to end, I'll be happy to speak to you then," Moses said.

"You'll come with us now or I'll call in backup and we'll take you to the police station," Ben said.

A slight intake of breath came from Rev. Morel who, however, said nothing.

Moses glared at Ben for a few long moments. Then he ripped the microphone from his lapel, tossed it to the floor, and led the way to the pastor's office. Ben, Rachel, and Rev. Morel followed.

As soon as the door closed behind them, Rachel turned on Joshua Moses. "You killed Lincoln Nix. He threatened to blackmail you, and you killed him."

Moses had arranged his face into an expression of exaggerated innocence and complete bafflement. "I don't believe I know..." he began.

But Emory Morel interrupted him. "How did she know that?" he asked.

"Shut up!" Moses snarled in a low voice.

"Know what?" Ben asked.

"That this Lynx character had tried to blackmail Joshua," Rev. Morel said.

All eyes turned on Rachel. "It's what he did for a living," she said. "Of course, he tried to blackmail a father who meant nothing to him."

"Rev. Morel, would you please tell us what you know about all this?" Ben asked.

"Emory, you keep quiet," Moses hissed.

But Rev. Morel was not intimidated. "I got a phone call from someone calling himself Lynx the day Joshua was due to arrive," he said. "Lynx said Joshua was his father and Lynx had some private business to conduct with him. He wanted Joshua to come to his home at 1809 Tomlin Street that evening."

"What day was this?" Ben asked.

"It was a week ago Wednesday," Rev. Morel answered. "When Joshua got here, he said he didn't have a son and wasn't interested in meeting some other man's b...." He paused and looked at Rachel. "Well, he didn't want to go. When I insisted, he agreed to go if I accompanied him."

"What time did you reach his house?" Ben asked.

Rev. Morel had to pause and think about it. "It was between 6:00 and 7:00, but I can't pinpoint the time exactly."

Ben nodded. "Go on."

"Well, this fellow - Lynx - said he was the son of a Jess Hurley and a Rachel Ellison. He claimed Joshua was Jess Hurley. He said he might be persuaded to keep this information quiet if Joshua was willing to pay. Naturally Joshua stormed out and I followed. The whole idea was preposterous!" Rev. Morel hesitated, looked at Rachel, and added, "Well, I thought it was preposterous at the time."

Ben waited for him to go on, but he had nothing more to add.

"What else?" Ben asked.

"Nothing else," Rev. Morel shrugged. "I asked Joshua about it in the car, and he said it was a vicious hoax. He'd never heard of Jess Hurley or...Rachel Ellison."

The entire group looked at Rachel. "What was your maiden name?" Ben asked.

"Ellison," she said softly. Then she turned to Moses, "And you didn't even remember me." Weeping, she left the office.

"Joshua Moses, a.k.a. Jess Hurley, did you kill Lincoln Nix?" Ben asked.

"Of course not!" Moses scoffed. "You heard Emory. The boy was alive when we left his house."

"You could have gone back later," Ben said, "after you left Rev. Morel. Where have you been staying in Deepwater - in a motel or in someone's home?"

"In a motel," Rev. Morel supplied.

Ben shrugged. "So it would have been simple for you to return to Tomlin Street and murder Lincoln Nix."

Moses gave him a pitying look. "Detective, I've read a few newspapers since I arrived. I'm aware that this Lynx character died when a helicopter attacked his house with missiles. Are you suggesting that I have a helicopter hidden somewhere?"

"That's right!" Rev. Morel said excitedly. "We talked about it the day we heard about it - how amazing it was that this very same person should be killed right after he tried to blackmail Joshua!"

"So you see," Moses said calmly, "even if I wanted him dead - which I didn't - someone else did the deed."

Ignoring this remark, Ben turned to the pastor. "Rev. Morel, how much longer are you going to be holding services conducted by Rev. Moses here?"

Emory Morel gave Moses a dark look, then said firmly. "They're over."

Moses looked surprised, but said nothing.

"How long are you planning to be in town, Rev. Moses?" Ben asked.

"Actually, I've arranged my schedule to stay until the Fourth," Moses said. "I understand your town is planning a big celebration this year. I'm looking forward to it."

"Good," Ben said. "I may have more questions to ask you."

"Any time," Moses said to his back. Ben was on his way to find Rachel.

Driving Rachel home, Ben asked, "Do you really think Hurley forgot you?"

She grinned. "I don't much care. But *Emory* cares."

Ben considered her words only a moment before he grinned, too. "I see," he said. "Good work!"

They spent a few satisfying minutes, as they drove through the darkness, imagining the scene in which Rev. Morel gave Rev. Moses a piece of his mind. But Ben's thoughts soon returned to his case. "How did Lynx know Joshua Moses was his father?" he asked.

"I don't know," Rachel said. "How did he know *all* the secrets he knew? It was partly because he was...what do they call it, a hacker?"

Ben nodded. "That's right."

"But he liked 'hands on' snooping too. Do you know what he looked like?"

"No," said Ben. "He has been a deep, dark mystery to me until now."

"Well, he looked like Caspar Milquetoast. He was a little guy - much closer to my size than Jess's - with wire-rimmed glasses; brown hair; green eyes. I bet he could walk into any office in the country and get any information he asked for, just because he could look like a timid lamb. I had told him his father's name was Jess Hurley. He must have found out Jess's new name the same way you did."

"I found out from a private investigator," Ben said.

Rachel shrugged. "Well, however *he* found out, then."

"A timid lamb...," Ben mused. "That wasn't the picture I was getting from the things you told me this afternoon."

"Oh, he didn't always look like a lamb," Rachel said. "He could look like a lynx too - very still, watching, waiting, poised to pounce. He could be terrifying."

Ben nodded, then changed the subject. He had to try one more time to convince her to tell him where Patrice was. "Mrs. Hudson," he said, "I *must* speak to Patrice Lacey. Can't you see how important it is for me to talk to her?"

Rachel sighed deeply. "She'll be on an 8:00 A.M. flight to Dallas Wednesday."

"How do you know?"

"Because I took down the blouse I had hung in the window of my room at Paul's parents' house. She goes by the house every day between 5:00 and 9:00 P.M. to see if it's still in the window. When she went today, it was gone, so she knows it's safe for her to come home. She'll make her flight reservation for Wednesday morning."

"But it's not safe!" Ben said. "There are at least four men waiting for her to return."

Rachel turned wide eyes on him. "But I thought Jess Hurley killed Lynx. Everything matched. Lynx was killed the same night Jess came to town. And Trevor was taken to the police station, for God's sake. Who else but his grandfather would take care of the child after he'd just committed murder?"

"Hurley may have killed Lynx, but some of his blackmail victims annihilated his house early Saturday morning. Now they want whatever evidence he had that implicates them. They seem to know Patrice has it."

"How do you know they know Patrice has it?"

"They're watching her apartment," Ben said.

Rachel stifled a scream. "I have to go back," she cried. "I have to go back to Green Bay and hang the blouse in the window. When she comes tomorrow and sees it there, she'll cancel her flight."

"Mrs. Hudson, she'll never be safe until she comes back and tells me where she put Lynx's notes. Maybe then I'll have enough information to make some arrests."

Rachel began to cry. "I don't know what to do," she sobbed.

Ben patted her arm. "It's not your problem any more," he told her. "I'll make sure she's not hurt. What about the baby - Trevor? Will she have him with her?"

Rachel shook her head. "He's with Patrice's grandmother - not Paul's mother, but her mother's mother. She won't bring him back here until she's been here herself and knows it's safe." Rachel wiped her nose with a tissue she'd found in her purse. "It nearly scared her out of her mind when she couldn't find him that morning."

"Mrs. Hudson...Rachel, you've been a big help today," Ben said, pulling to a stop in front of her home. "I want to thank you."

"You're sure you can keep Patrice safe?" Rachel asked.

"I can't make any guarantees, but I'll do my best," Ben promised.

"Well, then, I guess you're welcome," Rachel said, looking anxiously at her home.

"Are you going to tell him about Lynx?" Ben asked, seeing her nervousness.

She nodded. "Everything. I guess it's about time."

Ben got out of his pickup and lifted Rachel's suitcase out of the back of the truck. "Come on," he said. "I'll walk you to the door."

Chapter XVIII

The week of the Fourth passed in a blur for Tobi. The number of last minute details requiring her attention were endless. She was on the road to Midland Tuesday, driving a Granville Industries pickup to get more materials for floats, when she remembered she had never told Ben about seeing Audrey Mansett in Dallas. She dialed his number and told him about the brief encounter.

"Thanks," Ben said. "I haven't been able to reach her. I was beginning to wonder if she had skipped the country with Kent."

"I don't think she would do that, even if he asked," Tobi said. "She's mortified by his behavior."

"Listen, Tobi, you know you're always welcome at our house, don't you? You didn't come over Saturday night to sleep, and I was so involved in this case that I forgot to insist."

Tobi laughed. "I'm so involved in this parade that I forgot to be afraid."

"Well, if you hear any creaks or squeaks or booms or bumps in the night, don't hesitate to call," Ben said.

"Thank you, I will," Tobi promised. "What about the case? Have you learned anything new?"

"Too much to tell you now," Ben said. "And you'll never guess where I am right this minute."

"Where."

"Pulling up to the curb at Rachel Hudson's home."

"You mean she's back from Green Bay?" Tobi asked.

"She came back with me yesterday," Ben said. "And today she's going to help wrap this case up if I have to spend the whole day with her."

"Better you than me," Tobi said. "I'll pray for you."

"Thank you. Oh, and Tobi," Ben said, suddenly remembering, "I guess you don't know - it turns out that Rachel Hudson and Joshua Moses are the parents of Lincoln Nix."

The phone went dead, and Tobi stared at it with her mouth open. "No way!" she told it.

It sounded like a party was going on at the Hudson's home. Ben followed the sounds into their big two-car garage where he found a bevy of people creating a dairy farm on a low trailer. Rachel, wearing tattered shorts and an old shirt, was in the middle of them, painting the barn red. The dark circles under her eyes were gone, and she was as beautiful as ever in spite of the old clothes. Seeing Ben, she introduced him to the other workers, then led him inside to the kitchen where she poured two cups of coffee and sat down at the kitchen table. "Next question," she said smiling.

"You look relaxed," Ben observed. "Dr. Hudson must have taken your news well."

Rachel's expression grew serious. "Yes, he did," she said. "I never realized until last night what a wonderful man I married."

Ben grinned. "Well, that's a good thing to know."

She smiled back. "Yes. Very good."

"Okay," Ben said. "Here's what I need from you today. Please help me figure out what Patrice Lacey did with the material she took from Lynx's safe. Tell me everything she did from the time she found his body until the two of you boarded the plane for Green Bay."

Rachel nodded and paused, thinking back to that day. "She got here... between 8:30 and 9:00, I guess. Joel had already called me, so I knew what had happened to Trevor. Of course, I didn't know why until Patrice arrived and told me Lynx was dead. We went straight to the courthouse. I parked on one side of it and Patrice parked on the other. You already know what we did."

She looked at him with sad eyes. "I'm so sorry for that. We didn't know how to get Trevor back without answering a lot of questions. And Patrice was about to fly apart at the seams, not knowing where he was." She hesitated before she asked, "Are we in trouble for taking him? For breaking and entering, you know?"

"Technically, yes," Ben said. "But the lady who was going to keep Trevor was so distraught that her son came and took her home with him to San Diego. She may be so grateful Trevor is safe that she won't press charges when she gets back."

"She must be a very nice woman," Rachel said.

Ben smiled. "She's a grandmother."

"I know we caused her a lot of grief," Rachel said. "I'll write her a note apologizing and thanking her for taking care of Trevor. And I'll pay for the window, of course!"

"I think that would make her feel better about everything," Ben said.

"Anyway, as soon as we had Trevor," Rachel continued, "we packed and got out of town. Patrice would barely let me out of her sight. She was terrified that whoever killed Lynx had seen her at his house, followed her, and was going to force her to give him everything from the safe."

"Are you saying she wanted to keep it for herself? Was she going to take over Lynx's blackmail business?"

"Of course not!" Rachel cried indignantly. "She wanted to give it to the police or the FBI so his 'clients,' as he called them, could be notified to quit sending him money."

"Then why *didn't* she?" Ben asked. "Why didn't she trot herself down to the police station and say, 'Here's all this evidence and I want my son back'?"

Rachel gave him a guilty look. "I wouldn't let her. We were so confused and terrified that I told her we had to get away from it and think about it. I was afraid she would be blamed because she...wanted him dead. I was hoping we could manufacture an alibi for her. I don't know. We were so frightened we barely knew what we were doing."

Ben nodded. He could understand the terror that had driven them. "Okay, back to your story - where did you catch a plane?"

"At the Midland/Odessa airport."

"How did you get there?"

"In my car."

"Is it still at the airport?"

"No, Paul had the girls from his office drive over and get it."

"Okay. We'll need to search your car," Ben said, making himself a note.

"And Patrice's car," Rachel said. "I know where the spare keys are."

Ben looked up from his notepad, frowning. "I'm afraid we won't need them," he said. Patrice's place has been trashed. The car was searched and the upholstery was slashed."

"No!" Rachel gasped. She got up, went to the sink, rinsed her coffee cup, and drew a cup of water, which she gulped down. Finally, she returned to the kitchen table. "You can't let her come back here! What will they do to her?"

"Nothing if we get them first," Ben said.

"Can you do that?" Rachel asked doubtfully.

"*We're* going to do that," Ben said. "You and I are going to do that."

"I?" Rachel's eyes were wide and frightened.

"Yes. *You* are going to help me figure out where those notes are!"

Rachel nodded. "I'll try, but where do we start?"

"Well the information wasn't in her apartment," Ben said, "because the men who were looking for it are still hanging around. So we have to think where else it could be."

"Okay, we're going to check my car," Rachel said. "Where else?"

"Were the two of you ever separated after you got to the airport?" Ben asked.

Rachel shook her head.

"You say she arrived here between 8:30 and 9:00?"

"Yes, I'm pretty sure that's right. Joel called about...oh, 8:15, I guess. I'm sure it was 15 minutes or more after he hung up before Patrice came."

"What time was she due at work?"

"Seven forty-five."

"Then she must have gotten to Lynx's house by 7:30 at the very latest," Ben said. "Does that sound right?"

Rachel nodded.

"She finds Lynx dead," Ben said, speaking more to himself than to Rachel, "then she searches the house for Trevor. That's what? Ten minutes?"

It was obvious he didn't expect an answer so Rachel simply listened. "We've got a good hour - probably more - unaccounted for." He looked at Rachel suddenly. "Did she say - was the front door locked?"

"Yes," said Rachel, "but not the dead bolts, just the one in the door knob that you could lock from the inside. And the burglar alarm was disconnected."

"You know what she did?" Ben asked, sounding excited.

"What?" Rachel asked.

Ben thought a bit longer, then said, "She took everything from that safe, went out the back door in case someone was watching the house, and took it somewhere. Now where would she take it? A safety deposit box?"

Rachel shook her head. "Not that early in the morning."

"Where, Rachel?" Ben asked earnestly. "You're the only one who can tell me."

But she was ahead of him. "I know!" she cried. "It's in our locker at the health club."

"Where is the health club?"

"About six blocks from Lynx's house. She could get there by going down back alleys most of the way!" Rachel said.

"That's it!" Ben exclaimed. "That's it!" He was so excited he would have hugged her and whirled her around if she had been DeeDee or Tobi. But he contented himself with wringing her hand. "You've done it! Now, all we have to do is figure out how to get to it without being seen."

Rachel's excitement was replaced with alarm. "What do you mean? Is someone watching this house?"

"I expect so," Ben said. "And I'm sure I'm being followed."

He thought a few minutes, then said, "Okay, here's what I want you to do. I'm going to have you give DeeDee the name of the health club, the number of the locker, and the locker combination." He already had his phone out, dialing his home phone number.

"Who's DeeDee?" Rachel asked.

"Hmm?" Ben gave her a distracted look. "Oh, my wife."

When DeeDee answered, he told her what he wanted her to do. "I'm going to put Mrs. Hudson on in a minute to give you the locker number and combination," he said. "But listen carefully. I'm going to have Rawls drive by the house in a patrol car. Don't leave the house until you see him go by. Then he'll follow you to the health club and to the police station. He won't get close, but he'll make sure you're not being followed."

"Me?" DeeDee squealed. "You think someone is following me?"

"Of course not," he said. "If I did, I wouldn't send you. Okay, any questions?"

"You want me to go to a health club, open a locker, get some stuff out of it and take the stuff to the police station," DeeDee said. "I think I can handle that without straining too many brain cells."

"I know you can. That's why I married you," Ben said. Then he handed the phone to Rachel.

After they had finished talking to DeeDee and Ben had spoken to Don Rawls, he asked Rachel, "Did you or Patrice ever actually see anyone following you before you left for Green Bay?"

She shook her head. "No. We were watching every second, and we never saw anything suspicious, at all."

Ben nodded. "Do you know what I think that means?"

To his surprise, she was nodding her head slowly. "Yes," she said. "Jess Hurley."

An hour later Ben's desk was covered with more evidence than he had ever wanted. Lincoln Nix had kept meticulous notes about every diabolical scheme he carried out - or failed to carry out. He had been a master computer hacker and a dedicated researcher. As a result, he knew intimate details about some very wealthy people. He had used this information to commit crimes - from embezzlement to murder - and frame his wealthy targets. Then sometimes he stumbled across information he could use outright for blackmail, as in the case of Kent Grantham's group of murdering conspirators.

Typically, once he chose a victim, Lynx would travel to the city where he or she lived, and put his target under surveillance. When he was confident that he was in control of every detail, he would commit the crime, creating a piece of evidence to use against his target. He didn't make mistakes, and he didn't take no for an answer. Communicating with them by phone, email, or in disguise, he demanded monthly cash payments. Those who didn't comply, died mysteriously. Newspaper accounts of their unsolved murders were collected and used to persuade future victims.

Ben paused to ponder this paradox. Lynx went to great pains to obtain or create evidence to blackmail his victims; yet he punished their noncompliance by murdering them instead of following through with the blackmail threat. Why?

When no answer occurred to him, Ben returned to his reading. He found one group of files labeled, "Jon-Benet Syndrome." Frowning he read through a couple of case histories. Apparently, Lynx believed that he could kill a child in the home, then hide the body in the home, and the police would automatically blame the parents. It was simple to obtain a parent's shirt or shoe and drip blood on it, then blackmail the parent.

Ben pushed all the files away from himself, leaned back in his chair, and closed his eyes. He was feeling nauseous. It had been a game to Lynx and children were pawns in his sick game. Ben was sorry Lynx was dead - dying was a fate too gentle for him.

Five minutes passed. Ben sat motionless, afraid if he opened his eyes or moved a muscle he would begin retching or weeping. Neither behavior was acceptable in a homicide detective. "Lord, protect the babies and the children," he prayed, as he waited for the nausea to recede. "Dear God, please don't let Davy or Allison or DeeDee ever cross paths with a soulless monster like Lincoln Nix."

When he began reading again, he skipped over most of Lynx's grisly accounts. He was eager to find the evidence against Kent Grantham and his cronies. Finally, in a folder labeled "Omega Group," he found what he was looking for. Kent was named, as well as Matt Tatum, Harry Marcum,

Ike Simmons, Lyndon (Zorro) Deatherage, and many others. Heading up the group was Texas state senator Nelson Kirby.

Ben glanced through the file. He found copies of e-mails, letters, and financial records, all printed out from computers Lynx had hacked into. He also found photos, each bearing the date, the place, and the circumstances of the photo. Barely daring to hope for more evidence against Kent Grantham, Ben looked through the pictures and was richly rewarded. Kent seemed to have been a pet project of Lynx's. There were pictures of him - apparently taken with a telephoto lens - actually aiming a rifle at his targets. Invariably, these pictures were followed by photographs of his dead victims, one of whom was Nelson Kirby's mistress - Missy Sheridan - in New Orleans the previous February.

Ben paused to reflect on his own trip to New Orleans in May, where he had learned for himself that Kent Grantham had murdered Missy. He had been trying to clear Tobi of Hugh Mansett's murder at the time. He wondered if Hugh ever had an inkling that it was his own stepson who had executed Senator Kirby's mistress.

He looked through the rest of the material in the file - it was very damaging information. No wonder Kent and his group were determined to silence Lynx. And to get their hands on this evidence.

Ben straightened all the folders, put the Omega Group file on top, and dumped them into the tote bag Patrice had used to haul them to her health club. In one hand he carried the tote bag; in the other he carried two grocery bags, each half full of hundred dollar bills.

The Chief of Police was drinking a cup of coffee when Ben appeared in his door. "You been shopping, Walling?" he asked.

"Not exactly," Ben said, dumping his load onto the Chief's desk. "I think we need some help this time." He took the Omega file out of the tote bag and set it in front of the Chief. "Especially with this one."

"Well," the Chief said looking over Ben's offering and picking up the Omega file. "Now we're getting somewhere."

Ben sat down in a chair opposite the Chief's desk. "I'd better warn you," he said. "After you've read a few of those files, you may feel like giving this man's murderer a medal."

The Chief looked at Ben over his reading glasses. "That can be arranged," he said.

"Well, don't arrange it," Ben growled.

Leaving the Chief talking to the FBI, Ben drove to the Church of the Living Vine. Lou, the secretary, was the only person there. "When do you expect Rev. Morel?" Ben asked her.

"In 30 minutes or less," Lou told him. "Is there anything I can help you with?"

Ben started to shrug and leave, then decided she might be the very person he needed to talk to. "The black limo outside - who drives it?" he asked.

"Visiting evangelists mainly," she said. "Of course, the pastor or one of the elders usually drives it to the airport to pick them up first. Then they give the evangelist the keys and let him use it while he's in town."

"Then, why isn't Rev. Moses using it while he's here?"

Lou's eyebrows went up. "He refused it - says it's too *grand* for him."

"Do you believe that's the real reason?" Ben asked.

"Let's put it this way," she said. "I don't think that man believes *anything* is too grand for the likes of him."

"Why do you think he refused it?"

Lou thought for a long time, then shook her head. "I haven't been able to figure that one out. He says he likes a convertible better, but I'm not so sure."

"Because..."

"Well, he's so fussy about his appearance. Every time he drives it, he has to stop in the bathroom and repair the damage - comb his hair, straighten his tie, whatever."

"Okay, let me get this straight," Ben said. "The guy arrives on a Wednesday, right? Wednesday of last week?"

Lou nodded.

"Did Rev. Morel pick him up at the airport in the limo?"

"Right."

"And Moses takes one look at it and says, 'Not for me. I'll rent my own car!' Is that the way it happened?"

"No. They came back to the church in the limo and Rev. Moses drove it to the Dream Country Motel where he's staying," Lou said.

"So he had the use of the limo Wednesday night?" Ben asked.

She nodded. "And then he brought it back Thursday and said he had phoned for a rental car. He wouldn't be using the limo any more."

"What did the pastor think of that?" Ben asked.

"He was angry, actually," Lou said. "He's proud of that car, and he likes for our evangelists to be seen driving it."

"Has the limo been driven since Rev. Moses returned it last Thursday?" Ben asked.

"Nope. Just sitting there, gathering dust," Lou said.

"Is there any way to tell how many miles he drove it?" Ben asked.

"Certainly." Lou turned to her computer and began tapping keys. In less than a minute, she said, "Hmm, looks like he drove it 45 miles that night." She looked surprised.

"How far would you have expected him to drive?" Ben asked.

"It's five miles to the motel," she said. "So ten would have been about right. Anything up to 20 would allow for him to get lost and search the whole town until he got back on track. But 45 miles? What's that?"

"Maybe he couldn't sleep, so he got up and went for a drive," Ben suggested.

Lou looked at the number 45 again. "Okay, well 10 miles to the motel and back to the church. So he drove an extra 35 miles - 17½ both ways. What's 17 miles from here?"

"Cow pastures," Ben said. "Cotton fields. Oil wells."

Lou looked up with a bright expression on her face. "Your choice," she told him. Then looking beyond Ben, she added, "Here's the pastor now."

Rev. Morel was not looking happy that bright July day. "Detective Walling," he said, shaking hands. "I'm glad you're here. Please, come into my office."

When they were seated, the pastor asked, "How can I help you?"

"I was talking to your secretary about Rev. Moses and his dislike of 'grand' cars. How do you read that - is he really so humble?" Ben asked.

"The one thing he's *not* is humble," said Rev. Morel. "I don't know why he wouldn't drive our limo."

Ben nodded. "Okay, the first thing I have to know is where you stand. There are a few things I'm not ready for Moses to know. Can you convince me you're not going to report everything we discuss to him?"

Rev. Morel gave Ben a steady gaze. "I want to know the truth about this man a thousand times more than you do," he said. "He has been preaching in *my* pulpit six nights, and his ministry has been, to say the least, unusual. If he's not what he seems, I have to know."

"How did he take it when you cancelled the rest of his services?" Ben asked.

Rev. Morel looked grim. "He flew into a rage."

The pastor's words and sober manner seemed to persuade Ben that he was being forthright, so he went to the heart of the matter. "What Moses doesn't know," he said, "is that I know Lincoln Nix was already dead when his house was destroyed."

The pastor sat up straighter in his chair. "What are you talking about?"

"Lincoln Nix - Lynx - died Wednesday night; his house burned early Saturday morning. Because his body wasn't found before the attack on his house, we have no way of determining a time of death. But I was in the vicinity late Wednesday night - between 11:00 o'clock and midnight, I'd say - and I saw a black luxury car, traveling without its lights, turn off Tomlin Street."

"Are you suggesting that the black car was this church's limousine?"

"It's a possibility," Ben said.

"How do you know Lynx died Wednesday night?"

"The mother of his child found him dead Thursday morning," Ben said.

Rev. Morel fell back in his chair, aghast. "You're not saying that Joshua Moses killed his own son, are you?"

"Yes," Ben said. It was the first time he had stated it positively, but the moment he learned Moses was driving the limo the night of Lynx's murder, he had been convinced. "That's exactly what I'm saying."

"It's impossible!" Rev. Morel moaned. "It has to be impossible. This could destroy my church. We received Joshua Moses as a man of God and he has won the hearts of my people. My people and many more besides."

"What does that mean?" Ben asked coldly. "Are you going to try a coverup? Try to protect him for the sake of your church?"

Rev. Morel didn't answer immediately. Apparently, it was a possibility he had to consider. Finally he said with a deep sigh, "No. If I did, how could I live with myself?"

"Then I'd like permission to examine the limo," Ben told him.

"What would you be looking for?"

"Blood."

Rev. Morel's eyes widened. "But Lynx was blown up. Even if you found blood, you couldn't prove it was Lynx's blood."

Ben nodded. "That's true. But why would there be blood in your limo?"

"Oh." With another heart-rending sigh, Rev. Morel said, "Do it. I have to know, too."

Chapter XIX

Patrice Lacey was waiting in line to board an airliner for Dallas, Texas, on Wednesday morning when a young woman stepped into the line beside her. "Patrice Lacey?" she asked in a low voice.

"No," Patrice said, "I'm...I'm...uh, Rachel Hudson." She held up the airline ticket she had purchased in Rachel's name.

The woman pulled a police shield out of her pocket and, keeping it between their bodies, showed it to Patrice. "Rachel Hudson is in Deepwater, Texas," she said quietly. "So I know you can't be Mrs. Hudson."

Patrice nodded, looking defeated. "Are you here to arrest me?" she asked.

"Of course not. I'm here to protect you. Alyssa York." She held out a hand to Patrice. "I'm pleased to meet you."

Patrice took the proffered hand limply and let Officer York shake hers warmly.

"I won't be sitting with you," York explained. "If you'll sit toward the front, I'll be able to find a seat behind you." Seeing Patrice's frightened expression, she said, "We don't believe anyone knows where you are; I'm merely a safety precaution. Also, I'll be flying on to Midland/Odessa, then driving to Deepwater in your place. The homicide detective from Deepwater will meet you and drive you home from the Dallas/Fort Worth Airport."

"How will I know who he is?" Patrice asked.

"You don't need to," York said. "He'll recognize you from a picture. *Don't worry*. His name is Walling. Mrs. Hudson sent him. She said to tell you that you can trust him."

Before Patrice could ask her another question, Officer York had stopped walking and was falling back in the slow-moving line of people.

Watching for Patrice's face in the line of deplaning passengers in Dallas, Ben hardly dared to believe she would appear. But she did. On first glance, Ben thought she was a teenager. On second glance, he saw that her eyes looked haunted and weary. When she reached him, Ben took her arm and said, "This way, Ms. Lacey. I've been waiting for you."

She looked at him fearfully. "Who are you?" she asked.

He showed her his I.D. "Ben Walling, Deepwater P.D." he told her. "I've been wanting to meet you for a long time."

They made a stop to pick up Patrice's suitcase, then Ben led her outside to the borrowed car he was driving. "That's not a police car," Patrice said, staring at the battered blue hatchback, in which Ben was stowing her suitcase.

"Actually, the car belongs to the wife of Don Rawls, a buddy of mine on the force. I wanted to be sure I got out of town without being followed," Ben explained.

Patrice nodded and got in. She still seemed uncertain about him, but resigned to her fate, Ben thought. "You look exhausted," he told her. "Let's get a bite to eat and then you can take a nap. When you wake up, you can tell me about Mr. Nix, the Lynx.

"I don't know if I *can* sleep," she said. "I'm tired enough, but I have trouble getting myself to go to sleep."

"Is Trevor safe?" Ben asked.

She nodded. "I think he is."

"Then you have nothing to worry about. The police woman who made contact with you in Wisconsin is armed. She's going to enter your apartment, just like she's you. There will already be two FBI agents in there. When the bad guys come to get you, they'll be arrested. As for you, you'll be staying at the Hudsons' until we're sure it's safe for you to go home. So! What else is keeping you awake?"

Patrice considered his words, then gave him a hesitant smile. "Nothing, I guess."

After a quick lunch, Patrice crawled into the back seat of the car where Ben had had the foresight to put a pillow and light blanket. She was asleep almost instantly. Ben studied her sadly. She looked as innocent as a child, curled up under the blanket with her dark, tousled hair framing her pale face. It was hard to believe she had her own child and her own adult responsibilities.

They were nearly at Abilene, traveling 70 miles an hour on interstate 20, when Patrice sat up, looking rested. She was ready to talk.

After Ben made a pit stop and Patrice moved into the front seat, she began her story. "I met Lynx because of Rachel," she said. "He boldly rang the doorbell one day and told her who he was. I happened to be there at the time, so I knew he was her son, but she never told Uncle Paul."

"He knows now," Ben said. "She told him when she got back from Wisconsin."

Patrice's face brightened. "I'm glad! I always wanted him to know, but I didn't think I should be the one to tell him. Anyway, Lynx seemed shy and lonely. I felt sorry for him at first. He latched on to me and seemed so smitten with me that I was flattered. And he treated me like his queen. Pretty soon I decided I was in love with him, and I would spend the night with him occasionally."

She paused and Ben looked at her questioningly, so she continued. "I was *so stupid*. He was out of town more often than he was *in* town. And he never explained why. Now I know he was off trapping victims in blackmail schemes. But I never asked any questions and he liked that about me.

"Pretty soon I was pregnant. More stupidity on my part. I should have taken precautions, but I was embarrassed to admit to anyone, even a doctor, that I needed birth control. When I told Lynx I was pregnant, he refused to marry me. So I broke up with him. We stayed in contact because of Trevor, and he probably thought of us as friends but, after I found out what he did for a living, I was terrified of him."

"How did you find out?" Ben asked.

"He started bragging about it," Patrice said. "He was a blackmailer. I mean, blackmailing was his whole profession. I don't think anyone else in the world knew what he did. And he wanted someone - me - to know how clever and ingenious he was."

"You didn't ever consider turning him in?" Ben asked.

"Every day," Patrice said. "Every day, a thousand times a day."

"And...?" Ben prodded.

Patrice's hands began trembling. "He told me if he was ever arrested, he would get out on bail. And when he did, he would disappear and take Trevor and me with him. I believed he could do it. And he never actually said he would torture or kill us, but he used to spin tales about how he would treat anyone who betrayed him. He used to say, 'I would let that mother watch me kill her son - a slow, lingering death.' And then he would gaze at me with his cold, hard eyes." She shivered. "He was evil to the core."

"How did he get away with it?" Ben asked. "It's about to drive me crazy trying to understand why his victims didn't go to the address where they sent the blackmail money and find out it was coming to Deepwater, then have him arrested."

Patrice sighed before she spoke. "He took care of that problem first. His earliest blackmail victims were supervisors of mail rooms in big stores or companies. So the blackmail money would be sent to a certain made-up name at the company. The mail room supervisor would re-package it so that it was no longer recognizable and send it on to Lynx, again not in his real name, but to some alias. A stranger couldn't just stroll into the mail room behind the postman to see what happened to his package. And if he tried to watch for it coming out, he wouldn't know it because it had been repackaged."

Ben whistled. "It's brilliant, I guess, but it seems awfully risky. How could he trust the person in the mail room to keep his secret? And to keep doing his dirty work?"

Patrice shrugged. "The same way he could trust his victims to send him money every month. He convinced them he would turn them over to the authorities for some crime he had framed them for. Or he threatened to kill them or a family member. He could be terrifying - his voice would go low and angry and his eyes would turn into green ice, and I would believe him if he told me he was going to kill the devil."

She paused, but Ben sensed she would continue if he waited. And he was right.

"I guess his main safeguard was that he moved often. He once told me that as soon as he got settled in a place he began looking for the next place he would live. He stayed in Deepwater longer than most places, but he told me last week it was time to go because his house was going to be fired on by missiles early Saturday morning."

Ben nearly drove the car off the road. "He knew?"

Patrice nodded.

"How?" Ben asked.

"I don't know," Patrice said. "But I do know that his burglar alarm had gone off in the night twice in the last two months."

Ben frowned. "I don't remember hearing that. Someone should have mentioned it to me in light of everything that's been going on."

But Patrice was shaking her head. "No, his burglar alarm didn't go to the police station or anywhere else. The only person it warned was Lynx."

Ben glanced at her. "You mean he was...armed?"

"Yes. And he was pretty sure he had wounded a man who tried to break in one night about...oh, about two weeks ago, I guess. There were two of them, and they ran when he started shooting, but he found blood on the porch the next day. He was furious that he hadn't killed them. 'I should have waited,' he told me over and over. 'And I would have, but I didn't know how many there were. If there had been enough of them, one of them might have gotten through and taken me out. So I shot too early.' "

"I should think he'd be glad he missed. He didn't seem like the type who would want police crawling all over his property, because he had killed an intruder."

"No, he wouldn't!" Patrice agreed. "But he wouldn't have reported it. He would have tossed the body in the basement or buried it in the back yard."

Ben nodded. "Of course."

"Anyway," Patrice continued, "he wanted to keep Trevor one more time because he was leaving Thursday and might never see his son again. I prayed it was true - that Lynx would move on and never come back." She paused to weep before she added through her tears, "When I walked through the door and saw him lying in a pool of blood, I thanked God that he would never be able to bother us again."

Suddenly she laughed wryly. "I wasn't happy long. I nearly went berserk when I couldn't find Trevor."

Ben considered her words. "That's right. You didn't know where your child was when you hauled all that evidence to your health club."

Patrice gave him an excited look. "You found it then? I'm so glad!"

"Yes," Ben said. "Mrs. Hudson figured out where it had to be. But how did you have the presence of mind to salvage it when you didn't know where your baby was?"

"Desperation," Patrice said. "I was sure one of his blackmail victims had killed him and would come back looking for any evidence he had against them. But I wanted *all* of his victims to be free of him. I thought if I got the information to the police, they - *you* might be able to undo some of the evil he's done."

"That was very courageous, Patrice," Ben said gently.

She wept heart-wrenchingly then. "I don't feel courageous," she told him through her tears. "I haven't felt like anything except a coward for the past two years." She pointed out the window at a pump jack in a pasture they were passing. "My life was like that pump - bobbing up and down, up and down, going nowhere forever. I wanted to die, but I couldn't because of Trevor. And I wanted Lynx dead so bad I wasn't sure I hadn't driven over there in my sleep and killed him myself."

After she had calmed down and mopped her eyes, Ben asked, "What was wrong with him? Do you have any idea?"

Patrice stared at the highway a long time before she said, "He wanted to be a tiger."

"A what?" Ben asked.

"A tiger. He wanted to be a tiger. He said a lynx was just a big pussy cat. Tigers are fierce and powerful. They're feared by man and beast. And Lynx wanted to be a tiger."

"Are you saying that if he did enough evil - enough violence - he would feel like a tiger instead of a pussy cat?" Ben asked.

Patrice took her eyes off the hypnotic highway and looked at him. "Maybe. His whole house was decorated in black and white and gray. He wouldn't let any other colors come in, except for one huge picture of a black-and-gold Siberian tiger that hung in his living room. Sometimes he sat there staring at it like he was in a trance."

She paused a few moments - remembering - then continued. "He had tiger pictures in every room of the house, but all the other tigers had black and white stripes. And they were snow pictures with black or gray frames. I guess he wanted his house dark and shadowy like a lynx's lair, but it seemed drab to me. Sometimes I stared at the Siberian tiger too, just because I wanted to see some color..."

"Why did he live in such a poor neighborhood?" Ben asked. "What did he do with all that money?"

"Oh the house and the neighborhood were camouflage," Patrice explained. "Everything inside the house was beautiful and expensive. He lived like a king."

"A king who wanted to be a tiger," Ben said musingly.

"Yes, and he never understood what a pitiful little weasel he was," Patrice said.

"Well, he came by it honestly," Ben said. "His father is one of the lowest pieces of scum I've ever had the misfortune to meet."

Patrice looked puzzled. "His father? Who's his father."

"The Rev. Joshua Moses, a.k.a. Jess Hurley," Ben said.

Patrice's eyes widened. "You don't mean...?"

Ben nodded. "That's right - the revival speaker at the Church of the Living Vine for the past six nights."

She thought about it for a few moments, then said quietly, "Tell me, please."

So he did.

When they were close to Deepwater, Ben called Don Rawls to find out what had happened when Officer Alyssa York arrived, pretending to be Patrice.

"Two goons were at the door of the apartment three minutes after she arrived," Rawls reported. "When they threatened her, the FBI took them into custody, plus two others - those guys working on the float."

"How about Moses?" Ben asked. "Is he still in town?"

"Yep. Living the life of Riley," Rawls said.

After Ben hung up with Rawls, he smiled at Patrice. "Everything went according to plan. Officer York is safe and the thugs who were waiting for you have been arrested."

"I'm so grateful," Patrice said. "I was a fool not to go to the police as soon as I found Lynx's body."

"I can't argue with you there," Ben said, but his voice was kind. "Listen, what about the physical evidence Lynx collected - like blood-stained shoes and clothing? Did you leave it behind because it was too much to carry? Or was it stashed somewhere else?"

"It didn't exist," Patrice said. "What I mean is, he always sent it to his victims. He would claim to have more evidence, but he never did. He didn't want to keep up with a lot of blood-stained shoes and clothes. So..."

Her voice broke and she paused to take a couple of deep breaths before she finished. "So he killed them if they didn't do what he wanted. Once... once he killed a man's grandchild, instead of killing the man himself - just for revenge." She was weeping again, but she managed to ask through her tears, "How could anyone be so evil?"

Ben didn't have an answer. But he thought he knew her deepest fear, and maybe he could help her with *it*. "Patrice," he said, pointing, "look up at the sky there."

She had to wipe her eyes to see but, when she did, she saw a graceful hawk riding the air currents far above them. "You mean, at that bird?" she asked.

"Yes," Ben said. "I want you to forget the pump jack going nowhere forever. It's behind you now. Be like that hawk. Be free so you can help Trevor be free."

He paused and prayed God would give him the words she needed to hear, then continued, "His heritage from Linx and Jess Hurley must feel like an impossible burden..."

"From my parents too," Patrice said softly.

Ben nodded. He hadn't thought about *her* parents. She must feel her son was cursed from both sides of his family. "All I know," Ben said, "is that God loves both of you. He loves you enough to die for you. And his power is greater than the power of genetics."

Patrice's gaze was glued to his face. "What are you saying?" she asked.

Ben took a deep breath. He couldn't make promises for God, but he would not believe Patrice's son was a lost cause. "That the Lord loves Trevor more than we can understand. And there must be a way to help him be like his heavenly Father instead of his earthly father." He glanced at her sympathetically. "You'll have to find that way. I don't know how you'll do it, but I do believe there is a way. And I believe God gave Trevor to you because you're the one who can find the way."

Patrice was nodding. "I'll try," she said solemnly. "I'll do my very best."

They were in Deepwater now and Ben headed for the Hudsons' home. "Detective Walling," Patrice said, "would you do me a favor?"

"If I can."

"Well, I haven't told Rachel everything about Lynx. I mean, he's her son, and I didn't want her to know how horrible he was," Patrice said. "I was hoping you would..."

"Do the same?" Ben asked.

Patrice nodded. "If you can."

Ben shrugged. "You're the one she's going to be grilling for information."

"I know," Patrice said, "but she may come to you if she thinks I'm holding out."

"I see," Ben said. "Well, if it happens, I'll tell her I can't discuss it."

"Thank you," Patrice said. "And thank you for everything. Today is the first time in nearly two years that I'm beginning to feel safe again."

"Well, Patrice," Ben said, stopping at the curb in front of the Hudsons' home, "that's what makes my job worth doing."

He carried her suitcase to the garage where a crowd of laughing people were listening to the radio and putting last minute touches on the Wisconsin float. Paul saw them, at once, and came out to give Patrice a hug and take her suitcase from Ben.

"Officer Walling," he said, with Patrice still tucked safely under his arm, "please tell me what we should expect. Are Rachel and Patrice going to be charged with obstruction of justice or breaking and entering or kidnaping or...anything?"

Ben looked pained. "That's the D.A.'s decision," he said. "But I'll tell him how much they helped my investigation and how terrified they were." He looked at Patrice's young, somber face and smiled at her. "If all else fails, I'll show him a picture of Trevor."

Patrice smiled, too, at the thought of her son.

"But if you tell the D.A. they shouldn't be charged, he won't charge them, will he?" Paul asked.

"Probably not, but I can't make any promises."

Paul nodded. "Do you think this nightmare is ever going to end?" he asked wearily.

"Yes," Ben said. "Very soon."

Rachel looked up, then, saw him and waved. Ben gave her a smile and a salute, then hurried back to the car. He couldn't wait to see the lab report on the limousine.

When he got to his desk, the report was lying on the top of his In-basket. He reached for it eagerly. "They found blood in the limo," Don Rawls said, coming over and sitting on the edge of Ben's desk. "Lots of blood."

"I knew it!" Ben cried. "Moses killed Lynx, then he heard the baby - heard Trevor cry. So he took Trevor downtown to the police station in that limo while the blood on his shoes and clothes was still wet. He probably got blood on the baby's pajamas, too, and that's why he took them off before he left Trevor in our lobby. Then he went back to the house to make sure he hadn't left anything that would incriminate him."

"And to wipe off his fingerprints," Rawls said.

"Right!" Ben said. "And he was leaving that second time when he nearly ran over Davy and me. He did it! But how do we prove it?"

"Beats me," Rawls said. "But I think you have a bigger problem right now."

Ben looked up surprised. "What's that?"

"The float - what was it - Arkansas? Those four fellows were pretty hot when they were arrested. It wouldn't surprise me if they called in a helicopter to blow up that barn, just for revenge."

Ben sighed. He wished he didn't care if the float *was* blown up. But he did. And Tobi would be heartbroken. "So where do you suggest we put it?" he asked.

"A one-car garage wouldn't hold it," Rawls said, musingly.

"Nope. It would take a two-car garage," Ben agreed.

"Well, I might know someone who would be willing to park their cars on the street overnight," Rawls said, "so the float could get a good night's sleep before its big day."

Ben looked up, trying to read his friend. "Really?"

"And," Rawls continued, "we'd need your pickup to pull the float. I don't believe I want to try it with my car."

"Where *is* my pickup, by the way?" Ben asked, realizing he hadn't seen it outside.

Rawls shrugged. "Well, it might be busy dragging a parade float across town."

"You dog!" Ben laughed, slugging Rawls' arm. "Where would I be without you?"

"Sunk up to your armpits in some slimy swamp," Rawls said. "Now, if you'll be good enough to give me my keys, I'll go check on the progress of our float, and get your pickup back to you."

Ben tossed him the keys and asked. "I guess I'd better come along and help, huh?"

"Why? Don't you think we can handle it without you?"

Ben glared at his buddy. "Get lost, Rawls! I have work to do."

Rawls tossed the keys into the air, caught them, and went out whistling.

Ben paused one moment to thank God for Don Rawls before he consulted his notebook and called Tyson Banning. Tyson was his last hope for putting Joshua Moses behind bars.

"Listen, Tyson, I want you to think really hard," Ben said, after they exchanged greetings. "I know who killed Lynx, but I don't have any way to prove it."

"Gee, Officer Walling, I've told you everything I can think of," Tyson said regretfully.

"I know, but I want you to give it one more try. Not right this minute but, when you're taking it easy, let your mind wander back to Wednesday night. Don't strain. Just be relaxed and get a picture in your mind of the street that night. You know what I mean?"

There was a pause. Then Tyson said, "You mean Friday night, don't you?"

"No, he was killed Wednesday night."

There was a longer pause this time. "Look, Officer Walling," Tyson said finally, "I don't mean to be a smart aleck, but that helicopter shot up his house Saturday morning."

"Tyson, he was already dead! He died Wednesday night," Ben said. "I didn't realize you didn't know that."

"Gee," Tyson said, "I remember everything about Friday night and Saturday morning, but I don't remember Wednesday, at all."

192

"That's okay," Ben encouraged him. "Don't worry about it. But think about it occasionally and let me know if anything comes to you."

He hung up the phone with a sigh. He should turn in his badge. He hadn't even bothered to inform his best witness - and his last hope - when Lynx died. He had to get away from this place before his job turned him into a blooming idiot.

It was after 9:00 o'clock when Tobi staggered into her house, carrying two bags of groceries, her purse, and a handful of mail. She was almost too hot and weary to breathe, and she sank onto her sofa to cool down while she shuffled through her mail. When she came to a letter bearing the return address of Audrey Mansett, she turned on a light, opened the envelope, and read:

"Dear Tobi,

"Again, I thank you for your kindness to my son and for your kind words to me. These things will not soon be forgotten.

"I have seen Kent. In the middle of Saturday night he sent some of his associates for me. After a long drive, we came to him. He had sent for me to say good-bye because he was about to leave the United States. I don't know where he went or whether I'll ever see him again but, if I do, I will tell you. I did not call the police because he assured me he would be out of the country before his confederates delivered me back home.

"I am writing now because Kent asked me to send you the enclosed note.

"Please pray for him and for me.

"Yours very truly,

"Audrey Mansett"

With a lump in her throat, Tobi looked at the second page, bearing Kent's scrawl, and read:

"My dearest Tobi, I saw you last Saturday. I was hiding in a stall in an old barn south of town when you came to see the float being built there. I had been sent back to Deepwater in case my particular talent was needed for the job underway there at the time. The fools building the float mentioned my name, thinking it would be a kick to frighten you. I was furious at them and abandoned them to their infantile antics as soon as you were out of sight. I'm still furious, and may even do as you urged me, and renounce my association with this group of buffoons. I'm out of the country as you read this, but it is my eternal hope that one day you will meet me in Holland during tulip season. Kent."

Tears were cascading down Tobi's face when she finished reading. She wept long and hard for Kent Grantham. Not because she loved him. But because she didn't love him. And because he didn't love Jesus.

She must have cried herself to sleep on the sofa because a ringing phone wakened her. Her eyelashes and hair were still wet when she went to find the handset. Looking at the caller I.D. number, she saw that it was Joel.

She took a deep breath and tried to sound natural when she said, "Hi, Joel."

"Whoa!" he exclaimed. "What's wrong?"

"I'm tired," she said.

"And?"

"And I got a note in the mail from Kent's mother, and a message from Kent."

"Saying?"

"He left the country. He may break off with the group of thugs he works for."

On the other end of the line, Joel hesitated, trying to decide what to say next. Finally, he asked, "And that upsets you?"

Tobi snorted. "Why would it when I don't know if anything he says is true?"

Another pause followed, then Joel said, "You don't want to talk about it, do you?"

"Not now," Tobi said gratefully. "Later, when I'm not so tired."

"Should I hang up and let you get some rest?" Joel asked.

"No!" Tobi cried in alarm. "Please, don't. My ears are starving to hear your voice!"

"Really?" Joel smiled in relief - she sounded like herself again. "Well, I like your ears. I may have to kiss them tomorrow and tell them how lovely they are."

"Mmm," Tobi said. "They'll be looking forward to that." She went into her bedroom and settled herself against a pillow. "I'm looking forward to it too."

"Me too," Joel agreed. "However, I'm glad I came here."

"Will you go back next week?" Tobi asked.

"No, I think I've probably taken more than my share of Caleb's time although he has been great about it. He's given me the titles of some books and some internet addresses that will help me study on my own. And he says I can call him any time I want to. So I'm thinking it's time to get on with my life."

Out of Darkness

"I'd like to read your books sometime," Tobi said, "and get the internet addresses. I'd like to know more too."

"Your mentioning Grantham makes me think of something interesting Caleb told me this week," Joel said obligingly. "I was telling him about Grantham's group - these kooks who think they're going to take over the world, and he said it wasn't surprising. He said several would-be messiahs arose around the time Jesus lived because the Jews knew from prophecy it was time for Him to come. And now that we're starting to look for His return, it's not surprising that there are people like Jim Jones and David Koresh and Kent Grantham rising up and trying to be messiahs."

"That's scary," Tobi said, "when you think how many people are willing to following those guys."

"Yes, and follow them to death," Joel agreed.

"Or to murder in Kent's case," Tobi said. "Joel, does it disturb Caleb that Charismatic doctrine is becoming so popular, or am I worrying about nothing?"

"He's plenty disturbed," Joel said. "And it's not just Charismatics. As he sees it, the root problem is Gnosticism."

"What's Gnosticism?" Tobi asked.

"I can't give you a definition without going and looking it up," Joel said, "but I can tell you why it's a problem. So-called Christian Gnostics believe they have a special relationship with the Holy Spirit, and He is feeding them exciting new secrets and ways of doing things. It doesn't bother them that their new things are unscriptural. They develop a sense of specialness, of being more spiritual than traditional Christians because they have this deep, intimate relationship with God."

"And so they come up with ideas like the Toronto Blessing and believe they got it from the Holy Spirit?" Tobi asked.

"Yes! That's exactly how it happens."

"Why can't they see how evil and foolish it is to behave the way Joshua Moses was teaching them to behave?"

"I guess there are as many answers to that as there are people buying into it," Joel said, "and I'm no expert. But I can think of a few reasons. Maybe some have 'itching ears' - they always want something new to amuse them. Maybe some are too proud to admit they missed God. Maybe some aren't saved, and they can't possibly know any better."

Tobi was nodding as she listened. When Joel ran out of reasons, Tobi said, "I'm sure all those things are true, but I believe I've known people who didn't fit into any of those categories. Including me. And you. What were we doing in that horrible heresy?"

"Going astray," Joel said. "Just going astray."

Chapter XX

The Fourth of July dawned gray and cloudy that year. The prospect of rain was always a treat in West Texas, but Tobi eyed the clouds with agitation. "Dear Lord, please let it rain, but not until after tonight," she prayed as she drove toward the farm where the Arkansas float was located. She hadn't been able to contact Harry or Matt that week, and she had to know everything was in order.

"Oh, and Lord," she added, "please keep me safe and don't let Ben know I came out here by myself." She smiled to herself as she prayed, but it was a nervous smile. And she felt the pocket of her blue jeans shorts to make sure Joel's cell phone was there.

No military helicopters had flown over Deepwater the previous night and shot missiles at the farm where the Arkansas float had been built, but someone had torched the barn. The old structure had burned to the ground in record time. When Tobi arrived, she found a neighbor, raking through the ashes to make sure all the embers were out.

"No!" she cried, running from her car to the ashy ruins. "No! No!"

The old gentleman from the neighboring farm gave her a puzzled frown. "No, what?" he asked.

Tobi took a deep breath and forced herself to speak calmly. "What happened? Where's the float they were building in this barn?"

The old man shrugged. "The barn burned in the night. That's all I know."

"What about the float?" Tobi insisted.

"What's a float?" he asked.

She wanted to give up. She wanted to go home and cry herself to sleep. How could they have a parade without Arkansas? She sat in her car trying in vain to think of a way to produce a new float in eight hours, then drove to her next stop, battling tears all the way. She thought she couldn't possibly deal with the ache of loss and failure over the burning of the Arkansas float.

And then, all of a sudden, the cell phone in her pocket was ringing and DeeDee was demanding to know where she was. "Let's see," Tobi said, looking around. "I guess this is New Hampshire."

"New Hampshire!" DeeDee cried. "You promised you would be here for lunch. I told you I had a surprise and you promised you would be here. I don't care if you're in Timbuktu - you're supposed to be *here*!"

"Calm down, DeeDee," Tobi said. "I'll be there by 12:00. I promise."

"By 12:00," DeeDee shrieked. "How is that possible when it's 12:45 now?"

"No, it's not," Tobi said, looking for a clock. When she didn't see one, she grabbed a passing wrist and checked the time. It was 12:50, according to that watch.

"DeeDee, I'm sorry. I had no idea it was so late, but I can't possibly get away now. There's this beautiful float made up to look like polling booths for the Republican and Democratic primaries. But the lettering on the signs faded. If we don't get them repainted, nobody is going to understand what..."

"Hold it," DeeDee interrupted her. "You wait right there."

Tobi heard her saying to someone on her end, "Here, you talk to her. She won't come for me."

Tobi grinned. DeeDee must have invited Joel for lunch too, and he was there. Goody! She would hurry and...

"Hey, Baby Sister," said a familiar voice. "Where are you?"

"Julius?" Tobi gasped. Her older brother was a prominent lawyer in the Houston area and rarely had time for visits. "When did you get here?"

"Last night. Joyce and I drove by your place to say hello, but it was dark. So... I understand you're not coming to my birthday dinner?"

"Your birthday? But your birthday's not until the 15th."

Julius laughed. "Doesn't matter. You know your sister - if it were April, she would have made me a big birthday dinner, knowing I wouldn't get back again in July."

"I *am* coming," Tobi promised, "just as soon as I can. I can't wait to see you!"

As she put the phone back in her pocket, someone drew the paint brush out of her other hand. "You scat," said a grandmotherly woman. "I thought it would be so hot today I wouldn't last past 10:00 o'clock, but look at those nice clouds." She pointed upward at the thick cloud cover. "They're keeping it cool and I'm still going strong. You run along."

"Are you sure?" Tobi asked. "I could come back later to finish."

The woman shook her head. "You go. You've done your share."

So Tobi went - straight into the arms of her idolized older brother and his charming wife Joyce. Auburn-haired Julius, at 55, was looking more like their father every day, which endeared him all the more to Tobi. And Joyce, whose brown hair was rapidly turning white, was still the sweet, vivacious woman Julius' family had loved from the day they met her.

Tobi was still hugging Joyce when the doorbell rang. Davy raced to answer it and soon led Joel, Gloria and Grace to Tobi for another flurry of hugging.

Ben, in the backyard tending hamburgers, hots dogs, and steaks on the grill, never thought to tell Tobi the Arkansas float had found a new home. And Tobi didn't mention it because she had forgotten all about it.

But she remembered it at 5:00 o'clock, as she and Joel drove toward the block where the floats were to begin lining up. "Oh!" she gasped, putting both hands over her mouth. "Oh no!"

"What?" Joel asked.

"Arkansas!" she cried. "Arkansas burned last night. I didn't know what to do about it. Then I forgot. And now it's too late to do *anything*!"

"You mean that Arkansas?" Joel asked, pointing toward a float that looked exactly like a hot spring and wore a banner proclaiming, 'Hot Springs, Arkansas, where Americans go to bathe their cares away!' It was being towed slowly and carefully toward the starting point by Ben Walling in his powerful little pickup.

Tobi threw open the door of Joel's SUV, sprang out, and ran to Ben's pickup. She jerked the door open and threw her arms around his neck. "Ben Walling, you wonderful man! How...? Where...? What...?" she sputtered unintelligibly.

"Woman, are you trying to get killed?" Ben gasped. He put his gear shift into Park and got out with Tobi still clinging to his neck. "What *is* your problem?" he asked.

She pointed at the float. "I thought it burned up," she said.

"Burned up!" Ben exclaimed. "Are you nuts? Why would you think it burned up?'

"The barn burned last night," Tobi said. "I thought the float was in it."

"Well, what do you know?" Ben said. "Rawls was right."

"About what?"

"Grantham's buddies. He said they were so angry when they were arrested, they might call in a helicopter to blow up the barn."

"They were arrested?" Tobi gasped.

"Yesterday," Ben said. "And you can thank Don Rawls for saving your float. I never would have thought of it. He hauled it over to his grandparents' garage yesterday evening."

"Is anybody going to ride on it?" Tobi asked.

"Sure, he rounded up four or five people who want to bathe their cares away."

"It's perfect!" Tobi cried. "How am I ever going to be able to thank him?"

"Don't worry about it," Ben said. "His grandparents were so thrilled for a chance to participate in the parade that they've thanked me at least 30 times so far. They'll be two of the people riding on the float."

There were tears in Tobi's eyes when she climbed back into Joel's SUV - tears of gratitude and joy. Laughing and crying at the same time, she told him what Ben had said, finishing with a reverent, "Thank God!"

With 50 full-size floats in the parade, Tobi expected a logistics nightmare as the participants began to converge on downtown Deepwater. But they had been given precise times and locations for their arrival and, under the expert direction of Deepwater P.D. officers, the huge procession began to take shape.

"You know," Tobi said with sudden realization, "it's out of my hands now. I don't really have anything else to do except watch."

"Then let's find a good place to watch," Joel said. "Where do you think?"

Tobi shook her head. "I don't know if I'm going to be able to see it or not."

"Why not?" Joel asked in surprise.

"I'm afraid I'll cry all the way through it," Tobi said. "It's so beautiful - it may be the most beautiful thing I've ever seen!" As she spoke, she was gazing at the Alabama float, which had been turned into a 1950's city bus. Those who would be riding it were milling around now, but she could already imagine the scene as she watched a tall white man help a little black woman onto the float. Tobi had to smile. They were the stars of the Alabama show. When the parade began, they would be locked in angry conflict, as a dignified Rosa Parks and an irate white businessman who wanted her seat.

Joel watched Tobi watching the parade come together, and his heart ached with love for her. Putting an arm around her and pulling her close, he whispered in her ear, "I'm so proud of you I could bust."

She flashed him a smile. "Don't be silly. Dalton did all the hard work."

Just then a roaring in the sky turned into a helicopter. Alarmed, Joel looked around for safety. "What going on?" he yelled over the racket.

Tobi was calm. "Dalton hired a television station to make a video of the parade. They're going to get an aerial view of all the floats as they line up, then do the rest of their filming from the ground. That way, the noise of the helicopters won't interfere with the music of the marching bands," she explained, yelling over the drone of the chopper.

As she had predicted, Tobi did weep softly through much of the parade. But she wasn't the only one who wept. The approach of many floats brought forth either tears or cheers from the onlookers. Rosa Parks and the Alabama float brought both.

Alaska, heralded as the "Adventure Capital of America," portrayed fishing, hunting, dog sledding, spelunking, and nature tours. California, the "state that brings laughter and encouragement to America," bore larger-than-life figures of Mickey Mouse and Ronald Reagan. Florida, "America's Retirement Paradise," featured the amazing variety of wildlife found in the Everglades - alligators, sea turtles, cougars, deer, flamingos, and blue herons. And so it went through all the 50 states.

The New York float drew the most emotion. On it, a police officer and a fireman stood head and shoulders above scaled-down skyscrapers. Side by side, as still as statues, they marked the place where the proud twin towers of the World Trade Center had once dominated the New York City skyline. A banner read, "In New York City on 9/11, Tragedy + Courage = Unity. God bless our American heroes." The float was followed by a hush and floods of tears.

As the Texas float approached, Joel observed, "Well, somebody didn't strain themselves on our float did they?"

Tobi followed his gaze to the float where an oil derrick stood on a mainly unadorned trailer. A patch of bluebonnets along the back of the float and a Texas flag flying from the top of the derrick were its only decorations. The equipment was being manned by two Hispanic and two white workers. The banners, both fore and aft, read simply, "Texas, the Lone Star State."

"Dalton was in charge of that one," Tobi told Joel. "He was worried that, if he turned Texas over to someone else, they would go overboard. Try to make a float bigger and better than anyone else's, and then we'd have a 'lopsided unity.' That's what he called it, a lopsided unity."

Joel grinned. "He's probably right. I've known a few Texans like that."

As Wisconsin's dairy farm rolled past, Tobi looked beyond Wyoming's Yellowstone National Park with Old Faithful spurting, and asked, "What's going on? Wyoming is supposed to be last."

Within seconds she could see the answer for herself. The Wyoming float was followed by a float honoring the U.S. air force. Sitting in a World War II vintage fighter plane, proudly wearing an airman's uniform, sat Dalton Granville. He gazed stoically ahead as if he really were flying a mission over Germany or Japan, while all around him people cheered and clapped.

Tobi was too flabbergasted to move for a moment, then she began to laugh and wave and shout Dalton's name. He couldn't have heard her, but his eyes found her in the crowd. Breaking his pose for a moment, he waved and blew her a kiss. She pretended to catch it and press it to her heart. They beamed at each other for the briefest moment, and then he was gone.

Then Tobi was crying again, barely able to see the army tanks, the marine helicopter, and the naval aircraft carrier passing in front of her eyes. Only a handful of men and women rode the floats, but they symbolized the thousands who had suffered and died for freedom. "Oh Joel...," Tobi whispered suddenly intertwining her fingers with his.

"What?" he asked.

"Men are so wonderful!" she said, smiling at him through tears. "We want you to go out and defend us, protect us, provide for us, then come home and be all soft and warm and involved. And the amazing thing is that lots of you actually pull it off!" She hugged him. "Thank you for being wonderful!"

Before Joel could respond, the last and largest float in the parade appeared before them. It was a stage, carpeted in red, white, and blue floral sheeting. In the center of the stage was a flag pole from which a huge American flag waved gently in the breeze created by a hidden fan. The "Star Spangled Banner" was being played over a sound system mounted somewhere on the float. And signs attached to both the back and the front in huge letters read, "*E pluribus unum*." Then underneath the Latin words was the translation "Out of many, ONE."

Instinctively, Joel and Tobi put their hands over their hearts as Old Glory fluttered past. "...O say does that Star Spangled Banner yet wave, o'er the land of the free, and the home of the brave?" the solo voice sang.

"Yes! Oh thank God, yes!" Tobi whispered.

"Dear Lord, may it ever be," Joel prayed softly.

The parade's slow march took it to the baseball fields on the far side of Willowdale Park. The floats made a giant circle in the parking areas surrounding three baseball fields, and crowds of people followed them to get another look or take pictures. Some of the parade participants were giving away free samples from the states they represented, such as leis from Hawaii; red chili pepper key rings from New Mexico; agate, obsidian and other rock samples from Utah; and Wisconsin cheese.

Ben Walling got out of his pickup and stretched. He was grateful the slow-moving procession had finally ended. But he hadn't seen the parade, so he began walking past the floats, enjoying the elaborate artistry. He wished DeeDee were with him, but he couldn't blame her for wanting to spend time with the brother she rarely saw. Feeling a little blue and lonely, he had reached the Florida float when Tyson Banning rode up on his bicycle at breakneck speed and threw on his brakes in a spray of dust and pebbles.

"Tyson!" Ben cried in irritation.

But Tyson dropped the bicycle and pulled some photographs out of a plastic grocery bag he was carrying. "Look!" he ordered.

Ben looked. What he saw was a nighttime picture of Joshua Moses carrying Trevor Lacey toward a black limousine parked in front of 1813 Tomlin Street. And another of Moses putting Trevor into the back seat. And finally, a perfect picture of the limo's license plate.

"Tyson, where did you get these?" he gasped. Then before Tyson could answer, he warned, "You'd better watch out. I'm about to kiss you."

Tyson beamed. "You know Mr. Grimshaw...," he said.

"No," Ben interrupted. "Who's Mr. Grimshaw?"

"He's a biology teacher who lives next door to me," Tyson said. "You were talking to him that night - you know, the night Lynx's house blew up."

"Oh, right," Ben acknowledged. "What about him?"

"He borrowed my camera," Tyson said excitedly. "I forgot that I'd taken a couple of pictures with it before he borrowed it. Mr. Grimshaw just got his pictures developed and he brought these to me this afternoon. As soon as I looked at them, I remembered Wednesday night."

"You remember that these were taken Wednesday night?" Ben asked tersely.

Tyson nodded. "Yes, because I went to pick up Lynx's mail Wednesday night and Friday night last week, and I took those pictures the same night I picked up mail. I know it wasn't Friday because I remember Friday. So it had to be Wednesday. Besides, Mr. Grimshaw had the camera Friday night."

"Why did you take these pictures?" Ben asked. "He's not even parked in front of Lynx's house."

"Didn't matter," Tyson said. "I took pictures of every stranger I saw anywhere in the neighborhood. I didn't even realize the baby the big guy was carrying was Trevor until I saw these pictures."

Suddenly Ben wrapped Tyson in a bear hug. "Tyson, buddy," he said fervently, "you are my hero!"

He pulled out his cell phone, then, and made the call he had been longing to make for days. "I have the evidence," he said. "Pick up Joshua Moses. Suspicion of murder."

He hadn't even put his phone away before it rang. "Gimme' a break," he muttered, but he answered it, scanning the crowds for Moses all the while.

"Sorry to bother you on a holiday," said the voice on the phone. "Mac Bolton here."

"Hey! Good to hear from you," Ben told the detective. "What's up?"

"Two things," Bolton said. "Moses' itinerary has changed dramatically since last week. When I took this case, I printed off his entire web site. He was scheduled for meetings in ten cities in six states in the next three months. Today, his schedule shows two meetings in England for next week, with tentative meetings being discussed in France, Belgium, and Germany."

Bolton paused and Ben said, "Good work! What's the second thing?"

"I've just learned that Moses always wears a hunting knife strapped to his left leg. Down low, just above the ankle, on the inner leg so he can get to it fast," Bolton said.

"Bolton, you couldn't have called at a better time! I just got the goods on him and we're about to pick him up. I'll call you tomorrow and let you know how it went." Ben put the phone away and said to Tyson, "Help me spot the guy in the photograph. I don't want you anywhere near him, but you've got bright, young eyes. You might see him before I do."

Sure enough, Tyson saw Moses first. "There!" he cried, pointing toward the Washington float. Moses, walking hand-in-hand with a pretty young blond, had just passed the West Virginia float. Looking, Ben saw two uniformed officers closing in on Joshua Moses and his date.

Moses saw them too. He said something to the blond, disengaged their hands, and casually bent over as if he were brushing dirt off his pant leg. He came up with a knife tucked in his right hand, which he turned away from the approaching officers.

And then Moses disappeared, as a large group of people moved between him and Ben. Ben thrust the precious photographs at Tyson. "Guard these with your life," he said before he raced toward Moses and his fellow officers.

Pushing through the throngs of people, he was unable to reach the officers in time to warn them about Moses' knife. But he did witness Moses thrust the knife into the belly of the police woman who had stepped forward to tell him he was under arrest. Keeping his grip on his knife, Moses heaved the officer into her partner who staggered backward under her weight. Before he could flee, Ben tackled him. Moses hit the ground hard and the knife flew out of his hand.

Joshua Moses was a big man, and a strong one. He might have flung Ben aside as easily as he had the police woman, except for Rachel Hudson.

Rachel had been watching Moses ever since he strolled past the Wisconsin float where she was helping give out samples of cheese. When she saw the police officers approaching him, she abandoned her post and moved in on him too. She wanted to know what was going down.

When the knife flew out of Moses' hand, Rachel pounced on it. Before Moses had time to catch his breath, she turned it on him. "Don't move," she warned him in an ominous tone. "I would love to sink this knife into the middle of your black heart."

Rachel's intervention gave Ben, who was less shaken by the fall than Moses, all the time he needed to jerk the big man's arms behind his back and apply hand cuffs. Leaving Moses on the ground, he called to the crowd of onlookers, "Has anyone called 911?"

At least ten people raised their hands or their cell phones into the air.

"Thanks!" he yelled at them.

He glanced at Moses' date. She was staring at the big man with wide-eyed astonishment and gave no indication that she might try to help him. He turned to Rachel next, grinned, and said, "Don't use the knife on the big ape. I've been told he's not worth it." Then he went to check on his fallen comrade.

She was lying on the ground, still and white. "Is she...is she...alive?" Ben asked.

"Sure," her partner said. "She's just keeping still so she doesn't lose so much blood, but she'll be fine after the docs finish with her."

"Stella," Ben said, bending over the young woman. "This place seems to be swarming with heroes today. How does it feel to be one of them?"

Stella opened her eyes and smiled weakly. "I can think of things I'd rather be."

"Well, if it makes you feel any better. You helped us get a bad one," Ben said. "We've done the country a great service by getting this thug off the streets."

Stella's smile widened then. "I'm always proud to serve my country," she said.

As dusk gathered, the lights in the center ball field were turned on and patriotic music was played from its speakers. Many of the people who had been admiring the floats took the hint and began filling the stands. Among these were Joel and Tobi.

"Dalton's going to speak," Tobi told Joel. "Let's go see what he has to say."

As they approached the baseball field, they met Rev. Emory Morel, walking toward them from the opposite direction. When they were face-to-face, Joel said, "Good evening, Emory."

Rev. Morel looked up with a start. "Oh, Joel, hello," he said absently. Then his eyes moved to Tobi. He glanced away and back again. "It's *you*!" he exclaimed, focusing on her face.

She gave Joel a quizzical frown before she replied uncertainly, "Hello, Rev. Morel."

"I want to know everything Joshua Moses told you," he said urgently, searching her face with troubled eyes. "I don't understand...I can't understand why the Holy Spirit would use such a man..."

"He wouldn't," Tobi said softly.

Emory Morel gazed into her eyes as if he were probing her soul. "May I see you one day next week?" he asked. "And Joel, too, of course. I wouldn't ask you to come alone after...after what Joshua did..." His voice trailed off.

Tobi touched his shoulder sympathetically. "Monday afternoon," she said. "Will that be all right?"

"Yes. Thank you!" he said eagerly. "Any time Monday afternoon. I'll see you then."

He shook Joel's hand and wandered off, looking like a little, lost puppy.

They watched him for a moment, wishing they knew a way to lighten his load. Then Joel took Tobi's hand and led her through a gate and into the bleachers.

When the stands were full, Dalton, still wearing the airman's uniform, walked onto the field where a speaker's podium had been placed. When he was ready to speak, the music stopped and the crowd grew quiet.

"People have been telling me all day that it was going to rain on my parade," Dalton said, speaking slowly and distinctly. "But I wasn't worried. I wasn't worried because I believe God is pleased that we are celebrating this beautiful country of ours. I believe He is pleased because we are celebrating founding fathers who conceived of a nation that honors Him and His Word. And I believe He is pleased because we are celebrating liberty.

"I have always loved liberty. I have been grateful to live in a country where I could be free. And when my son died in a prison in a country that does not understand the meaning of the word liberty, I decided I wanted to throw a parade in honor of liberty."

He paused while the crowd cheered.

"But a funny thing happened on the way to my parade," Dalton said, cutting the cheering short. "I found out that in my long life I had never understood liberty, at all. A beautiful little girl named Tobi Kirkland walked into my hospital room last week and taught me what liberty is all about. She showed me how I could be free from the cruelest slave owners I've ever known - sin and death.

"I have served those two cruel masters for over 70 years. But today I know that if I lived in the darkest dungeon in the world, I would still be free because I am free from the bondage of sin and death. Jesus Christ died on a cross in terrible agony to earn that freedom for me. And for you. I have to tell you these things because we're celebrating liberty today. And Jesus Christ is the greatest liberator in the history of mankind."

He paused to blow his nose, and the crowd waited in respectful silence.

When he spoke again, his words rang with joy and hope. "I love my country. And I love the God who made my country possible. I'm proud to be an American. God bless you all. And God bless the U.S.A.!"

As the crowd clapped, Judith escorted Dalton off the ball field. Then the mayor of Deepwater took his place. "Folks," he said, "it's almost time for fireworks! Less than 30 minutes now." The crowd cheered. "The fireworks will be set off on Homerun Hill. You are welcome to stay in the baseball stands. You may come down and sit on the baseball fields. Or go over to the park to watch - as long as you don't get under one of the willow trees, you'll be able to see it all. There are booths selling food and drinks. Please throw your trash away in the proper receptacles. And let's give one more hand to Dalton Granville who has purchased for your viewing pleasure the biggest display of fireworks this town has ever seen!" The crowd applauded with gusto.

Joel and Tobi met Dalton and Judith at the gate. "You were beyond magnificent!" Tobi told him, giving him a hug. "And why didn't you tell me you were going to be in the parade? And about those last five floats? They were *so* beautiful!"

He smiled happily. "Just a little surprise. I didn't want you to know *everything* about the parade."

Joel put out his hand, then. "I'm Joel Trent," he said, "and I want to thank you for this wonderful day. I've never seen anything like it."

Dalton shook his hand, smiling. "So you're the young fellow who puts the sparkle in Tobi's eyes. Well, you just make sure you're worthy of her."

Joel looked nonplused. "But I'm not," he protested. "And I don't know how to be."

Dalton laughed. "Well, as long as you know it, you'll be all right."

"Don't listen to him," Tobi objected. "He's much too good for me."

"I don't believe that," Dalton said. "But you two can work it out. I'm going home to watch the fireworks from my own porch."

"And I'm going with him," Judith said. "My husband is already there and if we don't chase him out of the house, he'll watch some stupid ball game without even noticing it's time for the fireworks."

"Judith, would you bring the car?" Dalton asked, lowering his lanky frame onto the lowest row of the bleachers. "I'm feeling tired, and I'd like to talk to Tobi one more minute."

"Of course." Judith hurried away, and Tobi and Joel seated themselves beside Dalton.

"This could wait," Dalton began apologetically, "but my heart is so full tonight that I wanted to tell you what it has meant to me - that first time you came into my hospital room and suggested I use my money to feed hungry children..."

His voice broke, and he paused to wipe away a tear and regain his composure. Then he continued. "I didn't want to be alive after Gabe died, and now I'm glad I'm alive! But it's more than that. I'd never let myself think about it before, but I've felt like a worthless old coot all my life. I don't anymore. If the good Lord in Heaven can use me to help children have better lives...then I'm not worthless any more. Tobi, I'm not worthless any more!"

Tobi put her arms around his neck and held him. "You never were, Dalton. You never, never were. If you had ever been worthless, you wouldn't care about children."

He gazed at her through soggy eyes. "Do you really, really think so?"

She gazed at him through her own soggy eyes. "I really, really do."

Joel and Tobi met Ben, DeeDee and Davy, Julius and Joyce at Willowdale Park. Gloria, Grace, and Alison, of course, had long ago joined their friends to enjoy the festivities with more compatible companions than their parents. Ben had insisted that Tyson Banning spend the evening with his family, and Tyson had shyly agreed. But, when Alison came around looking for money, she had taken his arm and drawn him along with herself and her friends. "Come on," she had said. "You don't want to hang around with the *old folks* all night, do you?"

The moment DeeDee spied Tobi, she cried, "Ben got him! They got Joshua Moses!"

"You're kidding!" Tobi cried. "For what?"

"Murder," Ben said. "The murder of Lincoln Nix. *And* the attempted murder of a police officer. He won't be causing trouble for anybody else, anytime soon."

"You're a genius," Tobi said, giving him a long hug. Then she gazed into his eyes to add, "Thank you."

He gave her another quick squeeze, then accepted Joel's outstretched hand. "Way to go!" Joel said. "You're the greatest!"

"Coach Trent," Davy said, pulling on Joel's sleeve to get his attention. "My Mom said you brought lawn chairs for us to sit on. Can I help you get them?

"*May* you," DeeDee corrected him automatically. "*May* you help him get them?

"*May* I help you get them," Davy asked.

"Of course," Joel said. "I could use some help."

He and Davy walked toward the parking lot while Ben and Julius went to buy soft drinks all around. Joel and Davy passed Paul Hudson on the way and Paul hailed Joel. "I have received my wife's official blessing on my middle name," he said happily. "I am and will forever remain Paul Avery Hudson."

"Hey! How did that happen?" Joel was amazed.

"I don't know," Paul said. "I didn't do it. I think the Lord was working on her while she was in Green Bay by herself, worrying about Patrice and Trevor."

"I guess that proves God still does miracles," Joel said.

"Oh you haven't heard the best part yet," Paul said. "She's decided she wants to have a baby with me! And she says we'd better get on with it - she's not getting any younger."

Joel's mouth fell open. When he recovered his power of speech, he asked, "How did you do *that*?"

Paul shrugged elaborately, raising his shoulders *and* arms. "Again, I didn't."

Joel shook Paul's hand heartily. "Congratulations, Paul! You're going to be a great father."

"Look, Joel," Paul said earnestly, "I'd like you to know that if my child loves me half as much as your daughters love you, I'll be a happy man."

"Thank you for saying that," Joel told him, fighting the tears that wanted to form in his eyes. "It means a lot."

"I can only imagine," Paul said sympathetically.

When Joel and Davy began pulling lawn furniture out of a caddie, most were regular chairs or chaise lounges. But one was a double. "Look," Ben said, pointing, "a love seat for the love birds."

"Not necessarily," Joel said. "Some of you old married folks are welcome to use it."

But Tobi's family insisted that she and Joel should have the love seat, and they didn't object. So when the fireworks began and the attention of the group was drawn to the splendor in the sky, Joel was able to pull Tobi close and say quietly, "I believe your Mr. Granville thinks we're going to get married."

Tobi, her eyes on the sky, nodded. "Probably."

"So do Gloria and Gracie," he said.

Tobi smiled.

"And DeeDee."

She looked at him, then, realizing he was leading up to something. "Yes, it's her main goal in life right now."

"What do you think?" Joel asked. "Do *you* think we should be engaged?"

"No!" Tobi's answer was so emphatic that Joel's stomach took a nosedive.

"Oh," he said forlornly. It was the answer he wanted, but it would have been nice to know she felt some of the same longings he did.

"Joel, any romance can be rosy for a month or two," Tobi said seriously. "Neither one of us is ready to make that decision yet. What brought this on?"

"The way I feel," Joel admitted. "Plus I saw Paul Hudson a few minutes ago. He told me he and Rachel are going to have a baby, and Rachel says they'd better get on with it because she's not getting any younger. I couldn't help thinking - we're not getting any younger either. And I don't know whether you want... Well, we've never talked about..."

"It's not time to talk about it," Tobi said. "But thank you for telling me how you feel."

'But I didn't tell you how I feel," he protested. "The way I feel is - sometimes I think I'm going to die of longing. I want to be married to you now. I want to be married to you ten years ago! Twenty years!"

Tobi's arms went around his neck softly. "I feel the same way," she whispered. "I really do. But I *know* it's too early to decide yet. I decided too early when I married Kyle, and that marriage was a nightmare."

"So how are we going to know when it's the right time?" Joel asked.

"I don't know but, for the first time since my divorce, I'm beginning to believe the right time *could* come. I wasn't so sure of that for a long time."

"What changed?"

"Look at them," Tobi said, nodding toward her family.

Julius and Joyce were holding hands, quietly enjoying the fireworks. Ben's arm was resting across the back of DeeDee's chair, and they were laughing and talking to each other and Davy, encapsulated in their own little family world.

Joel nodded. "What about them?"

Tobi smiled. "I've spent a lot of time trying to figure out why it was so easy for them to make good marriages, and so hard for me. I think I understand now, at least part of it."

She looked into his face and saw that he was listening intently. "I hope I can explain this right," she continued. "Let me go straight to the bottom line - one reason is that they were never involved in the Charismatic movement."

"So?" Joel's face showed his confusion.

"Well, in the Charismatic church I attended we were trained to turn off our minds. We were taught to follow impressions and impulses. I believed that's how the Holy Spirit was guiding me. So as soon as I got some lustful feelings toward Kyle, I convinced myself God was telling me to marry him. And I did."

Joel said nothing, but Tobi could see that he was deep in thought. Perhaps he was remembering his decision to marry Rachel. She waited until his eyes engaged hers again before she continued. "In those days, I was walking around in perpetual night. I was like a pinball, bouncing from a feeling to an impression to a passing whimsey and believing they were all the Holy Spirit. When you're a pinball, if you bump into somebody in the darkness and they say, 'Hello, I'm Joshua Moses, and I have all kinds of good feelings for you from the Lord,' you don't think about it. You just follow him."

"And then you're following someone who is blinder than you are," said Joel. "It reminds me of the plague of darkness God sent against Egypt - a darkness so dense they could feel it."

"Yes," Tobi said excitedly. "But now we're using our minds. When we use our minds, God's Word lights our path, and we can see where we're going. We don't have to be pinballs any more because we can see! Joel, we can see! It gives me such hope just knowing I've been delivered from that dreadful, Charismatic darkness!"

"Me too," Joel said soberly, "but it terrifies me to remember how determined I was to spend the rest of my life in it. I'll be indebted to you forever, Tobi, for showing me the way out."

There was a tear rolling down his cheek, and Tobi gently brushed it away. "No, not to me, Joel. Jesus led you out - I was just a vessel."

"Then thank you for being a vessel," he said with a grateful smile.

"I'm the one who should be thanking you," she objected, "for all the wonderful things you shared with me while you were in Dallas."

Joel considered this a moment, then said, "Okay, I have a proposal. I propose we make a pact that we'll continue helping each other find our way out of darkness."

Tobi studied his face. "Do you mean we would help each other understand God's Word? We would help each other walk in *light*, instead of darkness?"

"Yes."

Tobi was radiant. "Oh, Joel! I would love that!" she said eagerly.

"And how do you think we should seal our pact?" he asked with a wink.

"How about a kiss?" she asked.

"My thought exactly!"

So they sealed their pact with a kiss as sweet and gentle as love itself. And above their heads the black satin sky blossomed with spangles of light in every color of the rainbow.

B.J. Aaron

About The Author

Life was simple for B.J. Aaron during the long, sweet days of childhood in a small West Texas town. Faith in God was simple then, too. But during her college years, B.J. heard and followed the siren song of the Charismatic movement. This destructive philosophy consumed 20 years of her life.

After she was delivered from "charismania," B.J. was dismayed to observe that traditional Christianity is doing nothing to warn its laity about this enticing heresy. Her desire is to use fiction as a vehicle to warn and inform the Church about Charismatic doctrine. *Out of Darkness* sheds light on several passages from I Corinthians in the context of a romantic mystery.

Printed in the United States
51256LVS00004B/262-270